Avonelle's Gift

Avonelle's Gift

Nova Scheller

Amma's BREATH

Design by Meadowlark Publishing Services.

Photos on p. 280 courtesy of Missouri State Archives.
Other photos courtesy of the author and her family.

Cover painting by Chloe Corrigan.

Published by Amma's BREATH LLC.
www.ammasbreath.com
info@ammasbreath.com

Manufactured in the United States of America.
ISBN 978-1-4951-6810-9

Published 2015

To all my ancestors, both known and unknown.

Honoring our lineage allows us to draw upon our
ancestors' strength and good wishes. Then we stand
on their shoulders rather than carrying them on our
backs.
Paraphrased from Bri Maya Tiwari

... it is the [Open] Heart which allows the mind
to discern clearly.
Nova Scheller, *The Open Heart Meditation*, 1997

Contents

Preface

I wear a locket filled with my grandmother's bones. These remnant bits carry the essences of her father and mother, my great-grandparents. Their life stories were lost because she never knew them. I didn't know my grandmother because she died eight years before I was born. My mother's stories about her permeated my life. Grandmother's strength and fortitude as an abandoned orphan during the early 1900s have been fundamental to knowing who I am. I couldn't escape her reach; she arranged our first encounter after my mother died. She has been gently guiding me ever since.

My mother's people, on her father's side, came from English and Scotch-Irish who immigrated to America in the late 1600s. The succeeding generations gradually migrated westward from North Carolina to Tennessee. The Civil War years tested family loyalties and one brother left, taking a westerly turn into southern Missouri; my mother's father, a great storyteller, was his grand-child. The need to tell and retell these family stories lies within our DNA. My grandfather told his stories, my mother told her stories and now I tell our stories. All my maternal great-grandparents met at the turn of the twentieth century. What flowed from their unions continued through the Great Depression, World War II, and on into my own life.

This book was written as a blend of fact and fiction. The facts were told by family or found in old documents, letters, newspapers and emails exchanged between my half-uncle and my mother. In one case, a death certificate revealed a name but I was unable to find anything more. Images and scenes formed as I meditated on my great-grandparents and grandparents. In 2011, I traveled to Missouri several times to research my grandfather's checkered past and visit places and homes where I knew my people had been. That geographical arc encompassed Bootheel towns including Kennett, Hornersville, Campbell, Malden and Poplar Bluff; extended northward to Cape Girardeau and St. Louis, and westward to Jefferson City and Lake of the Ozarks. Among these places I visited two former family homes, schools, the St. Louis church where my grandparents married, Jefferson City's State Archives, the defunct Missouri State Penitentiary and the Osage River. Instinct, inspiration and reverent inquiry drove my exploration of these vibrant people, all of whom brought me into this life.

My mother died days after my fifty-eighth birthday. As I sorted through her possessions, I uncovered both of my parents' earlier personal histories. Old bank statements, dairy-farm logs, love letters, and photos were stored for decades in paper grocery sacks and an ancient leather valise. Unfamiliar photographs of my father and my mother, carbon copies of my father's typewritten correspondence and his exquisite love letters to my mother—his only love—catapulted me into their lives. Bit by bit I began seeing my parents not as Mom and Dad, but as Silva and Arno, before I was even a thought in their minds. How precious to see the complex humanity of each parent.

My mother's family shaped me from the moment of my conception. My mother's death was like a starter pistol shot: my time had arrived to understand the patterns and meaning of my maternal ancestral past. My search for meaning requires me to reclaim those who were forgotten, rejected and excluded. Family stories alone cannot reveal the family soul. Only when the unseen are witnessed and accepted as bearing their own individual fates can the family soul be experienced in its fullness. My inner ear is cocked and my heart's sensibility is tuned to those who brought me here. With love and reverence I have sought out the where, when, who, why and how of my family soul. Each of us has one, and this is mine.

The Bootheel Region

This part of my family's story begins in 1900, in southeastern Missouri, where a rectangular "heel" pokes down into Arkansas. In those days, the Bootheel region contained more than two million acres of swampland and was called "Swamp-east." This northernmost part of the Mississippi delta was home to abundant wildlife including bear, wolves, panthers, and wild boar. These creatures roamed freely and fed on game like deer, rabbit, squirrel, possum, raccoons, and wild turkeys. Fowl were as diverse and the rivers, creeks and marshlands contained seemingly endless fish. Life teemed, and mosquitoes were active nine months of the year. Vast bogs of cypress, tupelo, oak and sycamore made larger human settlements impossible, but smaller groups settled on the highest narrow strips of land that remained dry enough for farming. Over hundreds of years settlers included Native American tribes (including the prehistoric Mound Builders), the Spanish, French, and finally the Americans.

Humans penetrated the watery forests by dugout canoes or bateaux. Many settled deep into the various swamps, living on houseboats or in simple cabins built on stilts. They emerged infrequently with furs to trade for coffee, sugar, flour, gunpowder and whiskey. The region stayed waterlogged year round. Boats were commonly used for traveling across the grassy wetlands. The few roads ran the length of the highest dry land, where the first towns were established in the early 1800s. As the population slowly grew, new roads were built from wood. Planks straddled huge logs that were laid end to end across marshy stretches. Before these lowland roads were built, horses, mules and oxen struggled through deep mud, especially when the spring and summer rains flooded the already wet ground. Avoiding marshes and watery forests made travel from one county to the next lengthy and never direct. The few ferries crossed the larger rivers, such as the St. Francis, when their waters were not at flood stage.

The Swamp Reclamation Acts of 1850 and 1860 allowed the state of Missouri to sell swampland acreage to large investors. The significant economic potential the virgin woodlands offered led directly to the land "improvement" efforts of timber companies and railroads. Harvesting the timber required a staggering amount of human and animal labor. Only the railroads and lumber mills were mechanized and strategically located. Cutting, pulling, and carting the raw timber were done manually with axes, saws, mauls, wedges, poles, and hooks; mules or oxen pulled the skids and carts to either a waterway or a railroad spur. Yet even after millions and millions of board feet were logged, milled and shipped, much of the cleared, stump-riddled swampland still lay under water. "Swamp-east" Missouri was one of the last regions in the continental United States to be civilized into agricultural productivity.

Although some of the cleared lowland could be farmed, yields were unpredictable because of frequent and severe flooding. The soil's fertility, however, was second to none because the unwanted waters deposited fresh nutrients on the floodplain every year. Crop yields were among the nation's best, yet only about ten percent of the land could be farmed.

In 1905, several county governments, property owners and businessmen met to plan a comprehensive headwater diversion district that became known as the Little River Ditch Project. Work on drainage channels began in 1912. Timber harvesting was winding down and the Little River project would offer new jobs for the next sixteen years. The effort would remove as much dirt as had been dug for the Panama Canal. Completed in 1928, the five-hundred-thousand-acre Headwater Diversion District channel system drained 1.2 million acres across six counties. Afterwards, just three percent of the usable land was not farmed.

Inside of sixty years the largest inland bottomland wetland forests in the United States had been cleared, drained and converted to some of the Midwest's best farmland. Not surprisingly, little of the once-abundant wildlife remained. When this story begins in 1900, the timber industry is past its heyday and the Little River Ditch project has not yet been conceived. People traveled in

ox wagons or horse-drawn buggies. Telephones were just beginning to be available in towns, and railroads were the only rapid
form of transportation. Most Bootheel acreage was rural and iso-
lated. When the story pauses sixty-five years later, this family's
humanness and its members' hearts remain much the same, but
set in a vastly different time in American culture.

Part I

Chapter 1

When Walter Willard flicked the reins, his heart began to break. The wagon wheels started to turn and the cart lurched forward. It was a hot, muggy June afternoon in 1905, in southeastern Missouri. Tears filled his eyes. He refused to look back but his mind's eye saw his four-year-old stepdaughter Ethel standing on the worn porch, watching him, as he rode away. He shook his head. Maudie would not want him leaving Ethel here. Maudie had been the girl of his dreams, too much to have hoped for, now gone forever. Ethel was not his blood, true, but she was the reason why Maudie had married him in the first place. Not being the first man for Maudie: well, that had been all right, too.

When the baby died the week before, everything had crashed down around him. Maudie's sister, Mae Baker, had assisted Doc White during the birthing and made sure the household kept running. She cooked, and watched and soothed little Ethel as Maudie's labor kept on. But things went terribly wrong. The doctor delivered the baby but Maudie was too weak. She had lost too much blood. She died. The baby boy was sickly. With no mother and no nursing milk, the tiny little one whimpered and struggled. The day after drawing his first breath, he drew his last. Walter had the bodies of a dead wife and his firstborn to bury. And he needed to find someone to take Ethel. He loved the child like she was his, "'cause she was Maudie's." But she was not of his own.

After the burials, standing in the Bakers' small parlor, his mother-in-law Mary Baker had spoken plain. She refused to take her granddaughter Ethel. Something about tainted blood and the look of the child. Walter never knew who Maudie's lover had been; she'd never said. He looked over at John Baker and Mae, father and sister, and saw their shocked looks. Even if the child's parentage was questionable, Ethel was their kin. She was part of their sweet Maudie. In front of Walter, though, they spoke not a word. Their silence spoke loudly. With nothing more to say, Walter rose from the armless chair, his hat in hand, and walked out the front door.

After he climbed onto his horse cart, he heard footsteps running towards him.

Mae's eyes were swollen from crying. "We both loved her, Walter. I'll be by later." Nodding, Walter shook the reins. The cart jerked forward, its wheels churning up dust as he drove away. Thoughts of Ethel, images of Maudie and his dead baby, and worries about the remaining farm chores arose and then faded one after another, again and again. Exhaustion slowed his stunned mind and body, as the monotonous rhythms of cart wheels and hooves rolled and clopped along. He jerked back into alertness when the cart came to a stop and the horse nickered at the barn door.

That night, after supper, Walter's middle-aged aunt Mattie set down two cups of weak coffee, heavy with cream and molasses, on the cleared kitchen table.

"How'd it go?" she asked. Mattie never minced words.

"Mrs. Baker spoke and said no." Walter spoke softly, shaking his head.

"No surprise, there. She never came here all the years with Maudie. Seemed she was thawin', though."

"She was nicer after Maudie was expecting. But that's all gone now." Walter sipped his coffee and ran his finger around the rim. He continued, "John and Mae said nothing, just kept looking at

Mrs. Baker. Then Mae came running out when I got to the cart. Said she'd come later."

"Be good to see her. I like her. Spunky girl. Was good with Ethel and Maudie." Aunt Mattie put her cup on the table. "Now, I been talking to Mrs. Olsen, from the church. There's a place for such as orphans and motherless. A farm on the other side of Malden, over by Risco. She says it's church connected, 'n' called Mercy's Place. Children work there doing what's needed. Field-work, or in the house, what keeps everyone eating and warm. 'Ts not family, but will do. She'll be fine. Think on it. I'm turning in. Try to sleep tonight." Mattie stood, leaned over and put her hand on Walter's shoulder for a moment and then emptied the balance of her coffee into the waste pail, rinsed out the cup, dried it and put it back into the dish cupboard.

Walter sat a while in the empty kitchen, his eyes mindlessly glancing at the cupboards, the dish tub, and the curtains framing the window. The kerosene lamp cast a dreary light that made everything appear muted and faded. Just like he felt. Dread began to touch his stomach and as the feeling grew, Walter's deep innards started to twist up. He knew what he had to do. Tomorrow he would take Maudie's daughter, Ethel, to Mercy's Place.

Chapter 2

For the Baker family farm, the year 1900 proved to be one of the best ever. Spring brought the necessary rains for spring planting and early crop growth but no floods. John Baker was grateful. Twenty years of farming had ranged from bad ones, which meant fending off hunger, to better ones, when some crop losses still allowed a modest return. Between the abundant game that lived in and about the nearby swamp and cash from Mary's egg and milk business, the family eked out a living through hard times. Many farmers struggled during the flooding years. Farming in the Missouri Bootheel was unpredictable, but the good years were good indeed. While flooded swamps could destroy a year's planting and harvest, they also provided succor for humans determined to cultivate the adjacent, drier land.

Just west of the Mississippi, the Bootheel, as southeastern Missouri is commonly known, contained two million acres of bottomland grassland and forests. Newcomers would hear about the New Madrid earthquake eighty years earlier but most farmers and small businessmen were focused on the future, not long-ago events that'd made the land and swamps what they were. When John and Mary took over their farm in 1880, railroads and timber companies were snaking into the Bootheel to harvest the massive oak, tupelo and sycamore trees from the marshy forests.

Wherever a railroad spur ended, huge logs were loaded onto railroad cars and carried to the nearest sawmill. These mills created jobs, small towns sprang up about them, and the big investors knew they were well under way to "reclaiming" the vast acreage. Tree by tree, acre by acre, the swamps were being tamed.

A mild-tempered, hard-working man, John Baker had settled in Cotton Hill Township, about ten miles from Malden, the largest town in all of Dunklin County. Most viable farm property was on or bordering a narrow strip of land known as Crowley's Ridge. Cutting north-south through the Bootheel, the strip began in northeastern Arkansas, with floodplains on both sides. During the early 1800s, the first towns were built on Ridge land, as its elevation rose a few hundred feet above the marshy flatlands. Adjacent prairie sections sloped towards the watery lowlands and were farmed with risk of occasional flooding. The Bakers' acreage included both prairie and swamp. Like his farming neighbors, John never knew what each spring would bring.

He was fortunate to have married Mary Montgomery. She had proved to be a strong partner in their life together. Their five children had all survived and were healthy. During the hard years, no matter the difficulty, Mary faced their problems squarely and always came up with a plan that worked. The Bible said men were the leaders of their family, but John knew Mary was his family's captain and that was all right. Their family's solid reputation in the small community around Malden was of utmost importance to Mary. In public, she was always deferential to her husband. At home, though, she was a firm mother, and had little patience with her children not following rules.

Both mother and father were born during the Civil War. Mary came from Arkansas. She was the last child born to Gladys Montgomery. Two of her brothers had been old enough to be conscripted into the Confederate ranks. Just before Mary was born, Gladys had been notified that both her boys had been killed in battle. Mentally delicate, she coped poorly and could not care for her newborn baby girl. Despite the pain of her milk-filled breasts, she would not hold or nurse the infant. Her oldest daughter took over most of the cooking and laundry, running the house and raising the newborn. Mary's earliest memories of her mother were of a grieving woman who sat hour after hour in her upstairs bedroom, embroidering and frequently weeping. The youngest Montgomery regarded her oldest sister as her true mother. The family stories her mother told always circled back to the deaths of the brothers Mary would never know. Gladys, ever applying her needle to any available scrap of cloth, remained a stranger to her youngest child.

Years after she and John married, Mary would say sparks flew when they first saw one another. He was visiting relations and they met at a church dance. Theirs was a love match in a time when, despite the newspaper romance serials, most rural folk married someone they had known since childhood, usually from no more than a few miles away. Second and third cousin weddings were commonplace. And anyway, country folk didn't spend a lot of time reading romance stories. Mary knew John would be a good provider. Like many young women, she left her home and community behind when she wed. Anyone who knew the couple could sense John's devotion to her.

By 1900, the oldest Baker children could assume their parents' workloads when John and Mary were needed elsewhere. Mae was the oldest at nineteen and the first son, Asa, was seventeen. Their second daughter Maudie, Mary thought, was a dreamer. Whenever Mary saw the faraway look in her fifteen-year-old's eyes, unbidden memories arose of grief-stricken and distracted Gladys. Maudie's abstractions sometimes felt like Gladys had come visiting. Mae, on the other hand, was more like Mary was, good with details, but tender-hearted like John. The last two children were Esther, eight, and Zeke, six. They were just now starting with the lighter farm chores but had been helping in the house for the past couple of years.

The warmth and length of summer days kept their agrarian life endlessly busy between taking care of livestock and tending to their own needs. Days began about five, when either Mary or Mae got up to light the woodstove. John and Asa left to feed their horses, mule, pigs and cows. John Baker could keep his personal livestock to a minimum because he and Asa often hunted in the nearby swamp. During the warmer months, the slowly moving waterways between the tall cypress yielded good catches of fish. Winter's cold iced over the waterways. Then they hunted larger game for their main meat. Meat from deer or a rare bear was eaten fresh, and the remainder was salted for long-term use. Killing larger game was laborious. The men had to "dress" the carcasses before bringing them back to the house. Skinning, gutting, bleeding and partial butchering out in the swamp allowed the women to lend a hand. Smaller game like squirrel, rabbit, fowl and coons were brought home intact. The un-skinned or un-plucked carcasses were easier for the women to handle but getting to the raw meat required more of their time.

A couple hours after each day's beginning, Mary and the older girls would have breakfast ready. The stove heated the kitchen and a bit beyond, but the house was drafty and chilly in the winters, hot and stale during the summers. John and Asa kept enough logs split and dried to fuel the stove year round. Daily, one of the children was assigned the task of keeping enough wood stacked next to the stove. Breakfast was simple but generous, made from everything they raised or grew, except for coffee, flour and sugar. Eggs, cornmeal biscuits, and some sort of meat filled several serving bowls. Everyone was hungry for the day's first meal. Once their plates were emptied, the men returned to their outdoor chores and the women washed up the dishes, pots and pans and began preparing the next meal. The children brought in buckets of well water as needed throughout the day. Any hot water needed for cleaning, washing, cooking and bathing was heated on the stove.

Keeping the family's clothes washed and mended was a major chore. The men's outside labor was rough on overalls and shirts. The laundry piled highest during winter. Everyone wore layered clothing. The males wore double overalls and long johns while the females wore leggings or some sort of bloomers under their skirts. Washing, scrubbing and rinsing garments and sheets were time-consuming and laborious. Getting everything to dry inside the drafty house during bad weather required small washes several times each week. Summer's heat and humidity drove everyone to wear as little as possible. Men wore only overalls and went barefoot unless specific outdoor chores needed boots. The females wore their long cotton dresses or shifts with only an underslip. Summer laundering went more quickly: smaller amounts of washed laundry were hung outside and dried quickly. In these rural areas, no one wore underwear as people do now. They bathed maybe every week or two during the cold, with daily sponge bathing typical.

John knew that when more than one pair of his overalls became too far gone with rips and tears to be passed down, a trip to Malden was approaching. During one particularly good harvest season, he bought a cast-iron shoe form, leather needle, and other cobblers' materials to keep the family's heavy boots and shoes in fair repair. When shirts, coveralls, dresses, aprons, socks and sweaters could no longer be mended, patched, or passed along, they were torn into pieces and used for rags or patches. Nothing was wasted. Ever.

Every couple of months John traveled with Mary or Asa to Malden for foodstuffs. Sometimes he brought along damaged farm tools for the town blacksmith to repair. Twice each year new shoes or clothes were purchased. In profitable years they even brought home hard candy for the children. A journey to town was a major undertaking that began just after dawn; the exhausted travelers returned home after dark. Horse-drawn carts made about eight miles each hour on good roads, but the way to Malden wandered. Few roads ran off the narrow Ridge, and established paths, which might be dry or muddy, wound along the edge of the marshy bottomlands. These shallower grasslands stood in several inches of water. Travelers who tried more direct routes were delayed when their cart wheels sank into the watery muck, which might swallow half the cart. Getting help could take many hours or even days before the cart was retrieved. The Bakers lived ten miles away from Malden. Traveling the rutted trails took three hours in daylight and longer after nightfall.

It had been a long, steamy day during the hottest month. Maudie looked furtively over her shoulder as she neared the kitchen's back door. Months earlier, she, Mae and their mother had spent an afternoon rendering bear fat after a lucky hunt. The boiled fat became tallow, which could be stored and was used to make candles. When evening fell, candles were used throughout the house, letting the kerosene bought in Malden last longer. Today, Mary had announced that she wanted to make more eggshell candles than usual, as she planned to give some to friends at church. That morning the girls carefully cracked open the breakfast eggs so each empty shell could hold enough tallow for several nights' use. Melting the tallow, and positioning each wick just right, was hot, tedious work. Maudie became restless, hoping to leave after supper's cleanup. Mae offered to finish the candles so Maude could begin cooking supper. Finally, when the dishes, pots and pans were clean, and no one was about, Maude burst out the door to head towards the cornfield closest to the swamp.

The sticky, thick but cooler air of the August evening caressed her face and arms while she walked through the corn rows. The stalks were taller than she was and their scent wafted in the dense, still air. At the field's edge, the tall cypress trees bordering the watery channels beckoned to her. She started to feel cooler. Her tense body began to relax as she let out a deep breath. The day's endless kitchen heat was behind her. In the swamp, Maude escaped the endless daily house and farm chores. Being able to leave the closed-in house at day's end was her good luck. Many farm children could not. Summer was the best time with the longest days and warmth. When winter's cold came, her only escape was inside her head. During those short days and long nights, there was no quiet and no being alone, housebound with all the others. Spring took forever to arrive.

The dark shady swamp was a magical place. The tall cypress and tupelo guarded its watery passages; canoeing through the arching trees transported Maudie. Her father and brothers came there only to hunt and fish. The Bakers had survived poor crops partly because of the swamp's game. When their flooded fields could not be planted, the swamp protected and shielded them from a farmer's greatest fear: not taking care of his own. Staying on remained possible. Farmers' complaints about wet bottomland woods and the inevitable flooding made her knot up inside. The idea of no swamp, no canoeing in its hidden and shaded waters, was terrible. She was part of the swamp, and felt tenderly held when she watched all creatures, large or small, drinking along the banks. If they looked up at her, she *was* one of them. Sometimes when she trailed her fingers in the water, she felt the fishes' soft nibbles and she smiled. While most folks felt the mingled odors of rotting leaves, fallen branches and soggy, spongy soil to be unpleasant, for Maudie the smells revealed the swamp's heartbeat and soul.

She was almost at the marshy bank where the canoe lay when a low whistle sounded behind her. Looking back, she saw the dark stranger boy who had come to the farm with his father the day before. She waved to him and he called, "Wait up!"

Maudie studied the youth as he made his way to her. A black hat with a broad brim crowned his head, a dark coat and pants clothed his form. Despite his heavy boots, he walked quickly but with a slight limp. When he had come close he silently gazed into her face. In the boy Avonelle's eyes she saw reflected her own, big blue eyes. Were strands of hair escaping from the dark-blond braid that she'd wound into a topknot, she suddenly wondered? She felt a hot flush on her cheeks. Her eyes fell. Never before had a boy looked at her so fully. She suddenly felt very alert and jittery.

"Where you goin'?" He had a special twang in his words, not the way folks round Malden parts spoke.

"Just getting to the swamp ways for a bit." Maudie nodded towards the canoe.

"Kin I come? I row," he offered. She smiled and nodded.

The two walked to the grounded canoe, through marsh reeds that mingled with shorter, flatter, compact greenery; their footsteps sank into the spongy soil. The canoe straddled both land and water. Bird calls echoed as Maudie stepped into the boat, which easily carried two. Avonelle followed her and using a paddle, he pushed the craft onto the water. The two faced each other as the youth skillfully dipped the paddle soundlessly into the water, and raised it for the next stroke.

She watched him drinking in the sights of her watery woods. His almost coal-black eyes wandered from one cypress trunk to the next. His skin was dark, not like darky slave folk but like the milky coffee her father drank. He had the sureness of a man older and knowing of the world. He cocked his head at the different bird calls, smiling at some and looking curiously at others. His mouth was broad with full, parted lips.

"I know the bayous," Avonelle said, "but these are some different."

"How different?"

"From where I come, same water, many same trees but birds: some same, some not. Feels good to be in the swamp. Papa and me are camped close. We know how to be in the swampland, but don't have no boat."

While the canoe moved slowly through the channel, a squirrel fight broke out on one of the cypresses. One chittered angrily, answered repeatedly with a guttural rasp from another.

"You know where we kin set this boat for a bit?"

Maudie nodded. "Close by is a good place." She pointed ahead to a clearing on the channel's edge. The boy brought the canoe to the shore, grabbed a hanging ropy vine and pulled himself up and out. After he gained his footing, he pulled the canoe onto the marshy slope. Tingling suddenly rushed through her body. She didn't know what to expect but waited. He sat back down into the canoe, facing her.

"This be the first time with a boy?"

She nodded.

"Come sit wit' me." He held out his hand and she uncertainly moved closer, but there wasn't enough room for the two to sit comfortably.

"Here," and he guided her to the canoe's center, where there was enough room for both to sit. Still, she knelt and he leaned towards her, looked into her eyes and moved to kiss her. She wanted to feel his lips but turned her face away and he caught her chin with his hand.

"No?" His eyes held hers and Maudie felt her face start to burn. She felt frozen but her head was swimming.

He smiled. "Umm, seems yes . . ." Avonelle slowly pressed his lips to hers and then he opened his mouth a little and his tongue ran over her parted lips, his eyes looking into hers. Maudie's eyes closed and his tongue softly entered her mouth. She was a little shocked, but it felt good.

She was caught in a current that slowly dragged her down, but she didn't know how to stop it. Her arms encircled the boy's shoulders. The two kissed deeper and Maudie felt a warmth and pulsing in her private parts. Her breasts started to tingle. As Avonelle probed her mouth and her teeth, she felt her body differently. She thought of blood and felt it everywhere. His weight sank onto her. She was not separate from him or from anything else. The channel waters, the tall cypress trees and all the swamp creatures pulsated as their presence swallowed her awareness. A hawk's scream sounded in the distance, followed by a splash near the canoe. Avonelle's hand reached down and started to pull her skirt up. She felt the evening air caress her exposed legs.

"Unhook my belt, will ya, girl?" he asked. He had become part of her sensing and feeling. Her right hand reached between them and unhooked his buckle.

"My pants . . ." He prompted her. She moved to reach for his fly, and felt a swelling. After she fumbled the buttons undone, his swollen member sprang free, with a sticky drop at its tip. The youth pulled away to recline as best he could on the canoe's bottom and guided Maudie's hand to his penis.

"Start pumping, like a well handle, girl." She lay next to him, grabbed him strongly. He returned to kissing her. But her mind was focused on her task. He watched her concentrated expression as she moved her hand up and down. His breath quickened and deepened as he started to arch his back and pulled away from her more. She slowed, to watch him.

"Don' stop, not now. More!" He urged.

She returned to her former rhythm and fixedly looked down as he shut his eyes. Suddenly he jerked forward, grimaced and groaned. The girl looked into his now unfocused eyes and felt his organ pulsing. She shifted her eyes down just as a milky stream shot up, with some falling onto her hand. Surprised, she thought, *Is this what happens when the bull joins the cow?*

The boy's body relaxed completely and he smiled sheepishly. Maudie kissed his lips tenderly. A light swamp breeze whispered to her that here was their watery nesting place. She sighed and nestled with Avonelle. The boy stretched out his arm around her while they listened to the early evening sounds of fish and frogs slipping in and out of the bog water's surface, followed by distant cricket choruses. The cicada's ringing saw-like rasp chimed in and the summer night's arrival slowly darkened the marshland. An egret's graceful wings carried its long slender body over the couple as it made its way through the parted cypress canopy. Tranquility cloaked all with the approaching night's enchantment.

After a bit Maudie stirred, thinking about returning home.

"Not leavin' yet, are ya?" Avonelle asked. He shifted and kissed her again, this time his hand between her legs.

Maudie drew back. "Time to go. My mother will be looking for me."

His hand continued to travel from her thigh to her private parts. She gasped and her breath suddenly quickened again.

"Wait a bit, girl, it'll be wort' it." Avonelle ran a finger along her moist, hidden lips. She sighed and gasped again.

"We're not done, if you stay," he offered quietly, looking deep into her blue eyes, his finger still softly stroking. Time stopped. What mother? What place to return to? There was only sensation and this boy who captivated her in this dark, fertile living place. Here Avonelle made her body sing, throb and spread wide open. He leaned over Maudie, still kissing her, as he worked his finger around her virginal tissue.

"This might be tender, girl. I'll stop if you need." She was too lost in her body to say anything. He nodded and hoisted himself over her, his penis erect again. He held his member with his right hand and stroked her cleft, working towards her hymen. Her head began to nod in rhythm with his movements. When he started to push inwards, she inhaled sharply and tensed.

"Girl?" Avonelle asked. She nodded her assent. He pushed deeper and she tensed again.

"Sure?"

She nodded once more; he pushed harder, more deeply. She moaned, and each time she felt her heartbeat. The boy pulled back farther, and with a last thrust tore through her hymen. She cried out. Virginal blood started to flow as he pulled back and re-entered her again and again. She still tensed but gradually released her clenched thighs. Little by little, she felt a loosening inside and intentionally relaxed to open more. He kissed her and his thrusting into her went deeper and faster. He pulled away to look her again in her eyes, reached under her hips, and pulled them to his groin. Her legs encircled his hips, her feet resting on the back of his legs. Maudie thought, *Is this the cleaving one to another in the Bible?* He sighed during his exertion and seemed to answer her question as they each embraced one another with both arms and legs. She felt the boy was lost within her, and Forever had claimed them both. He started to groan and with a low cry he pulled her tight against her, shuddered for a moment, and stopped. They lay motionless for a spell. Spent and quiet, both teenagers surrendered to the cypress bog's mysterious night songs. Twilight had further dimmed the day.

"I have to get back," Maudie pressed her lover. After setting their clothes to some order, the boy resumed his place in the stern and pushed the craft back into the water. Neither spoke as the canoe retraced the way back.

"Just ahead on the left," she said. Avonelle brought the boat to where they had started. Once out of the canoe, he reached out his left hand and helped her onto the more solid marshland.

"Maudie, girl, this seems a good place to be together. I come by here in the evenings to see if you're here."

"As I'm able," Maudie answered as she searched his face. Calmly, forthrightly, he returned her gaze. Her heart sang and her eyes softly narrowed. He stretched out his arms to her, and she stepped into them. They held each other for a time. She broke

away first and turned towards the farmhouse. The boy watched
her for a few moments and then sauntered the other direction
along the swampy edge of the Baker fields to where he and his
father were staying.

Chapter 3

Two weeks had passed since the first meeting between Maude and Avonelle. The early morning air was cooler for a change. Thunderstorms had come in the night and the sky was a soft pastel blue. Maudie knew the coolness would be brief. When the blazing sun climbed higher, the cloudless sky would deepen into a flat blue. But now, shaded by the roof's overhang, she looked over at Mae while both shelled beans on the back porch. After drying, some of the beans would be set aside as seed; the rest would become family meals. Daddy would have the girls sort through them, searching for the biggest and prettiest. These were separated for planting, those remaining stored for soups and stews. These past two weeks, to her fifteen-year-old mind, household and farm chores had felt less confining.

The several evenings she had spent with Avonelle had brought her across an emotional threshold, which broadened her tolerance for mundane daily tasks. She was crossing an internal divide that left childhood behind as she blossomed into young womanhood. Thoughts of her lover and her new feelings absorbed most of her concentration while she worked.

"There's a glow in your eyes, Maudie," Mae observed.

Maudie ducked her head to avoid her sister's direct look. "Think so?"

"Since you come back from your wanderings that night a couple weeks ago, you been changing."

"How changing?"

"You're not a little wild girl any more. Still wild, but not a little girl. You've not said much, but I know the visitors come from Louisiana. Daddy told. He said they come from what they called bayou country. Lot like the swamps we have here but even hotter. And I seen the way you and the boy looked at each other when first they came."

Maudie reached into the basket for more bean pods and laid them in her lap. "How you mean wild?" She focused her gaze on the beans popping out as she pried open each pod with her thumb.

"I know you been leavin' when you can at day's end and goin' off. I watched once and saw you go towards the swamp where Daddy sets his canoe. And when you came back, you smelled of that place."

"How's that wild?" Maudie persisted.

"Well, the swamp's wild, and you smell of it when you come back. I see how when we can't leave the house in the cold, you act penned up. Now you feel eased with your sometime wanderings. The last several days, somethin' else I feel. I think that boy has s a part in it."

Maudie started to tense as Mae went through her reasons. Of course Mae was right. *How does a body talk about things that don't seem to have words? They're feelings. In the body and heart?* She mused. Her sister's words fit a lot of what she had been feeling. "I do go along the swamp. I feel different there. His name is Avonelle. He says it's French."

"You know Daddy and Mother, if they knew . . ."

"Mae, if you say anything, they'll stop me. I do as good as I can here. But out there, I am more me," she begged. Mae stopped shelling and looked into her sister's face. Maudie spoke for what she wanted and needed. She knew Mae could hear her words. But would Mae keep her secret about the swamp, and, yes, the boy?

"Careful, little sister. I should say something. I don't want any harm to come to you. I hear all the stories about what can happen out there and you've no gun when you go. But I do feel the easing in your spirit when you come back from a-wandering."

Maudie's eyes started to fill with grateful tears. "I'm careful, Mae, I will be careful. Thank you." Maudie reached over to grab Mae's right hand. Mae smiled uncertainly.

"Careful with that boy. That can be another undoing!"

Maudie nodded, feeling her stomach lurch. That "undoing" happened each time she and Avonelle met. How could it not happen? They fit one another. The swamp shielded the two teenage lovers as they gave in to late summer's pulsing vibrancy.

"Well, I need to feed the hens and gather eggs for Mother." Maudie rose.

Mae nodded. "There's not many left. I can finish."

Maudie stepped off the porch toward the small, squat henhouse. It was just tall enough to allow a full-grown man to stand erect inside. The hens roosted in several shelves of nests. Most would voluntarily roost at twilight, but others had to be gathered up before dark and secured or only their feathers would be found the next morning. This morning, most of the hens were out and scrounging the yard for insects and grubs. Maudie reached into the little shed, pulled out a feed sack and started sprinkling handfuls of cracked grain around the hens and the strutting rooster. A little ways off, she noticed her father talking with Avonelle's father while the boy stood next to them. Both men were shaking their heads. No conflict was apparent but something was not right.

She had known the two visitors would not be staying long. Her father said so the day he introduced the pair to whomever was out in the farm yard. She had been gathering eggs then, too. Avonelle and his father were helping temporarily with the seasonal crops and any farm repairs or levee work before the next spring rains. The two young people had not talked much about how long he would stay in the neighborhood. They didn't talk much, ever. Each seemed to know what the other felt, without words. They just were. Now something had changed and it did not feel good.

She watched her father and Avonelle's father shake hands.

After her father shook the boy's hand, the two hired hands walked towards their horse-drawn cart. Maudie ducked behind the hen house, looking for her father. He was headed away to the barn and could not see her. She turned and ran after the others. Avonelle stopped and turned round first. "Papa," he said. The older man looked at both young people, shook his head, then nodded.

His words carried the same soft accent as Avonelle's. "Make it quick, boy. We gotta move on our way." He spoke briskly but not unkindly. "Your father, Mr. Baker, has been good to us. I let you two say goodbye." He continued to the loaded cart.

The two stood looking at each other, saying nothing. Maudie felt her heart splitting apart. Pain laced through her chest and her throat tightened. She saw sadness in Avonelle's eyes. His lips were trembling.

"I never knowed a girl like you, Maudie . . ." He stammered. "Our time here was to be short but this came faster than we knew."

She felt as if he had hit her. "What happened?" she choked out.

"Papa been asking for other jobs, to stay through the winter. Seems a new mill for wood is hiring in the Cape Girardeau."

"That is forever away," Maudie whispered. Her eyes started to sting. Tears welled up and ran down her cheeks.

"You make me feel somehow like my mama would do. I feel in my heart for you, with you. I feel anything good can be, with you. But my papa makes sure we stay together. I am his boy."

Maudie heard his words but the intensity of her feelings swallowed any comprehension. Avonelle embraced her carefully, being in his father's view. She burst into sobs as she buried her face in the boy's chest. She felt his breast heave as if he was trying to swallow his feelings.

"I come back for you, girl. Always, for sure. You the one I want. Have not much to offer for you now. I promise, I be back."

"I hope for that, Avonelle." She lifted her eyes and looked into his. "You make me all of what I am. Mae says I'm not a little girl anymore; I'm changed. 'S true. 'Cause of you. I look for your return."

She stepped back and Avonelle dropped his arms. They could not kiss, not with his father looking at them.

"Later, Maudie girl." He had spoken the last words she would ever hear him utter. He turned on his heel and strode purposefully towards his father, now waiting on the cart.

She stood watching as Avonelle's father shook the reins and his horse started pulling the cart. The boy kept his eyes on her face until the cart rolled out of the barnyard. She watched until it turned off the lane onto the road that would take them northeast to Cape Girardeau. As she watched, those many minutes until the cart was no longer in sight, her breaking heart became a dull ache. The eggs still had to be gathered. Somehow, she would get through the day. She would not let others see what she had lost and felt. Especially not Mother.

Chapter 4

Three and half months passed after Maudie watched Avonelle and his father leave John Baker's farm. After they left that late August morning, Maudie spoke to Mae about her loss. The sisters stood together washing up dishes, after the noon-day meal and before they would pick in the garden for supper preparations.

Mae had seemed to sense the younger girl's sadness, "Is something wrong? You seemed happy this morning."

Maudie burst into tears and her words came tumbling out. "They're gone, Avonelle and his father. They're goin' to Cape Girardeau for mill jobs. Avonelle said he'd come back for me, but knew he didn't have much to offer. Feel like I've lost my world, Mae."

Mae put her arms around Maudie, held her close and whispered, "You got in deep, didn't you, little sister?" Maude took several breaths as Mae stroked her back. Mae let her go, adding, "Be careful; but we can talk about this when you need."

But Maudie never again mentioned her heartbreak. While the evenings' warm weather lasted, she continued to visit the swamp. There, she wept freely. The heavy weight of her hidden feelings rolled away as she grieved. When she paddled through the channel waters she felt her love for the dark stranger boy rise up as she

recalled every detail from their times together. The swamp and
its creatures enfolded her; there she could accept consolation. Bit
by bit she saw how much more she now knew and felt. Loving
Avonelle had cost her, but another part of her was emerging. The
weeks passed, her heartbreak lightened and memories of their
time together became dreamlike.

In October, now that all the crops were harvested and stored,
Maudie, Esther and Zeke returned to school. By early December,
she became absorbed in thoughts of babies and of Avonelle being
the father. These comforting images on the colder, shorter days
made her housebound days easier. Her chores and homework
completed, she worked on her embroidery, thinking about the
swamp, Avonelle and what kind of baby they could have. She was
hungrier at mealtimes and sometimes beat out Asa's and Zeke's
grasping hands for the last bits in the supper serving bowls. Now,
all food tasted good. Her sleep was deeper. Sometimes when she
was frying certain dishes for meals, her stomach would turn from
the smell. These changes were gradual and she thought nothing
about not bleeding monthly. She had bled only once before she
was with Avonelle. Her mother had explained that girls her age
often were irregular in their cycles. Her dresses started fitting
tighter as her breasts and belly started to fill out.

One mid-December day, her mother Mary came upstairs to
the three sisters' small bedroom where Maudie was embroidering. The bed and a chest took up most of the space, as the highest
point in the wooden slat ceiling was the apex of the house's roof.
A small kerosene lamp lit the windowless room.

Mary sat down on the big bed next to Maudie and looked approvingly at Maudie's hooped fabric. "You're so much better at
needlework'n me. Never did have the patience for it. Your stitches
are so regular and tight. Just like my mother's."

Maudie smiled. Her mother seldom gave her compliments.

"I was thinking about your bleeding. You've not said anything
'bout another since your first last summer."

Maudie shook her head no.

"You should've by now. They get more regular after getting

a little older. And 'specially after a first baby." Mary looked at Maudie very closely, all over.

"Stand up, girl," she demanded. Maudie set down her needle-work and rose from the bed.

Mary's eyes ran up and down as she looked at how her daughter's dress was fitting. "I see you eatin' more at meals, daughter."

"True, mother, I've been hungrier. Food tastes real good. Have been sleeping harder, too." A look crossed her mother's face and Maudie's heart started to pound.

"Undo your dress, girl. I'm tryin' to figure what's goin' on. Strip to your skin so I can see better."

Maudie dutifully unbuttoned the back of her dress and let down her under slip so she was bare from the waist up. Mary looked hard at the girl's swelling breasts and then pulled the dress farther down to look at her expanding belly. She shook her head and told Maudie to set her clothes right. The girl complied and resumed her embroidery. Her mother hadn't spoken crossly to her, and she relaxed. Mary, however, seemed deep in thought. Maudie bid her mother good night when she left.

The next two days Mary spent visiting neighbors. Her mood was businesslike and she didn't explain what her visits concerned. In her absence, Mae took up the cooking, cleaning and washing tasks and other household chores. The family meals remained timely. On the second day, after the supper-time meal, Mary asked John and Maudie to come to the parlor. She seemed pleased but very serious.

Mary stood by the parlor door as father and daughter settled into their chairs and looked at her expectantly. After closing the door, she sat in her usual chair. The parlor was the only formal area. It held Mary's finest furniture. The room was kept clean but smelled a bit musty because it was seldom used. Only on important occasions did family or visitors spend time there.

"Christmas is almost here," she spoke, and both John and Maudie smiled at her words. "Maudie, remember when we talked a couple nights ago?" Maudie nodded as she shifted uncomfortably in her chair. After Mary apologized for discussing details of Maudie's bleeding cycles, she recounted their conversation to John Baker.

She ended by saying, "I cannot be sure what happened, John, but I think our daughter's expectin' a baby."

Mary paused, and her husband and daughter absorbed her words. John's eyebrows rose. His eyes opened wide. Shock froze his features. Maudie felt as if she'd been struck. Her muscles locked up while swirling panic coursed through her body.

Mary continued, "When I saw Maudie undressed, her body showed all the signs. She told me of her strong appetite, good sleep. Frying some meats seem to make her sickish. She's put on weight in the places that grow when expectin'."

Maudie saw deep sadness in her father's expression. After several moments he asked her, "How could this happen? You never leave the farm unless with all of us. I know none that're courting you. What boy? When?"

"Clearly this late summer, I think, John," Mary answered.

Maudie could not look either parent in the face; she kept her eyes on the floor. Avonelle was the father but if she said anything, then they would know of her secret swamp wanderings. She said nothing.

After several moments, Mary continued. "Since I cannot be sure and the girl doesn't say, I came up with a plan that saves our name and reputation for a time. If we wait and Maudie bears a child here, then all will know and we'll live with the shame wherever we go, to church, to town. Some'll shun us and perhaps neighbors might pull back from us. The girl may never have marriage prospects if a child's born here." She paused again.

For both the stunned father and the daughter the air seemed thick and difficult to breathe, yet Mary appeared very relaxed.

She resumed. "But there's a solution to our problem. Christmas is coming. The Lord's seen our need, this sad turn, and I've *good* news. I went to see the Willards yesterday, especially young Walter. Always he's had eyes for Maudie. When he brought her that blue ribbon for her embroidery at the County fair last year, I saw how he shifted one foot to t'other as he talked with her. A shy young man. He's a hard worker, and is taking over the farm for his agin' granddaddy. And Mattie, his aunt, is gettin' on.'"

As John listened, his tense face softened at Mary's words. Maudie remained so rattled by her possible pregnancy that she barely heard her mother's plan.

"My visit was as a matchmaker. Mattie and I visited a bit, and then Walter came in for his dinner. Mattie left and I told him I knew he'd feelings for Maudie. He's a young one who doesn't talk easy. I mentioned his hard work and how he and Mattie could use more help. Maudie's strong. She does work fine and now young Walter could have a family. Young farmers need sons to keep their farming sound and going. We would sign for Maudie, being she's not eighteen years. Also, with Christmas coming, it's a joyful time and a wedding would be good then."

"What did young Walter say?" John asked. He seemed calmer. Still subdued, he became very attentive to his wife's story and plan. Many times he had told their children that their mother always saw problems clearly and usually found a way to keep the family moving forward.

"The last thing I put before him," Mary answered, "was that I'd give him a day to think it over. Today I returned for his answer. Walter's pleased to marry our daughter by year's end at the latest. I offered he may come here at any time to court his betrothed and we, her parents, will sign for the marriage license in Kennett. We must make haste, there's fewer than two weeks before the New Year."

Maudie quickly glanced up to see the satisfied look on her mother's face. The girl then cast a furtive glance at her father, who smiled weakly. Mary continued and looked at Maudie sadly. "I been always worried about you, girl. Never felt I could understand you. I was right. Too much goes on inside you." Mary stopped and shook her head. "Just like Gladys," she murmured. Back to her previous volume, she continued. "Though soon you will have a baby, and every feeling in me says so, you'll be married. The child will be too soon for a proper birth but Walter'll be known as the father. People will talk but if the child is seemly in looks, 'twill be forgotten in time."

Maudie nodded quietly as she raised her eyes to meet her

mother's and cast them back to the parlor floor. She felt the truth of her mother's words. She knew her time with Avonelle had brought her to this point. Her father's deep disappointment and sadness made her understand how her impulsiveness affected her parents and her family's standing with their neighbors.

Mary finished, "But your time'll no longer be your own, in the small measures you have now. You acted as if you were a married woman. Now you will take on all the duties of a married woman. Soon, you'll have a baby to tend. This is the bed you must lie in, so young."

She stood up, walked to the parlor door, and waited for John to join her. "Maudie, when young Walter comes calling, be of a mind of how he's saving all of us from public shame. You, and all of us, owe him greatly." Both parents walked out of the parlor and Maudie sat still, trying to understand just what was going to happen in a few weeks, and then several months later.

Walter had always been kind to her. He was awkward, stammered some and his eyes seem to follow her whenever she was near him, either in the farmhouse or out in the yard. A girlfriend had submitted a piece of Maudie's embroidery to the housewives' needlework section at the Dunklin County Fair in Kennett. Maudie hadn't thought anything about the contest until a few days after the fair ended, when Walter brought her the first prize blue ribbon. His kind gesture had touched her but she had seen him only as an up-and-coming young farming neighbor who occasionally helped out her father. Afterwards, she became more aware of his attention. Mae was the oldest and should have been the first Baker girl to be courted.

Her mother was right about their good fortune of Walter wanting to marry her. She also knew Mary was right about her expecting. Her thoughts about babies and Avonelle as her baby's father had been streaming through her mind for weeks. But she hadn't known enough about her body to recognize she was pregnant.

Suddenly Mae burst into the parlor with wide eyes. Agitation rang in her words, "Little sister, Mother told the family about your comin' marriage. Why now?"

Maudie spoke, shaking her head with bewilderment. "It seems

I'm expecting. I will have a baby sometime next year. Mother went to Walter and he agreed to marry me and will be coming to court me. We're to be married by year's end." The younger sister shook her head in disbelief. "I just learned I'm having a baby and will be married in two weeks. I will have to leave this home, the family, and you. But if I didn't, my staying would shame us and everyone we know would turn away. I don't know Walter or his family. I will have to leave Daddy. So much to leave behind, all at once." She softly moaned, "Oh, Mae."

The older girl spoke slowly and sadly. "Little sister, I knew you were in deep with that boy. Now, this."

Maudie started to cry. Mae came closer, touched her forehead to Maudie's and hugged her. "Oh, Mae! We loved each other. This should be good news, if he was here. Maybe we could have married. Because of my wildness, you said once. It was love, Mae, it was. He's gone and I don't know when he'll be back."

Mae put her arm around Maudie's shoulders. "Walter's not far away. I'll visit as much as I can and help with the baby. Maudie, this is too much too soon for you. If anyone should be leavin', it should be me. At least taking on another's home wouldn't be so much for me. I've been stepping into Mother's shoes for some time."

The two held their embrace until the younger sister's weeping subsided. When she was quiet, Mae let her go. "Come, girl, time to go up to bed." The two left the parlor holding hands and started up the stairs.

Part II

Chapter 5

After fifty years of farming, Ezekiel Edley Dunn retired. His first wife had borne him seven children who lived, three girls and four boys. Although his two oldest were females, the boys' arrival made possible his staying on in Cotton Hill Township. His Dunn ancestors had arrived in America during the mid-1600s.

Born in 1849 in McNairy County, Tennessee, Edley was a fraternal twin. His sister was Uthena. He never knew his mother's name; she died when he was four or five. Twins ran in the family. Five years earlier his mother had borne another set of fraternal twins. Three of his siblings died before the age of two, including his older brother, one of the first twins.

His father, James Dunn, was a yeoman farmer. He moved the family to Tishomingo County a few years after Edley and Uthena's births, south of Tennessee line into northeastern Mississippi. McNairy County farmers knew this section of Mississippi was converting more and more to cotton cultivation. Cotton prices had been climbing steadily for some years and the hope of a better future for his children persuaded James to move. Most of his new farming neighbors were either yeomen or tenants who worked small plots of land. These farmers were a cautious sort, and most were economically stable.

James had inherited land in Tennessee, which he sold. He brought along his own farming tools, a mule, two horses and four cows to his new property. His first children, Jane and Will, were old enough to help him and their mother, Minerva, with farming and household chores. Another baby came in 1853, but sometime in 1854, both the baby and Minerva died. Jane assumed her mother's duties and Dunn family life continued. The newly arrived family had not fit well into their new home, and the Dunns received little acknowledgment from neighbors.

Edley remembered little of his mother. He did know he had been born in McNairy County. He had heard the place mentioned sometimes when his oldest sister, Jane, talked about the earlier years to their younger sister, Becca. What he did recall about his mother was the day she was buried. He had watched while his father and Will dug the grave for the crude coffin they had fashioned the day before. The hole was waist-deep for both men. When his father deemed the depth acceptable, they climbed out and returned to the barn to finish the long, narrow plank box. Edley remained behind and stood staring into the clay-colored cavity when fears of falling in swept through him. He froze. Only the sound of Will's voice calling him shattered his spell and he bolted, like a released spring. In the barn, his father and brother were finishing the last boards for the coffin's lid. Later, in the front room of their crude log house, he leaned over to kiss his dead mother's cheek. His lips felt how soft and cool her skin was. The weather was chilly; she still smelled like his mother. Sounds of the hammer nailing the coffin shut rang through the house. Each of the girls' bodies tensed at each blow when the hammer met each nail head.

Though Jane took over the household duties, Becca didn't hesitate to tell Edley and Uthena what to do, whether it was hauling in buckets of well water or fetching more wood for the stove or drying washed dishes and pots. The family continued on with daily life although its heart, their mother, was gone. A few years later, their father married a spinster, Margaret, but no more children were born. The marriage served each spouse's needs. James needed another companion and a mother for his family and

Margaret was able to relinquish her spinsterhood.

The occasional itinerant preacher on horseback would wander past Tishomingo farms but rarely was he invited to stop for a meal or conversation. Religion was not a strong part of the local farming community and the nearest town was far enough away to keep it at arm's length. People gawked when these messengers of God rode by and occasionally turned their backs. Edley never felt his father was truly hostile towards the travelers; rather, he was indifferent. The boy grew up knowing that work came first and, if any time was left over, maybe he and the others might sneak off and wander in the nearby woods, even during the winters. Mississippi winters were too warm for seasonal snow or ice.

James Dunn came to northeastern Mississippi as a non-slave-holding yeoman farmer. Tishomingo County's farming population was a blend of small farmers with and without slaves. Some rental farm properties came with slaves, tools and livestock. Since James had capital for land only, he never considered buying a slave.

When tensions between the North and South escalated in the 1850s, Dunn found himself aligned with a sizable minority opposing secession from the Union. Secession was in the interest of the large landowners alone. Their huge plantations were in western Mississippi, where the river delta soil was the best for raising cotton. Up until the last days before Mississippi formally seceded, the Tishomingo County minority vocally resisted. Once Mississippi seceded, however, James and other like-minded farmers understood how dangerous further resistance would be. At night, with flaming torches, secessionist vigilante groups slowly rode among the farms. Edley remembered lying in bed with his brothers during the spring of 1861, hearing shouts as the vigilantes rode their horses up and down the rutted clay roads. Torch flames glittered through the crude window panes, lighting up the opposite bedroom wall. He and the others held their breaths until the light and sounds finally stopped.

He was almost twelve when his life as a Mississippi farm boy forever changed. Both his father and brother Will joined the Confederate ranks. Tishomingo County was chosen to be a training

camp for almost ten thousand soldiers. Mississippi's outnum-
bered Unionists had no place to hide. The loss of the two oldest men put the burden of farming and the family onto Edley's
stepmother Margaret and his sister Jane. Life and farming grew
increasingly difficult as the war progressed. Shortly after coming
to Tishomingo, he had accompanied his father and brother to a
Mr. Alcott's farm, where two slaves lived and worked. Several
of the county's farmers owned or rented one or two slaves, but
not until two years after the war began would Edley have regular
contact with the black folk. The war dragged on, and boundaries
between farming families and properties began to dissolve as everyone struggled. Both white and black folk worried about having
enough food to eat.

Everyone kept a lookout for the Army men who appeared
sporadically, looking for boys old enough to be "recruited" into
the ranks. Many times both Edley and Jim had hidden under the
porch floorboards and listened to the recruiters' heavy bootsteps
and rough voices as they harassed Margaret and the girls. They
held their breaths, not moving a muscle as clay dust and small
pebbles rained on them through the cracks between the planks. If
word of recruiters came early enough, the youngest boys lit out to
the woods and watched until the dreaded visitors were clear out
of sight and sound.

His father and brother survived those four long years and returned to a shambles of what the farm had become. Only one cow
remained from James's pre-war livestock. The mule and hogs had
been either confiscated by wandering soldiers or butchered by the
family. Edley and Jim had taken over most of the plowing, planting and harvesting years earlier. The day James and Will returned,
one of the boys was in the fields. Sighting the very thin, weary
men, he sounded an ear-piercing whistle. Everyone came running from all over the farm. The next day, after sleeping in their
own beds for the first time in four years, James and Will walked
through their fields. Little fencing remained, and both roofs of the
house and empty barn were in bad shape. The Dunns' losses were
typical of their neighbors' farms.

Soon after, all citizens were notified that Mississippi, as a defeated Confederate state, was now governed by the Federal Fourth District, commanded by a Union general. The local farmers, never in favor of seceding from the Union, were subject to the same treatment as the vanquished secessionists. Until Mississippi was re-admitted to the Union in 1870, Federal authorities occupied and administered the defeated territory.

At the Civil War's start, cotton exports to Britain and other European markets had stopped. Britain started cultivating cotton in its Indian and Egyptian colonies during the 1860s, creating new competition for the South's cotton aristocracy. In the first years after the war, better crop productivity, high railroad freight charges, high interest rates and huge price markups by local storekeepers combined to create an economic trap for the South's small farmers. Tenant and sharecropper alike, no one escaped. Landowners commanded such large shares as rent from their tenants and sharecroppers that none could satisfy their debt. Sharecroppers typically owed landowners one-sixth of their corn harvest and five-sixths of the cotton. Tenant farmer shares were marginally better. Thirty years later, cotton prices were one third of what they had been in 1866, immediately after the war.

In his later days, Edley never talked about the immediate years after the war. His world stayed upended for about ten years, from 1861 to 1870. Very slowly the Dunn farm was brought back to proper repair and productivity. The war had destroyed the South's cotton economy and with cotton prices so depressed, the best many farmers could do was plant subsistence crops. Through barter and exchange, they replenished their livestock but the economic potential of the pre-war 1850s had evaporated. The two Dunn veterans said little about the war, where they had been, and in what battles they had fought. James Dunn slept poorly at night. His health was fragile. Will fared better physically but had taken to meeting up with other young veterans and drinking. He returned from the war with a ready-to-fight temper, which alcohol aggravated. Edley, hearing about work opportunities opening up in southeastern Missouri, left with his family's blessing in 1870.

He was twenty-one years old and faced a life of possibility. He left Tishomingo County with no cash but with his know-how about farming, logging and some carpentry.

His name next appears in the 1900 census, when he was counted among the residents of Cotton Hill Township, Dunklin County, during his fifty-first year. He had seen and lived through much of the Bootheel reclamation efforts, which were spearheaded by the railroads and timber companies. He never had the good fortune to make enough money to buy his own land. Like so many poor white farmers, he was caught in the tenant/sharecropper system established after the war.

It was 1901 when Edley took in his first grandchild, Virgil Lee Medling, son of his oldest child, Nettie. She had returned home to Cotton Hill a few weeks earlier, to have her second baby. She died in childbirth, as did the infant. Her older boy, Virgil, was eighteen months old and had no memory of the day when his father, William Marion Medling, handed him to Edley. His father never returned.

Whenever Virgil told the story of his arrival at the Dunns, he would comment, "Imagine the consternation my arrival caused my two spinster aunts, Mary and Bardie, and my many uncles, Will, Jim, Ernie and Fred. I have always felt I was much more a Dunn than a Medling."

The active, walking youngster was treated more like a pet, or a mascot, than as a child raised by a farm family. His sudden appearance landed on his aunts' watch, but even when he was underfoot, he never felt he was a nuisance or a burden. After his fourth birthday, he began to follow his uncles during their daily chores near the house or in the fields. Among the menfolk, he was treated just as indulgently. The boy arrived at a time when, years earlier, the work had been sorted out and divided among the remaining Dunn sons. Instead of burdening him with work, his young uncles taught their nephew how to hunt and fish and treated him as a sidekick. Years later he began to grasp how much time and labor farming required, none of which ever appealed to him during his Missouri years. Because the farm was well tended,

Virgil was free to attend school through all the grades, read and study as he liked.

When it became clear to the Dunns that William Marion had no interest in his own son, his aunts and uncles spoke openly. William Marion remarried five years later, and the quick birth of the newest Medling drew biting comments.

Virgil was eight years old when he heard his Aunt Mary and Uncle Jim talking. After the noontime dinner, Jim stood drying some pots while Mary sat at the supper table picking through dried beans.

"I heard Will Medling has had another child," Mary began.

Jim stopped drying the pan he was holding and looked at Mary. "Girl or boy?" he asked. Mary glared into the distance, her irritation apparent. The oldest sister, she was not tall or pretty. Her face was severe with a thin nose, small chin, and sharp cheekbones. Her wispy brown hair, pulled back in a bun, accentuated her thinness.

"Boy." She sighed, exasperated. "He has another son. 'Course, his first one, his oldest . . ." she looked over at Virgil "has been here all along, but he's never come back. Like Virgie isn't in this world. Certainly not in Will's world. Makes no sense and I'll never understand. What an example the preacher sets for his congregation!" She snorted in disgust and Jim grunted as he resumed wiping the pan.

Then the boy recalled earlier comments. He began to see how he fit within the two families—he didn't. He belonged to the Dunns and his father lived elsewhere. And when his father created his second family, his half-siblings were unknown to him. The Dunns' bewilderment, whenever they spoke of his absent father, was formative and fundamental.

Although the Dunns regularly went to the Baptist church in Malden, religion was not their first concern. Virgil's grandfather's farm in Dunklin County had been sufficient for the family. After

William left Virgil with them, however, the boy's needs absorbed any extra they had.

Learning his letters began his first exposure to religion. He practiced his reading with the family Bible. Immediately the boy felt drawn to the Word. Sunday sermons started to entrance him. Virgil watched the minister stand at the pulpit and listened to him thunder homilies and extoll the Godly virtues of seeking salvation and forgiveness to the congregation. By the age of eleven, he frequently asked to delay his return home. Could he stay behind and talk to the minister? Eventually, he spent at least an hour daily reading the Bible and began to memorize long passages. After a year, his diligence and demonstrated memory prompted the minister to ask him to help teach the younger children's Sunday school. Except for his military and college years, until 1938, wherever Virgil lived, he taught Sunday school.

He was fifteen when, on a hot summer day, he and Jim checked a couple of cornfields for harvest. Two children were working nearby in one of the Cleary family's fields. The girl was dark, but not Negro. The other was a smaller boy. They looked younger than Virgil. Jim had not seen them before but the field had lain fallow for a couple of years.

Back at the house, Mary and Bardie sat on the porch, breaking beans for supper. Both women wore dark, high-necked, ankle-length dresses with long sleeves. They sat in the porch's shade. Sweat beaded their foreheads. The fabric under their arms was darkly ringed and the strands that escaped from their tightly wound hair hung wetly about their brows. Virgil leaned against a porch post, hands in his pockets, and waited for a break in their conversation. Mary turned to him, expectantly.

"Mary, Jim and me saw two young-uns out on Cleary's place. They were picking. One, a gal, was dark-looking and the other, a boy. Do you have any knowing of them?"

"I'm not sure who you saw, but there's an orphan farm not too far off. The Clearys might've hired some help since they're expanding crops. There's a dark gal that's been at the orphan farm for some years now. When she was left there, lots of talk started." Mary paused to drink from her water glass. She shook her head.

"Lord, even in the shade here, it's hot!"

Bardie continued, "The girl was such as you, Virgie. Her mother died, too. She was married to, I think it was, to Willard?" She glanced at Mary.

Mary nodded. "Walter Willard. He married into the Bakers."

Bardie went on. "Walter Willard went to the mother's family, yes, the Bakers, to ask them to take the little girl, maybe three or four. Her grandmother refused. People saw the little girl looked not a bit like Willard. If she warn't kin to Willard's folk, and his wife's family said no, then only what could be done was, and he took her to Mercy's Place, for orphans."

Mary and Bardie looked at Virgil and then at each other. The sisters looked very similar. All the Dunns, male or female, had the same spare, angular faces—long, with high, sharp cheekbones and strong brows. Years of hard, ceaseless work with long seasons of sweltering heat and bone-chilling snows had worn away any softness of youth. They appeared somewhat like scarecrows, with minimal flesh and few curves. Their bodies were functional, not attractive, but he felt softness in their love, kindness, and affection. They gave him all the safety he needed.

"You think that's pitiful?" Mary asked. Bardie shook her head, looked down and kept breaking the beans. "There's even a sadder story. Sometimes proper things happen but far too late. A young couple who were too young to marry went together, there in Malden, where neighbors see everybody, all the time. The girl went away to have the baby, but someone in town adopted it. A few years later, the couple did get married." Mary took another drink of water.

Bardie took up the story, "The adopted girl found out she was their blood child. Her parents' family grew. Each child born was that adopted girl's full kin. The couple who gave her life knew she was their own and never said a word. Both families attended the same church on Sundays and sat on opposite sides of the church, never greetin' one another. The girl knew her brothers and sisters and parents sat across from her in church. The children went to school together." Bardie shook her head at the incomprehensibility of the situation.

Looking down at her almost empty bowl of beans, Mary said, "The whole town knew, and watched. Everybody knew."

At fifteen, Virgil saw the unfairness in both stories. Such consequences, though, were beyond his limited experience and he thought no more about it. Instead, the dark girl absorbed his attention. She was like him, with no mother, but she'd been put with strangers. A sudden curiosity about her and her life gripped him. What did she feel and think? What were her prospects? He had been thinking about his future. He resolved to meet this girl some time.

Chapter 6

S he stopped pulling corn from the waving stalks and watched the thin blond youth lean into the fall breezes as he walked across the field. The summer of 1916 had been plenty hot, but this afternoon was milder than usual for the Missouri delta. The moving air freshened her. The thin, cotton shift fluttered, removed any clinging sweat. Early that morning, she had grabbed the last hat as she ran to her ride for the day's work. There was not enough shared clothing for all the children at the orphan farm.

Sixteen-year-old Virgil Lee rustled through the ripe corn rows, and she quickly plucked more corn; his visits were never short. Local farmers hired her during the planting and growing seasons for help with their crops of corn, beans, potatoes and cotton. She had to finish harvesting by day's end; several bushel baskets remained empty. Virgil Lee came all times of the day to see her when she worked in the fields, but never came to the farmhouse.

Ethel Willard was fifteen, old to be living in an orphanage. Rural farming areas had no institutional orphanages. Extended family usually raised their younger motherless or orphaned relations. When her mother had died in childbirth, her legal father, Walter Willard, asked her mother's family to take the four-year-old Ethel. Her grandmother had refused, and Willard left her at Mercy's Place, the orphan farm outside Malden. Local people knew the girl's dark coloring was why Mary Baker refused to take in her own granddaughter. Any time the farm orphans came to town for Sunday church services, Ethel felt the sidewise glances and saw people's eyes shifting away when she looked back at them.

Virgil had started visiting her the year before. His first visit he peppered her with question after question about her life at Mercy's Place. Talking about life at the farm felt strange. Everyone she knew lived at the farm, where everyone knew what everybody else did. When answering his questions became tiresome, she asked him about his life and discovered his mother also had died in childbirth. But besides being born in the same section of the county, the two had little else in common. His mother's sisters and brothers had taken him into their home. In the countryside, it was unusual for a boy to attend all the school grades. While Virgil's uncles ran the farm, his time was occupied by reading books and newspapers and studying the Bible. His blond hair, blue eyes and light coloring blended in wherever he went. Ethel's days, however, were consumed with work. Orphan labor ran Mercy Place's farm. The orphans also worked for nearby farmers and their pay was either barter credits or cash that purchased necessities in town. The work of cooking, cleaning, washing and mending clothes was endless; household chores absorbed her other waking hours. Most of the orphans were poor readers, only good enough to follow church services and hymnals. Few could write more than their names.

When Virgil was closer, she saw that he held himself differently. *No idle chatter today,* she thought. He seemed filled with purpose. When he was several steps away, his words started spilling out.

"Ethel, the breeze is welcome, don't ya think?" Virgil's body bristled with energy. "Glad I found you here today because I have my plan. I figured it yesterday. I was sittin' on Grandpa's porch, musing and all of a sudden, I was struck like by a lightning bolt. It was so strong! Must be a message from the Lord . . ."

She tossed her last pulled ear into the nearby basket and waited uneasily. Glancing at the sky, she figured a couple hours more light was left. At dusk, her ride would come to help deliver the filled baskets and take her back in time for supper. Virgil's voice sounded as rushed as his arrival.

"What be the message, Virgil? I must have the field picked before Matt comes or I will have to walk back and miss supper . . ."

"Worry none 'bout that. I kin ask my uncles to borrow a cart and I'll get ya back. I came to tell you not only about my plans but our plans."

"We have no plans, Virgil. Whatever are you talkin' about?" Time was passing. Virgil was always thinking about tomorrow.

"I am hopin' you will consider a mutuality to the message that came to me, that it will be ours 'stead of just mine." His blue eyes bored into hers.

He is different, she thought. Her concerns about finishing faltered as her chest grew tight with a warning feeling. Virgil's earnestness demanded that she listen *now!*

"Tell me," she said resignedly.

The boy stepped closer to Ethel and grabbed her hand. They had never touched before.

"Ethel, I am thinkin' to enlist. My time as a man is coming and I have no future here in farming. All the land is promised to one uncle and there's not enough for all the Dunns, their children and me. 'Sides, I don't want to farm! With the war on in Europe, the papers all talk about America joining in. I want to join the army, be ready to go, and I then will get to Europe. How else kin I get there?"

Ethel, her hand in his, looked into his face. He was trembling and glowed like some preachers she had seen. Her body started to quiver with excitement, but his wanting to enlist frightened her. Men died in wars. He was too young.

"But your age?" she protested.

Virgil shook his head slowly, triumphant. "I'll change my birth year to 1898 and slip under the wire. Men been tellin' stories on their age forever to go to war. Been done all the time, in all sorts a' countries and here, like in the States' War, no way for them to find out! When I get back—and I will—then I will come back for you. Unless you don't want me to?" For a moment he looked like he hadn't considered that possibility.

"I never think about such things, Virgil. Why would I? I have to think about what and where, next. I am fifteen and getting too old to be on the farm."

"Ethel, the army barracks are in Saint Louey! There's factory work in Saint Louey! Ask about. Someone in town will know. We might not be in the war yet, but now we're selling things to Europe that they need to fight the Huns. Lots of country folk move to big cities for factory work and cash money. Saint Louey has factories helpin' what they call the wartime effort."

What little she knew about the war she had learned when the orphans attended Sunday services. Scattered bits of conversation among congregation members floated by when her group settled in the back pews. This boy was a fountain of information about things far beyond her daily life. Saint Louis, she noted. It was a starting point. "You feel different, Virgil. Never have you sweet-talked me." She glanced down at their clasped hands.

Virgil smiled, and she was caught in the netting of his plans. What he said made sense, at least the part about the factory work. Good with her hands, Ethel quickly had learned many needle-crafts: embroidery, crocheting, tatting, and quilting. How hard could factory work be? Her childhood had been spent planting and picking during farming season or helping indoors. When the weather turned cold, after completing household chores, she mended clothes and made quilts for her companions. Any leftover time allowed her to make finer items like tatted lace, embroidered linen towels or crocheted doilies for sale to customers in town.

Virgil leaned closer to her face and slyly peered into her eyes. "What do ya say, Ethel Mae? Will you wait for me? Will you write, least where you be or have someone write me so I'll know where you be, when I come back?"

She took a deep breath, irresistibly drawn into his plans—*oh, Lord, help me.* "I will wait for ya, Virgil. I will let you know where I am. My writing is poor, so I might need someone else to write for me. I will wait."

Virgil bent his head and touched his lips to hers. He pressed firmly—her first kiss. She started to pull away, but his arms wrapped tightly around her back and he pulled her body full to his chest. Tingling spread through her and she stopped resisting.

He stepped back from her. "Goodbye, Ethel Mae. I will be back before I leave." Turning from her, he walked back towards his granddaddy's farm, whistling a church tune, "How Great Thou Art."

Chapter 7

In early December, six months after arriving in St. Louis, Ethel stood at the small kitchen sink and washed up dishes from a late Sunday breakfast. By now the McFarland family, with whom she had come, were savvy city dwellers. In 1917, the big city demanded no less. Unaware newcomers might end up in its crowded streets as paupers scratching for tidbits. This day's leisure brought to her mind the past six months' milestones: the trip to St. Louis, living in an apartment, and her first factory job.

The new city surroundings had overwhelmed her provincial sense of proportion. Tall buildings towered over wide, noisy streets that surged with trolleys, horse-drawn buggies and automobiles. Stylishly dressed men and women crowded both sides of these thoroughfares. A single glance could not take everything in. The St. Louis factory district had no open spaces. Memories of open fields in the Bootheel, where skies revealed the time of day and incoming weather, flooded her mind. Two hundred miles north of the orphan farm, St. Louis skies seemed pushed higher and farther away. Walled-in streets cut the heavens into patches and channeled strong winds blowing in from the river. The only animals she saw were an occasional dog that trotted beside its owners or the horses that pulled buggies. Only the city park bordering the Mississippi River offered her respite.

There, tall stately shade trees stood above long thin strips of grass that framed arrangements of seasonal flowering shrubs. The park's view embraced the wide river. Both the park and the river gave her some relief from the unending urban stimulus. Birds sang, nested, and flew about the park and along the river, but it was not the same. Her life in the countryside had been hard, but there she could pause in her labors for moments of ease. Often wild creatures appeared in the fields and their presence was not threatening. On the contrary, during these encounters, any and all living forms helped her feel peace and balance. The big city's tireless energy excited her but people were everywhere all the time. She missed her moments of serenity and solitude.

The previous May, when she had set out on her journey with the McFarlands, she had been exhilarated but cautious, too. Auntie Grace unexpectedly had given her money saved from the last quilt she had sold.

"Here, girl, get you some city clothes to travel in. You're goin' to another world. Best t'arrive looking less country." Ethel had burst into tears; she couldn't remember anyone ever giving her anything that wasn't a necessity. Now, she was leaving the only home she had known for ten years to make her way in the world. Five years before, Auntie Grace had begun managing the farm, and living conditions had changed for the better. The orphanage matron rarely showed tenderness, but was always fair.

Grace, too, had grown up at Mercy's Place and had experienced the previous caretakers' harshness. Small missteps and infractions were punished severely, and the atmosphere had been dour. Younger children had struggled with tasks beyond their strength, and the older ones sometimes were forced to work without breaks or meals. When Auntie Grace became the caretaker, religion and the Bible were no longer used in punishment. While she firmly maintained routines that kept the farm running, the children knew she truly cared about them. Grace steadily cultivated the older children's chances to work for nearby farmers, and these efforts brought in more cash or barter credits.

Auntie Grace had encouraged Ethel to sell her needlework. Her designs and patterns acquired a reputation in Malden, where she sold her quilts, lace collars and cuffs, tablecloths, and doilies to townsfolk. Money from her goods came between the growing seasons, and was used for orphanage necessities. Until the day Auntie Grace had pressed the coins into her hand, Ethel did not know any of her earnings had been put aside.

The McFarlands had met Ethel at the farm the week before they departed. After Virgil Medling had suggested she go to St. Louis while he was serving in the Army, Ethel had left word in various Malden shops. The McFarlands heard of her interest and arrived at the farm in a dusty Model T Ford. The sight and sound of the black car halted all activity. The orphans and Auntie Grace gathered outside the house to meet these unusual visitors. They had seen passenger cars in Malden but this was the first one to come to the farm.

The car came to a standstill and the clattering motor sputtered to a stop. All the boys slowly walked toward it, as if pulled by an invisible force. They gawked at the twelve-spoked wheels shielded by front and rear fenders, which dipped down to the running board that stretched below the front and rear doors. Glowing brass trim outlined the grilled radiator. Mounted on each side were brass-rimmed headlights that looked like huge, colorless glass eyes. Dust from the dirt road had dulled the shiny hood, fenders and running boards and powdered the black canvas convertible top. The boys were enthralled. The girls hung back and whispered to one another. Auntie Grace stood with Ethel in front of the girls and stepped forward to greet the visitors.

Harold and Ernestina McFarland, accompanied by their two daughters, Carrie and Thea, met with Ethel in the Bible reading room. The McFarlands were all heavyset and wore town clothes. Harold was in his mid-forties. He had a florid face, weak chin and prominent jowls. His gray eyes matched his thinning hair. He looked soft both physically and in his demeanor. Ernestina was about the same age, and graying like her spouse. She wore a very imposing black hat. Never having seen such an extravagant, even disproportionate hat, Ethel found her eyes wandering from her prospective traveling partner's face to the hat. Its wide brim extended several inches from a broad-domed crown, generously wrapped with a wide satin ribbon. A delicate transparent veil hung from the brim, covering the upper half of her face. Plump like her mate, Ernestina spoke for the family while Harold silently nodded to affirm her pronouncements. All the girls were close in age. Mrs. McFarland addressed Ethel like a third daughter while eying the girl's cotton work shift and worn, scuffed shoes.

The family was moving to St. Louis because of Harold's poor health. With no sons to help, he couldn't keep up his farm. After he sold the property, the family had moved to Malden. Mrs. McFarland had heard about factory jobs in St. Louis, and Harold had relatives there. If she and her daughters found work there, some chance of prosperity was possible. Another person joining them made more cash available and could increase everybody's success. Mrs. McFarland explained to Ethel that, in exchange for their transporting her to the city and for the cost of her board, she would be expected to help with household chores and turn over her pay to them. In turn, they would give her money for her own needs. Ethel agreed, and the departure for St. Louis from Malden was set for the following week.

Excitement ran high at the farm. Ethel was the first ever to leave for a big city. Some girls had found work as house help for wealthier families in Malden. Boys often became hired hands locally or nearby in Stoddard or New Madrid counties. Luckier boys started at the Malden timber mill, or worked in warehouses or at the train station. When Auntie Grace had given Ethel the money, she also made sure one of the boys was free to take her to town. Ethel stretched her coins as far as possible. She returned to the farm looking like a stylish young lady from Malden way.

The McFarlands returned the next day. After saying her good-byes, Ethel sat in the Ford's back seat between Thea and Carrie. During the drive back to Malden, Mrs. McFarland turned around to Ethel and explained that the car had been lent to them. They would take a train to St. Louis after Harold bought their tickets at the station.

Then she added, "Ethel Mae, don't you look a sight! Seems you are ready for the big city." Ethel saw a hungry look cross the older woman's face. "We all are hoping for good fortune once we get to St. Louis, but your clothes!"

Not accustomed to being looked at, Ethel lowered her head, and hid her eyes.

"Yes, ma'am. Auntie Grace kindly gave me a little bit for proper clothes. We have so little at the farm."

Mrs. McFarland's expression was questioning. "Then you have nothing left to help pay for your ticket. You spent all she gave you?"

Ethel felt chided. "No, err, yes ma'am." The girl gulped before answering. "I bargained hard to get what I did from what I had. If I had known you needed the money . . ."

Mrs. McFarland shook her head and smiled sadly. The tone of her voice suggested that the girl had no thoughts but for herself. "'Course you didn't. We are a big group and our family has very limited cash for traveling. We'll manage somehow, but your ticket is part of what you owe, once you find your work. You understand, don't you?" The older woman sighed, shook her head and turned back to the front, leaving Ethel to view her grey upswept hair and large hat.

Sandwiched between the two stocky girls, Ethel gazed down at the old flour sack between her feet. In it were all her possessions: a set of crochet hooks, an embroidery hoop, her tatting hooks, some old socks, woolen long johns, a comb and cheap barrettes, a tattered old coat one of the older boys had given her, and a bit of crocheting she might work on during the train ride. She felt closed in. At the farm, she had known the rules, how things were done, She had helped teach the younger ones. None of the children were blood kin, but together they had formed a patchwork family, her family. Now she was an outsider, joining a real family with their own ways. Her new life with them would succeed only when she learned what worked with the McFarlands.

She sank into her thoughts. Excitement and occasional giddiness mounted: her first ride in a car! The engine's smooth rhythmic rattling, the soft, cushioned seat—there were no such cushions at the orphan farm—contrasted with how quickly the fields and trees flew by her as she looked through the windows. Riding in wagons was faster than walking, but either way she saw, smelled, heard and sometimes tasted what was carried by the winds and what fell from the skies. The car separated them from the outside, like a little motorized shed.

On either side of her the girls chattered constantly. At one point, Thea leaned forward and asked, "Momma, will there be time to stop for a sody before the train? I'm wantin' a sarsaparilla . . ."

"Harold, what ya think, kin we stop for sodies?" Mrs. McFarland looked at her husband. "Have we time enough?"

Straggling gray strands of hair escaping from Mrs. McFarland's hat caught Ethel's notice. Before Harold answered, her attention was drawn to a shifting roll of fat beneath his red neck, which was corralled by his shirt collar.

He cleared his throat. "Well, Tina, mother, if we return the car quick, we'll manage a visit to Rice's on our way to the depot."

Both daughters sucked in air before they started giggling. Their wiggling rubbed against Ethel. Such high-spirited laughter was new. Sometimes the new little orphans might giggle when gathered together. The farm's sober atmosphere had been focused on learning the right ways of doing tasks and being Godly. While laughter was not forbidden, there wasn't much to laugh about.

After Mr. McFarland returned the car, they strolled to Rice's General Store for sodas. At the soda fountain, Harold asked Ethel to choose a flavor. Not knowing what to choose, she deferred, so sarsaparilla was served to everyone. Her first soda was cold, foamy and sweet. The spicy carbonated fluid tickled her nose, danced on her tongue and almost burned when she swallowed. Exploding bubbliness expanded into her chest. She was so caught up in these unexpected but pleasant sensations that she barely noticed the walk to the train depot.

Mr. and Mrs. McFarland retrieved their suitcases from the depot storage and guided the girls to the waiting room. The station was spacious and airy and its ceilings seemed very high, unlike the dark and cramped farmhouse. Harold left them to go pick up their tickets. Ethel sat to one side of her companions and gazed about the waiting room. A few passengers sat nearby on polished wood benches. Some chatted with their companions or read newspapers. One woman was knitting, the only needlework Ethel had not learned. Yarn was expensive, unlike crochet thread. The time passed, and her body tingled with growing anticipation.

Many times she had heard train whistles during visits to Malden, but she'd never had seen a train. After an hour the waiting passengers heard the first whistle. Her heart started to beat very fast as the slowing Ka-chuka-ka-chuka-chuka of the approaching locomotive grew louder. The squeal of steel wheels against the track was piercing when the line of cars braked to a complete stop. The releasing steam whooshed for several minutes. A uniformed conductor briskly walked into the waiting room and announced that boarding for final destination St. Louis would begin in five minutes.

Their second class tickets allowed entry to a general passenger car, and there was enough room that Ethel could sit next to a window. The train pulled out of the station and the family talked among themselves while she hungrily watched the delta's flat farmland change to gently sloping hillsides blanketed in lush grasses and stands of oak, elm and maple trees crowded with late spring foliage. A few hours later, the train stopped in Cape Girardeau. From her seat, the girl saw the Mississippi River for the first time. It was so wide she couldn't see the other river bank.

Because their tickets did not permit entry into the dining car, the McFarlands had brought food with them. When sandwiches were passed around, Harold made sure Ethel was included. After eight o'clock, outside their train windows, the land lay in darkness. The train's gentle rocking lulled Ethel into a light sleep when she leaned her head against the window. Twelve hours after leaving Malden at five o'clock in the afternoon, Ethel and the McFarlands arrived in St. Louis at five o'clock the following morning.

It was still dark when the train's whistle jolted her awake. She looked over at the McFarland girls who were gently snoring. Harold was awake, and Ernestina's head lay on his shoulder. He nodded to Ethel, smiled and silently mouthed, "We're almost there." Ethel nodded and shifted her weight to sit upright. It was still too dark to see outside her window. So much had happened the last day before: what would appear next?

Train brakes let out an extended shriek when the cars came to a full stop in St. Louis Union Station. The McFarland women awoke. Mother and daughters sleepily gathered themselves. The lighter hues of dawn brought day's first light, which brightened quickly. The Malden travelers were unprepared for what they observed next. Thirty-two train tracks lay side by side as their train came to their arrival gate. The train yard felt as wide as Malden's central street was long. To the sound of hissing steam, all the passengers in their car began gathering their belongings and moved into the central aisle.

The girls in their group descended the car's door steps and entered a swarm of people milling about everywhere. The departure-arrival hall seemed wider than the entire Malden train station, with travelers streaming nonstop as they came and went. Clock after clock hung along the walls, each next to a sign posting train times to a specific city. Harold read out loud the names of each destination as the group slowly made its way down the crowded corridor. They came to the Grand Hall, through which was the main entrance to the street.

Upon entering the hall, all five stopped, spellbound. The ceiling was twice as high as the Malden depot's roof. Harold and Ernestina spoke softly in unison, "My Word!" The five slowly crossed the Grand Hall, and took in the frescos, gold leaf trim and Tiffany stained glass windows. The height and breadth of the space didn't seem possible. Was this real? A gigantic chandelier hung from the center of the Hall's vaulted ceiling; clusters of smaller chandeliers marked off its circumference. Arches were everywhere. Myriads of travelers flowed through the various arches, crossing through to the street entrance. Ethel shook her head as she gazed overhead. Like a tiered crown, second and third floor arches surrounded the Hall's perimeter and rose into the vaulted ceiling. People stood in these, looking down into the bustling hall. As huge as the Hall was, its scale could not reveal the enormity of Union Station. At this time, St. Louis had the largest and busiest train station in the whole world. The entire station, including passenger facilities, tracks and train maintenance, covered twenty acres. The Grand Hall, with its ornate walls paneled in cool green, punctuated by gold leaf medallions, numerous arches and seemingly endless marble floors, held more people in one place than the town of Malden. All of it overwhelmed her senses. As they stepped through the main entrance onto Market Street, the Bootheel travelers felt St. Louis welcomed them. Their new lives were beginning auspiciously.

The first weeks in St. Louis went smoothly enough. Harold's relatives had informed him which boarding houses were close to the factory district. They also had supplied the names of several clothing factories. Within the month all the women had found work. The girls were hired at a shirt factory. Their factory jobs required six-day work weeks with ten- to twelve-hour shifts. Sunday was their only day off. Mrs. McFarland found work in a retail store. Her mature comportment impressed her interviewer, and she was promised sales work once she had mastered her knowledge of the stock room's inventory.

Harold's health kept him from working, but he managed the money and found their permanent apartment. He shopped for food, which made preparing meals easier for the women. His soothing manner kept all the girls and Mrs. McFarland calm and settled.

One day, a few weeks after settling into the apartment, Mrs. McFarland came into the girls' bedroom. It was evening, after a workday, and both Ethel and Carrie were changing into their nightgowns. Mrs. McFarland was holding a couple of small packages wrapped in brown paper.

"Carrie, I have the belt for you. There's no telling when ya might start your course. Keep it with ya when ya go to work each day and take the nappie with you." Carrie nodded at her mother's words and started to blush.

Mrs. McFarland looked at Ethel. "Ethel Mae, I have an extra. Do ya want it?"

Feeling very puzzled about the belt, Ethel nodded. "Thank you, Miz McFarland . . ." Mrs. McFarland frowned. Ethel quickly collected herself. ". . . I mean, Ernestina." So hard to call her by her first name; *she's not Auntie Grace,* she thought. Mrs. McFarland's brow smoothed and she smiled a little.

"I got these in Malden before we left. Thea and I have been using them this past year. We feel so much cleaner. Now we're in the big city, it's best to leave the country ways behind. Working in the factories, with our city dress, it's nice to keep it from running down our legs onto our bloomers."

Ethel's mind was racing. What was Mrs. McFarland, no, make that Ernestina, talking about? "Good to know, and I'll use it, ma'am." Mrs. McFarland looked pleased, and handed Ethel her own paper-wrapped package.

She gave Carrie a hug, and kissed her on the forehead. "See you in the morning, girls!" and closed the door behind her.

Ethel looked at her package and then Carrie's. She looked into the girl's face, which was still bright red. She whispered, "Carrie, what's the matter? And what're these packages?"

Carrie seemed at an unusual loss for words. Ethel waited. Carrie's eyes fell to the floor and she whispered back. "Ethel Mae, you know . . . our monthly courses . . . the belts are for that."

Ethel remained mystified. "Monthly courses? What are those? Never heard about courses or monthly at the orphanage."

If possible, Carrie's face became even redder. "Every woman knows about, Momma calls it, monthly courses. I haven't started yet but she wants me to look for it. It's for when we can start havin' babies."

Ethel absorbed Carrie's words and asked, "What happens with a course? I don't understand and don't know what this belt is for." She waved the package at Carrie.

Carrie's eyes got very big. "You really don't know! A course is when we bleed from . . ." she mouthed ". . . down there." A thought crossed the girl's face, "Have you? Had your monthly course?"

A flash of understanding swept through Ethel. Courses were the bleeding and mess older girls and women went through. She nodded. "A couple of times." She stopped. Then she pressed, "And the belt?"

Carrie's face was a little less red. Talking about this taboo subject seemed to be lessening her embarrassment. "When we moved to Malden, Momma was lookin' in the Sears catalogue and found these"—she tapped her package—"they call 'em sanitary belts and they sell special cloth napkins with them." She opened the package and pulled out a white cotton belt with two cotton straps attached at the opposite ends. The straps had large metal fasteners. Ethel looked at the strange device, still not understanding.

Carrie pulled out a long cloth swatch and handed it to her. Ethel saw it was actually several folded thicknesses, sewn at the outer edges. Carrie continued, "See, ya pin the ends to the hanging down pieces and the blood goes on that, not yer bloomers."

Another flash of comprehension lit through Ethel. Like diapers, bleeding diapers for girls and women. "Thanks, Carrie." She touched the girl's arm. "I understand."

Carrie grabbed her hand and said, "I get so twisted up about this bleedin' and babies. Us women, girls, are not supposed to talk about this with boys and men around. Momma says we have to keep it hidden. It's the one thing I hate talkin', make that thinkin', about." The more she spoke, though, the paler her face became. Ethel could see Carrie was almost back to her normal self.

After all the girls had gotten into bed and the kerosene light was turned down, Ethel started thinking about the first time she bled. Country folk, make that country women, called women's monthly courses "bleeding," 'cause that's what it was. In the orphanage, things were scattershot. Maybe Auntie Grace thought to say something to the older girls, maybe not. In Ethel's case, she hadn't. After all, Grace wasn't a mother. Ethel's first contact with bleeding was helping with the laundry.

In the country, nothing special was done when a female bled: she bled into her clothes. In the winter, the females wore long johns, which if bled on, were always soaked and washed separately from the men's clothes. A couple of times, however, some clean, stained long johns got mixed in with the boys's laundry. The boys asked about the stains and the situation had been very awkward. The boys were never told and the matron raised Holy Hell with the girls for mixing up the clean laundry.

She'd been fourteen and a half when she first bled, and the second-oldest girl at the farm. She hadn't seen any blood-stained clothes in the gathered dirty clothes for a couple of years.

It was the summer before she'd come to St. Louis, and she was out in the fields, digging potatoes. It was a hot day, humid, and the sun was slowly baking the field. She had lifted the rows with a pitchfork, and knelt on the ground to begin pulling the loosened tubers. Her stomach had been crampy for a couple of hours. Once on the ground, she felt something slowly trickle onto an upper thigh. When she pulled her hand out from under her shift and under slip, she saw thick, dark blood on her fingertips. Her cramping worsened and she lay down on her side, hoping it would ease. Between the sun beating down, the twisting in her gut and the creeping stickiness on her thighs, she felt weak and beaten up. What was happening? She felt too awful to be afraid.

After a time, the cramping subsided and the sweaty, exhausted girl got back onto her knees and started digging again. Whatever this was, she knew she wasn't dying: several empty bushel baskets were waiting. Outside of death, there never was a good excuse for not getting a harvest completed when promised.

That evening, when Ethel got back to the farm, she said nothing. The cramping started again when she was in bed. Curled up into a ball, she waited for it to let go. She got drowsy and a couple of thoughts floated through her drifting mind. Adam and Eve with the apple: woman was the reason they had to leave the Garden of Eden—and the pain of childbirth. She sleepily wondered, was this cramping also part of that female pain? Was this why women felt they had to hide the blood from the men? Then she fell asleep.

A week later, Auntie Grace asked Ethel to help with the after-supper cleanup. She stood together with Lizzie and Ethel, drying the dishes, pots and pans.

The matron softly asked Ethel, "Ethel Mae, I was working the girls' laundry and found some dark stains on an underslip. Both

Lizzie and I bled a couple weeks ago. Was the underslip yours?" Ethel flushed.

Auntie Grace reached towards her. "Sakes, girl, there's nothin' to be ashamed of. I shoulda said somethin' to ya. But 'ts not any better than what I'd got as a girl, either. None told me before, only afterward. We never talked 'bout it. Partly, it's never to be spoken of around menfolk. Mebbe 'tis different in families with mothers. I wouldn't know."

She touched Ethel's shoulder. "You're a woman now. Rightly. You can have children because now you bleed. And the timing should be monthly but at the start, maybe a few more months before it happens again. You're all right?"

Ethel remembered the warmth she had felt when the other two took her hands that evening. She had joined something that, before now, had been only between Auntie Grace and Lizzie. Both of them embraced her when the older woman was done talking. She had crossed over a significant threshold, visible to other women but hidden from men. She bled again shortly after the New Year.

Now, months later, the concern and caring Mrs. McFarland had shown Carrie made another strong impression. *Maybe that's part of having a mother,* she thought. *What would it be like to have your own, to tell you about things before they happen?* She was not a family member, true, but she could learn from the McFarlands. The girls lived with both father and mother, both of whom were tender and looked after them. Maybe living with them could give her more than a place to stay. Maybe seeing how a real family worked and treated one another could help her when she had her own children. Then she thought of the sanitary belt and napkins. Coming to this big city was more than earning a wage. She was learning how to leave behind her country ways and become a modern woman.

Chapter 8

Many things had changed at the Baker farm in the seventeen years since Christmas of 1900, when Maudie Baker married Walter Willard. Both Mary and John Baker had died. Asa, the oldest son, was married, with three children, and ran the farm. Mae, now thirty-four, remained unmarried and stayed on. Her workload of endless housework and farm chores had eased considerably. Now, another brood of children helped with tending the livestock, cooking, cleaning and gardening in the summer and autumn. Mae was always busy, but an interruption in her work didn't disrupt the typical day's rhythm of meals and cleanup.

She sat in the sunny parlor, crocheting a tablecloth meant for her brother's wife, for their upcoming tenth wedding anniversary. Sunlight streamed in through the front windows and warmed Mae on this chilly November day. She looped three onto her hook, and crocheted each: treble, double and single stitches for the pattern. Her thoughts roamed; memories of Maudie surfaced. She shook her head sadly. Maudie had not fit into the family. She was a dreamer, quiet. What little she did say was only to Mae. The wedding to Walter Willard all those years ago had gone well, as their mother had intended. That day, Maudie had been in a daze and Walter beamed, having so easily attained the girl he was smitten with. Despite the pregnancy, undisclosed before the wedding, and the very early birth of Maudie's daughter, the couple seemed to get on well together. The marriage had solved the immediate problem of Maudie's pregnancy, for both the girl and her family's standing. Three years later, Maudie had been joyfully expecting another child and Walter was beside himself with hope for a son. Although Maudie had not loved Walter when she married him, their life together was a success—for a time.

Her childbirth went disastrously. The deaths of both mother and child had devastated Walter. A young widower at twenty-three, with no family nearby to help, he'd had to find another home for four-year-old Ethel. Mae shook her head again. Ethel, the sweetest, best-behaved young girl, did not look like Walter, not with her dark complexion. Walter was not her father but had regarded the girl as his own. If only things had gone right, if her mother had not refused her own granddaughter, sending the child away—Mae's mind lit onto the young dark boy Maudie had fallen for. He was Ethel's true father. He'd been a good-looking boy and a hard worker. He was never seen again.

The sounds of hooves and cart wheels coming up to the backyard intruded, then a barking dog. Mae's reverie dissolved. She called out to the visitor as she made her way through the warm kitchen. When she opened the kitchen door and saw who was standing there, her hand flew to her throat. She gasped. Hunched in a black coat in the cold November gusts stood an older version of the boy Maudie had given her heart to.

Avonelle shivered in the cold wind and nervously knocked at the back door. When it swung open, he saw Maudie's older sister, Mae. She was now a mature woman, no longer fresh-faced. She stood open-mouthed and wide-eyed, speechless at his arrival.

"This be the Baker farm?" Avonelle asked softly. His English still carried a hint of French but his years outside Lousiana had tempered his accent.

"It is, and I don't recall your name but I know your face.

You're the boy Maudie was with before she married Walter Willard. I'm Mae."

Avonelle nodded.

"Well then, come in out the wind. I was just thinking of you and Maudie and all that passed after you and your father left, long ago." Avonelle meekly entered the kitchen, startled at Mae's easy manner. He had anticipated a much more reserved response to his sudden visit.

"You are kind. And yes, much better in here than out there."

Mae took Avonelle's overcoat and motioned to the kitchen table. "Let me get you some coffee." He sat as Mae poured two cups. He wondered if his visit would remain so cordial. Mae took the seat opposite him.

"You never told me your name," she reminded him.

"Oh, yes. I am Avonelle Broussard, Cajun from Louisiana. Part Creole, too."

"I remember the Avonelle from Maudie. She declared it French," Mae responded. "Don't know about Cajun or what you call Cree-ole."

Avonelle nodded. "We Cajun come from Canada. French, driven out by the English and we travel to the bayous of Louisiana. The Creole are French also, but mixed, some with Spanish, some color gens, called the freedmen, darky. Also some Indian, like Houma, dat live there many, many years before white men come to the bayou."

Avonelle waited for Mae to take this all in. She looked steadily into his eyes.

"Mr. Broussard, why have you come back, after all these years?"

Avonelle swallowed hard. "Many years ago my Papa and I came back to Malden and asked about the Baker family. I was mebbe nineteen, and two years after we left from here. We hear stories. That Maudie married so quick to Willard. Also they say there was an early baby. I lost all hope of seein' her, with marriage to him. We moved on." Avonelle sipped his coffee. "My Papa die of consumption a few years ago and when I travel home to Louisiana, I stop through Malden again. Once more I ask for news of the Bakers. And I learn the saddest news . . . that Maudie is dead, from having a baby, also dead."

Mae nodded. A look of deep sadness crossed her face. "Things went very badly. I was there during her childbirth. The next day the baby died. And then there was Ethel." The mention of Ethel made Avonelle's heart leap.

"Umm, yes, the other child. She is not here?" he asked, knowing the answer.

"Walter came to our parents and asked that we take her. He was alone with no help and the child was not his kin. My mother decided we could not. It was the look of the girl. She was so dark. She looked just like us white folk, but so dark. If she came here, then there would have been talk about the father, the early birth and the rest. Better we be talked about for not taking the child." Mae stopped and her eyes started to fill with tears. "I loved Maudie, took care of her as she grew. And losing Maudie's first child grieved Daddy and me."

"With Maudie gone, who the father was, what matter?" Avonelle felt his throat tighten and his heart beat faster as Mae talked.

"Miss Mae, you ask why I come? I come about this child. Stories also say she was dark. You see me. What you think? Tell me true. I come for the truth."

"And what if she is yours? She's lost to us. Once Walter left her at that place, we Bakers never went to see her. I don't know where she is, even if she's alive."

Avonelle's heart felt as if it would burst out of his chest. He knew! This girl, if still living, was his own.

"Mr. Broussard, I do think she is—was—your girl. For she favors you in many ways. Same shiny black hair. Her eyes were lighter but her skin was like milky coffee. The last I saw her, though, she was just four years. Such a sweet, good girl. Never gave Maudie any grief."

Avonelle nodded. "My Mama, she was tender, sweet, like Maudie. Sure I fell for Maudie because she was the first softness I feel for so long. Mama died when I was eight years, also lost a young sister, to the cholera. My Papa took care of me. In time, I take care of him, later on. To have a little girl, with Maudie. No one, Miss Mae, touch me, touch my heart, like Maudie. Now I know there is more. There is a daughter from my swamp girl."

Mae answered, "The last time I saw Ethel, it was the night before, and next morning before Walter took her to the orphan farm. I would have gone with them, but Walter insisted he go by himself. We told her we were taking her to a place with other children and she would be taken care of. She wept at Maudie's burial and would cry herself to sleep at night after Maudie died. But she never made a fuss. She was much like Maudie, quiet and deep. I missed her terribly, for we were close. And I can never feel good about Mother refusing, we not taking her. It was wrong. My heart's always said so." Tears streamed down Mae's face. She got up to blow her nose and dabbed at her tears.

When Mae had composed herself and sat down, Avonelle continued. "You are so good, and answer all my questions, Miss Mae. Why?" he asked gratefully.

"Mr. Broussard, both my parents are gone. You come here now and look for your kin who was wrongly put elsewhere. Ethel should've grown up here, with her own kinfolk, regardless of her looks. Even though she was made outside of marriage. She's paid the price for what she had none to do with. I see you want to know."

Avonelle nodded vigorously.

"What will you do, if you can find her?" Mae asked.

"I need to see her, look in her eyes and tell her the truth she has not known. That she should know. We both have lost, me the father and she, my daughter. To meet her just once and then we see. I need to know where Willard took her, that farm, and go there."

Mae looked at him hard. After a pause, she nodded her head slowly. "This is a beginning, to set this wrong to a better place. We've no way of knowing what would make it right, ever. But your trying to find her is right, now."

Mae gave him the name and location of the orphan farm. It

was too late in the day to go there. Tomorrow was a new day and he would be fresher. The visit with Mae Baker had been exhilarating, but he was tired and needed to sort through his thoughts and feelings.

"You've been so kind to me, Miss Mae. Thank you for that. And for the coffee."

"Be well, Mr. Broussard. I pray the girl is alive and healthy and you two see one another. If you do, say none about me. I think saying anything about those who refused her during her deepest need could do more harm than good." Mae walked him to the back door. She waved as his horses pulled the cart through the farm yard and down the lane back to Malden.

Chapter 9

The Mercy's Place farm's acreage stretched out flat in all directions. Wooden fences partitioned the crop land into many fields. Scattered trees stood like sentinels, some solitary ones that seemed whimsically placed along the fencing. Oaks were the tallest, sometimes accompanied by scrawny scrub pines. The silhouette of clustered tree tops looked like huge saw teeth had ripped out chunks; most likely tornados had sheared them. Sun-bleached cornstalks and short scraggly cotton brush, the past season's spent residues, littered the fields. Avonelle stood on the dilapidated farmhouse's porch, while twenty-year-old memories of southeastern Missouri's delta crop lands swept through him. No swamp forest was visible here, and he had seen none on his way to the orphan farm. To the side of the farmhouse were a couple of small livestock sheds. Maybe hen houses? Beyond these stood a large, unpainted two-story barn with grey weathered walls. He saw young farm hands coming and going through the half-open barn door.

Well-worn by age and harsh weather, an uneven roof line crowned the house. Some windows were shuttered. Cracked glass panes filled the others. Under the porch overhang, plain gray benches stood on each side of the front door. As he walked from his cart, Avonelle noted that the house matched the barn, also unpainted. The porch floorboards squeaked with each step he took.

He had started early and the cart ride had taken most of the morning. The mid-day dinner hour would come soon. This November day was bleak, but absent were the winds that had chilled his bones the previous day. Gray skies hinted at possible snow. The coming change made his limping leg ache, where the barrel had rolled onto it twenty-five years before. The previous day's blustery winds had been tempered by Mae Baker's welcome. She had firmed up his hopes about his and Maudie's daughter. Now he was sure he was Ethel's father.

He hesitated before knocking, thinking about this place as his daughter's home. For more than ten years she had lived and worked here! In all that time she had never been touched, held, or kissed by family. If only he had known, he would have brought her home to the bayou, to his—and her—family. Maybe her presence as his granddaughter would have ended his father's perpetual need to keep moving. If only, somehow, he could have known. Pangs of regret shot through his heart when he thought of his swamp girl, Maudie. If they could have built a life together, Ethel would have been theirs. Their precious time together had been too brief. He took a deep breath as his hand knocked on the front door. Who and what would he find inside?

Voices of children sounded near the closed door but quieted when someone turned the creaking knob. The door swung open to reveal three young-uns. The smallest two, a dark-haired boy and a red-haired girl, each appeared to be about six years old. They looked up with wide eyes and serious faces. The oldest was a girl, maybe twelve, who stood behind them, a hand on each child's shoulder. She was big-boned and sturdy, strong but placid. Her braided chestnut hair crisscrossed her head like a coronet. She had a broad face, large blue eyes and rosy cheeks.

Bending to the younger ones, she encouraged them: "You know what to say; we practiced." Her words revealed a mix of Midwestern and foreign accents.

The smaller girl, curly auburn hair pulled back, eyes a startling green, stepped forward and firmly offered, "Welcome to

Mercy's Place. My name is Tilda." She looked over at her little partner and prompted, "Matt?"

Matt appeared to be tongue-tied.

"Come on, Matt, you know," Tilda urged him on.

"Umm, yep, this is Mercy's Place. Uh, ummm, 'm Matt." Clearly relieved that his part was over, he turned to his escort.

The big girl smiled approvingly at both children, and looked up into Avonelle's eyes. "Well, sir, you heard the name twice, so you know where you are. I am Chrissa. What can we do fer ya?" Her ease in guiding the little ones and receiving a stranger settled his nerves.

The children were clean, dressed in plain, functional clothes. Despite the November chill, the girls wore thin cotton shifts, topped with heavy sweaters, and long johns underneath. Matt's patched shirt and pants were too big for him; his heavy sweater was so big the sleeves were rolled up several times, letting his hands hang free. The orphans all radiated good manners and careful upbringing.

Avonelle smiled. "I'm the father of a young woman who has been here for many years. I'm looking to find her."

A startled look crossed Chrissa's face. She stepped back, the young ones flanking her, and she extended her hand to Avonelle. "Please come in. Auntie Grace's the one to see. The dinner meal is now close fer eatin'. Let me take you to the Bible-reading room and tell 'er you're waitin'."

Aromas of soup and baking biscuits wafted through the front hall. His mouth watered. Plain, unpainted planks formed the entranceway walls, running floor to ceiling. The worn wooden floors were scarred by countless footsteps over the years. Though warmer than outside, the house was drafty and cold. In summer, it would be oppressively hot.

The Bible room, perhaps once the front parlor, was dark. Chrissa lit a kerosene lamp, revealing roughhewn benches with no cushions or cloth covers, lined up in rows. The shuttered and uncurtained windows held cracked panes of glass. Maybe the shutters held the panes in place? At one end, on a tall bookstand, sat a large ornate Bible. Perhaps it served as a small pulpit for readings and services? Beneath the Bible was a large, intricate, crocheted doily. It was the only decorative item.

"Please wait, sir, and I'll get Auntie Grace," Chrissa said. The little ones followed her out of the room.

Standing behind the Bible, he turned to face the room and the rows of benches. During the bayou country's warmer winters, houses never needed boarding up or shuttering against the cold. There, it was the late summer and autumn hurricanes that demanded reinforcement of one's dwelling. What the weather requires, when life makes harsh turns, he thought. This is how children could be brought to a place like this, as a last resort. His train of thought vanished when a middle-aged woman came bustling through the doorway. Plain-looking, wearing eyeglasses, her grey hair was pulled in a bun. Her dress was as worn as the children's. She exuded competence. The questioning look on her flushed face was not unfriendly but suggested a need to return to what had been interrupted.

"I am Auntie Grace. Chrissa told me you're the father of one of our girls?" She spoke briskly and directly.

Relieved to meet the person in charge, he offered in a soft voice, "Yes, ma'am. I am Avonelle Broussard and my daughter is known as Ethel Willard."

The matron raised her eyebrows and exhaled slowly. "Ah, Ethel, yes." She paused. "Mr. Brew-sard, Ethel did live here for many years. She left several months ago."

Disappointment dashed his anticipation. His dismay deepened as he absorbed her words. "D'you know where she might be, Miz Grace?"

She looked hard at him, her eyes burrowing deeply into his. He felt her taking stock of him. Pursing her lips, she suggested, "Mr. Brew-sard, we are in the middle of cookin' the midday meal. I've a house full of children needin' to eat. 'Tis plain food, but you're welcome. We'll talk after." He nodded gratefully. "Well then," she continued, "come join us in the kitchen. It's warmer there. 'Twill give ya a feel of our place while we finish up for the meal hour."

Avonelle felt warmer as he followed her to the kitchen. Now

his coat was too heavy. A wide doorway joined the kitchen with the meal room, where benches surrounded two long cypress tables. All the furniture looked crudely handcrafted. The small, crowded kitchen's heat drove him into the eating room. Laying his coat on a bench, he straddled it, and watched the youngsters' comings and goings. Open cupboards lined the walls. The lowest shelves, within reach of smaller children, held stacks of mismatched dishes, eating utensils, and stacks of folded cloth. The kitchen was just large enough for a small table and two chairs, woodstove and a freestanding dry sink. A tall lanky girl, wearing only a thin cotton shift, worked in the ripples of heat that rose from the stove. She appeared all arms and legs: her flushed face beaded with sweat. Auntie Grace stood in the center of the room, directing.

"Chrissa, start getting the tables set. Lizzie, keep an eye on the potatoes, make sure they're not boilin' to a burn. Yep, pull the pot over to the cooler part."

Chrissa called out names. Lizzie, her blond hair caught at the base of her neck, stood far from the stove as her long arms shifted the potato pot. Avonelle thought she might tower over him. Raising the huge soup pot's lid, she inserted a spoon, large enough to be a small oar, and stirred.

"I think it's ready, Auntie Grace. D'ya want to check?" She was still holding the spoon. Grace shook her head, so Lizzie wrestled the huge pot to the stove top's coolest spot. "The biscuits are close, maybe a couple minutes more."

Auntie Grace nodded and stepped through the kitchen's back door. Seconds later, a dinner triangle clanged. Re-entering the kitchen, she said, "By the time the boys are here, all will be ready."

Chrissa escorted Tilda and Matt into the meal room. The little ones gathered flatware from the baskets. Chrissa lifted stacks of bowls and small plates onto the tables. Tilda started laying out her spoons and knives, glancing at Matt to check on his progress.

"Not so crooked, Matt! Let me do it. You start the plates. Those won't get cockeyed."

Matt willingly agreed, "Right, Tilda. You're better at straight'n me." Setting plates between the flatware where he thought they should go, the boy came to Avonelle. "'Scuse me," he said, and laid bowls in front of him.

Suddenly the back door burst open and a gaggle of boys pushed into the kitchen. Auntie Grace chided, "Hey, *hey*, HEY!" "I know you've not washed up. The tub of water and towels are'n the porch. Wash! Then we start servin'!"

Moans and groans trailed after the boys as they backtracked, leaving the door ajar.

Lizzie looked to Auntie, who nodded. Pulling pans from the oven, the girl quickly scored between the biscuits. Moving deftly, she drained the water from the big pot and dumped the cooked potatoes into a large bowl. By the time all was set for serving, the first boys had returned to the kitchen, waiting for Auntie's signal. Waiting for all to be present was clearly part of mealtime routine. When the last boys arrived, pushing the others into the dining area. Avonelle saw they ranged from about eight to fourteen years. They were thin, but healthy, full of rambunctious boyish energy. Auntie Grace, though, clearly ruled the roost.

"Seems we're gathered. Let's say the blessing. Peter, yer turn, and no short cuts!" A youthful masculine voice, occasionally croaking, began the blessing most farm folks used for midday meals. He clearly enunciated each word with no rushing. "Bless us, oh Lord, this day, for what we are 'bout to receive. For this and all other bounty, we thank you."

At the blessing's end, everyone chimed in with a hearty "Amen." The children grabbed bowls and plates and snaked back to the kitchen, lining up by the stove. Lizzie dispensed soup potatoes and biscuits to each child.

Auntie Grace called out, "Is there honey on the tables?" Chrissa stepped from her place in line, ran to a kitchen shelf and grabbed two half-full mason jars. These were passed hand to hand down the waiting line and set on the tables. The ease and flow among these orphans further softened Avonelle's earlier fears about Ethel growing up here.

He joined Auntie Grace and Lizzie, who served themselves and him. Chopped potatoes were spooned into his bowl of thick bean and onion soup and one of the last biscuits was added to his plate. Auntie Grace and Lizzie chose benches at opposite ends of the tables. The children shifted to make room. He followed Auntie Grace's nod and sat across from her. Sounds of slurping soup and twanging forks filled the room. No one spoke. Honey jars moved along the tables when the diners got ready to tackle their biscuits. Most of children saved their sweetened biscuits to eat last.

Tilda's clear voice chimed softly. "I'll do it, Matt. Might be trickles if you do." Avonelle spotted the two little companions sitting together at the far end of his table. They seemed the youngest. Next to Matt, Tilda expertly angled the honey jar. The boy clasped his small hands in his lap, nodding as he watched her drizzle his biscuit. Then he passed the jar along.

The food was ample, simple and just right for a cold autumn day. When most were close to emptying their plates, Lizzie called out, "The biscuits are gone but some soup and a couple of taters're left. Serve yourselves but no mess, please!" Two bigger boys with empty bowls got up and disappeared into the kitchen.

Auntie Grace looked about the tables and nodded. "Seems we're done. You know what to do. Back to the day's work."

The orphanage matron looked him in the eyes as she narrowed her own. "You believe you're Ethel's father. I wouldn't, if you looked other'n. She favors you." She looked down and paused, as she rolled her cup between her hands. "I don't remember any parent comin' to look for any of us." His look of surprise was noticed. Nodding, she continued, "Yes, I'm orphaned. I grew up here. Bein' country farmland, if no kin could take you, then this place was a refuge. Sometime older ones, eight or nine, was taken in by strangers, not as family, but for 'nother pair of hands. My own people died in a plague that swept through 'most forty years ago. No one knew my father's or mother's family because they were newly settled here. I was too young. Ethel is half orphan—one parent gone."

He offered, "Miss Grace, my mother died when I was eight. My younger sister, too, with the cholera. Only my papa and me were left. More family was lost some years later, then we left the bayou and come north. All we did was work and travel and work."

He drank from his water cup and continued. "Miz Grace, I

knew none of her, my daughter, for sure, 'til yesterday. My time with her mother was so short. My father with me, we stayed never long anywhere. I came back two times. First I heard Maudie'd married. Then a few years later, I heard she died, but there was a child. Last year, my father died, and I come back to Malden and heard Maudie's child was given away. I felt some question. Could she be mine? I always loved Maudie but my father never settled. I saw Maudie's sister yesterday."

At these words, Auntie Grace leaned in.

Searching the woman's face, Avonelle spoke calmly, "She spoke as you do, seeing me. She feels the girl, and her looks, to be my own."

Nodding, she sat quietly. He felt her taking in his words. "Mr. Brew-sard, very few of the children stay past fourteen or fifteen. Then it's time for them to leave and make their way as they can. Ethel stayed a bit longer 'cause she was such a hard worker, whether here'n the farm or workin' the fields for other farmers. Any earnings she made came to Mercy's Place. That gave the farm what little cash we have. She also worked the needle, crocheted, embroidered or tatted and made the best quilts. Some of these we kept, like that doily under the Bible. We need quilts for the winter cold. She never sat without doing somethin'. She did not know how. It was like her hands itched if they weren't movin'."

"It is good to know what you say," Avonelle said. "Tell me more?"

"She's slow to talk, shy-like. Quick with numbers but little book learning. We teach letters some in the winters, but we kin be here only through our labors. We work the farm here and for others. Ethel always knew what she was owed and no farmer could short her pay. She's fussy. Things have to be neat, stacked right. Her stitchin' on her quilts was the finest. She fetched the best prices because what she made, off the farm, was known. Sometimes, folks in town would give her their sewing scraps and thread, battin', and let her fashion a quilt her own way."

Avonelle thought of his mother's simple but beautiful taste, which showed in whatever she had crafted by hand. Then a memory about Maudie struck him. "Ethel's mother, Maudie, was good with the needle. She won a blue ribbon at the County Fair the year before we met. I never saw it because we spent our time outside in the swamp stream nearby. She tol' me." Shaking his head, his eyes darkened with sadness. It had been so long ago. Now talking about his daughter, the same age as when he and his Maudie girl were together and falling in love.

"What d'ya know about where she went?"

Auntie Grace nodded. "I know where she was headed. She'd a chance to go to Saint Louey, for factory work. When we went into town, Ethel would ask about that kind of work. There was something about the war and wartime needs. She left word at a couple of shops, that if she could get a way there, she was interested. We also asked at a Sunday service but we don't go often. Too much to do. A couple weeks later, the MacFarland folk came out to see her. They were movin' to Saint Louey and said they could take her. Some sort of arrangement they made, and Ethel left maybe five months ago."

Finding his daughter would be harder in the big city. "Miss Grace, you've been so kind. I pray God carries me to where I need go to find her. She lost everything when Maudie died. I see she was raised in a good place, even with no family. The children I saw today were bright, even loving." He thought of little Matt and Tilda. "The little ones that met me at the door—can you tell me some about them?"

"Matt's our newest one and he's been here for maybe a month. An orphan train from back East came through and no one took him. He was the only one left when they came to Malden, the last stop. One of the church folk stepped forward and offered the train folk that he could come here. Before him, Tilda was the newest but she has been here for 'bout a year."

"She seems to take care of him and help him like his sister, but older." Avonelle chuckled. "What I seen today is good and strong."

"This was a good day, Mr. Brew-sard. Everyone minded manners and tongues. It coulda been more trying. Thank you."

They both rose from the hard benches, and Auntie Grace led Avonelle to the front door. Once more on the porch, his broad-brimmed hat in hand, he faced the matter-of-fact matron and held out his hand.

As she took his hand, Auntie Grace nodded once more. "I pray you find her. She's one of our favorites. She's never mean and was good with the younger girls, teachin' em what she knew. If you two can see one another, 'twill be God's own gift. Safe travels!"

Avonelle walked to his waiting horse and cart while Auntie Grace watched. Once in the driver's seat, he shook the reins, clucked and the horse started forward. He guided the horse toward the road leading back to Malden, and turned, smiled, and waved to his hostess. Even though he still did not know where his daughter was, his determination to find her was stronger than ever.

Chapter 10

Sunday began as a typical day off. Ethel was in the kitchen cleaning up from the late morning breakfast when she heard one of the girls talking to someone at the front door.

Carrie came into the kitchen. "Ethel Mae, a man's waitin' fer you in the parlor."

She dried her hands, wondering who on earth could it be? Virgil had been sent out of the country. The only other men she knew were the factory bosses. She walked into the parlor and saw him. Dressed all in black, he stood with a broad-brimmed black hat in his hands. He looked worn from years of hard work and dressed country-like: heavy clothes and shod with dusty thick-soled boots. Although she never had laid eyes on him before, he seemed familiar. His face was the color of milky coffee and his almost black eyes shone. Thick, gray-streaked black hair crowned his head. The sight of him knocked the breath out of her.

"You be Ethel Mae Willard?" His soft words carried a mild and lilting accent. His eyes shot through her and she felt light-headed yet her legs held her up.

"Yes, I be."

He nodded his head as if he already knew what she would say. He limped slightly as he stepped around the short divan table

to face her, but he didn't come too close. "I am Avonelle Broussard. I knew your mother, Maudie Baker." His name sounded
strange and foreign. She recognized her mother's name. After ten
years of never hearing it, she had forgotten.

"Mr. Brewsawd . . ."

He smiled. "Call me Avonelle. It's easier for the Midwestern
tongue." There was a musical quality in his accented speech.

She nodded and swallowed hard. "Avonelle, what be your
business with me?"

He dropped his eyes. He looked up after a few moments, and
his eyes locked onto hers. "Ethel Mae, I am sorry for these strong
things to say, but . . ." She started to feel unsteady again.

"I knew your mother and we were very close. We loved each
other. You're our daughter."

He waited as the girl stood silently. All she could do was look.
His face, his eyes, skin and hair. *Just like mine.* She slowly reached
out her hand to touch his wavy, thick, hanging hair. He closed his
eyes and breathed in sharply when her fingers touched him. Feelings rushed through her with such strength that she felt bolted to
the floor. My father? *My father.* My father!

Several seconds passed and then he spoke. "How you be,
Ethel Mae?" His soft words cracked her heart open. She nodded
silently. She couldn't form any words.

"Should we sit?" He limped back towards the divan. She
joined him.

"I knew my comin' would be a shock, but once I knew, I had
to come." He looked at his hat as he ran the brim round and round
through his hands.

Her fascination with his features would not let go. "I see my
darkness in you," she whispered, and he smiled. She murmured
as if she was talking to herself. "All my life my darkness has been,
the Bible says, a stumbling block. Folks from all round talked of
my darkness and how my mother's kin wouldn't take me."

He nodded and softly smiled. "I didn't know of you until I
came into Malden after your mother died. I can tell you what I
know."

My father and now about my people? She nodded.

"May I hold your hand?" He held his hand out, and she placed hers in it, hungrily watching him. "My papa and me traveled and worked farms along the Mississippi. We started from bayou country in Louisiana where I was born. We came to the Baker farm where Maudie, your mother, lived. She and me were so young, she was fifteen and me, seventeen. Our time was short, maybe two weeks. It was late summer and Papa said we needed to find mill work in Cape Girardeau for the winter. So we left. I tole Maudie just before we went, and she cried and I said I'd come back for her. We come back almost two year later. I learned she'd married Walter Willard, a nearby farmer. I only saw him once."

Avonelle stopped for several moments. When he spoke of her mother, his face grew sad. Ethel could feel his love for her mother, from fifteen years before. She nodded, smiled. "Tell me more, please."

He sighed. "The talk said they were happy. That he loved her. That made me happy for her, but not so for me. Our time, hers and mine, would never happen again. A few years later, my father and me come through Malden again. I asked about Maudie and Willard. The news was bad. Maudie was dead, from havin' a baby. I heard about a little girl who Willard didn't keep."

Ethel jumped and he nodded, knowingly. "Yes, he went to Maudie's kin and asked them to take her, to take you. And they wouldn't. Some said 'twas your grandmother, that your looks . . ."

She started to cry. *I never cry, it never has gotten me a thing before,* but she could not help her tears. *Why, why am I crying now?* She covered her face with her hands and sobbed. Avonelle, her father, leaned close to her and put his arm around her. Next to him, she smelled his skin, felt the roughness of his whisker stubble, and sank against his chest.

"Ah, little one, shhhh, shhhhhh. I'm here now." His soft voice pulled all the sadness, aloneness, the years of feeling different and separate, out of her.

Her crying gradually eased, her tears slowed and started to dry. "To see someone who looks like me. This is the first time." His full-lipped mouth smiled broadly and his teeth flashed at her.

"My father, your grandfather, died two years ago. I went

back home to the bayou in Louisiana and spent time with family, your family. I lost my mama and younger sister when I was eight. Back in the bayou, I started thinking about the little girl, Maudie's daughter. I had to try to find you. You're ours. For you to never know of me and your mother? I couldn't accept that as long as I could look. Now you know."

"How did ya find me?"

"I talked to someone on the Baker farm. They said I had to be your father and told me of Mercy's Place. After talking to Auntie Grace"—Ethel smiled—"she let me see the place and we ate the noon meal together. She told me of the McFarlands and your coming here. I got here a week ago and I've been asking 'round sewing factories after the McFarlands and you. Then I found out where you all live."

She sat up straight. What did this mean? "Avonelle, you coming here. I am not sure; what do you want?"

"Ethel, I've thought about you as bein' me and Maudie's child for a couple of years. And you hear all this now, in one visit. The last months here, there've been many changes for you, coming to the big city? Now this." She nodded as he spoke. "May I come back to see you?"

Her tears started again. "Yes, please, you're the only kin I've known. I'd be sad to never see you again. I'm not small any more but . . . to see and talk to my father. Even if I never see my people, now I know something." He reached into his pocket and offered her his handkerchief. She laughed a bit and wiped her tears.

Her father stood. "I come uninvited this Sunday, so I leave now. But I'll be back in a few days. Nothing can prevent that, God willing." She followed him to the front door.

Before she opened it, Avonelle asked, "May I call you daughter, Ethel?" Her tears started again. "Oh, no, my daughter, no more tears. They are the past, for we see one another and know who we are for each other. I found you, and see you, the beauty you are. You're like my Mama—what I remember—and like Maudie, my sweet one. You look like Mama and your quiet way is like my Maudie. She talked not much, but a lot was inside her. You're her daughter."

Images of her mother suddenly flashed in her mind as she listened to his words. How they had sat together and her mother showed Ethel embroidery stitching, right before she died. Her mother's hair was so long it touched the floor when she sat and brushed it for bedtime.

"I remember little of her, I was so small."

Her father smiled. "Never forget her, what little you have. She was my life's love. May I hold you before I go?"

She stepped into his open arms and her body softened in their first embrace. They breathed together and his heart beat gently thudded against her chest. Then he kissed the top of her head and let her go.

Avonelle Broussard stood on the front door step and looked deeply into her eyes. "Until next time, God willing, daughter." He turned down the street, and Ethel reentered the apartment.

Joy pulsed through Avonelle as he walked, oblivious. The last time he had felt like this was with Maudie. Had it been that long ago? Loss had marked the years before and after they met. After he had lost his mama and little sister, the cholera had killed more kin a few years later: these deaths led to his leaving his home country. After finding Maudie, his father's demand that they leave, so soon, had crushed him. When he learned she was married, any possibility of reuniting with her died. The finality of her death broke not only his heart but his spirit. When he learned that their love had produced a child, however, his hope revived.

My daughter. The words rang through his mind. His own child had stood before him. She had his mama's cheekbones and looked a bit like his younger sister. Her quiet manner and slowness to speak reminded him of Maudie. Both Maudie and her daughter were well mannered and pleasing to the eye but their feelings lay deep. Ethel's big dark eyes, so like his own, radiated intensity. Her youthful skin glowed despite its dark tones. The Bakers' blood had lightened the darkness of his coloring but north of Louisiana, she would stand out. Bayou folk often had mixed blood and could be part French, Spanish, Indian, or even some Negro. He had heard his mother's kinfolk were a blend of all these. In the Louisiana countryside no one paid any mind to what people were, only how they conducted themselves.

On this November Sunday afternoon the city streets were filled with people and vehicles. Passersby repeatedly brushed by. Some bumped into him, tipped their hats and nodded in apology. He returned to the present, and saw he had missed the cross street to his boarding house. He began retracing his steps down Olive Street, a main boulevard with trolley tracks that ran down its center.

His thoughts resumed. She had touched his hair and stared into his face, not a muscle moving, transfixed. Her voice was low and soft, not shrill like some young women. He had held her in his arms and she had melted, her heart close to his heart, his daughter. Tears started to blur his vision.

He came a crossing point. On his side of the street, an automobile was headed towards him, next to the trolley car tracks. He decided not to wait, and began to cross. Back of him, two boys played catch on the street side. One missed a thrown ball, which bounced into the street. The other boy yelled. The voice broke into Avonelle's absorption; he startled and his game leg took a misstep. He teetered, and the auto behind him tried to swerve left but an oncoming trolley car was too close. The car hit him and knocked him flat. A buggy had been following the automobile. When the horse saw Avonelle's sprawled body, it spooked and reared. Semi-conscious and stunned, he heard the horse's scream and the driver calling out. A crushing pressure landed on his chest. Everything went black.

A couple of men rushed into the boulevard and carried his collapsed body to the street side. His chest was crushed, blood had started to run from his mouth, and his breathing was labored. A policeman ordered him carried to the closest hospital. After his body arrived, the doctor on duty pronounced him dead. When his clothes were searched for identification, only his mother's rosary was found. His body, tagged "John Doe," remained in the St. Louis police morgue and details of the accident were posted in the *St. Louis Post-Dispatch*. Within one week the unclaimed body of Avonelle Broussard was buried in a common grave for unidentified paupers.

Ethel was just closing the door after her father left when Carrie returned.

"Well, who was that, Ethel Mae? Seemed he was here for some time." Carrie always wanted to know what was happening. Her favorite pastime was spreading her news.

"He's a friend of a friend from Malden. He'd been looking for someone for a time and hoped I'd know somethin'."

Carrie's expression remained curious. "And did ya know somethin' or help somehow?"

I will not tell you what is mine alone, she thought, but she didn't lie. "No. He told me more'n any I could tell him. And 'twas old stuff from many years ago that I knew none of. Concernin' folk neither you or me know." Carrie accepted this and returned to her Sunday chores. Ethel finished the dishes.

Before supper time, Harold returned from buying an afternoon newspaper. He had walked by an accident on Olive Street; a man had been hit by an automobile and a spooked horse had crushed his chest. He died before the police could move him. These kinds of accidents happened sometimes. Between trolley cars, automobiles and horses, people on foot could get hurt. No one knew who the man was.

After dinner she found some time alone. The family gathered in the parlor to play cards and Ethel went to her shared bedroom. The apartment had two sleeping rooms, the kitchen and water closet, and a front parlor. All three girls slept in one room and Harold and Ernestina in the other. Time alone and privacy were rare.

She had never considered that she could meet her father. Now she had, and it was better than what she could ever have dreamed. It was better than anything she could hold or make or anything else she had seen here in St. Louis. *I saw my father.* She had no other words. Her feelings were so strong that her tears began again. Her heart swelled bigger and bigger. When she had fished or been out in the fields, there had been times when she felt she was part of something bigger, grander than normal, and her heart would overflow and peace would sweep through her. Now she felt some of that but she was . . . happy!

A small mirror stood on the chest of drawers. As she looked at her face, she saw his face. The reflection of her dark eyes brought back the sight of his gleaming, almost black eyes. Her eyes swept over her soft, olive skin tones and she recalled his darker-hued complexion; they were different but felt the same. Her hand lingered over her thick dark hair as she tried to remember how his heavy, wavy hair had felt. Mostly she hungered to hear his soft-accented voice calling her "Daughter."

Gratitude swept through her. She'd grown up with the knowledge that she'd been left by her own. She never tried to remember anything before Mercy's Place. Now she had some knowing of both parents. Seeing him had helped her remember a little something of her mother.

That night she dreamed of Avonelle. She usually didn't remember her dreams. Both of them were standing under a big old oak tree, in one of the farm fields. They were happy. He told her that no matter what came, he would be thinking of her. *Always, no matter what comes, daughter, we are together in our hearts. I will look and see you.* When she awoke, she felt he had visited her. The dream was so strong.

She dreamt of her father two or three more times, as she waited for him. For several weeks, Sunday afternoons were tense: she waited for his knock at the front door. But he returned only in her dreams. There she felt him once more. The days turned into weeks, and the only person who looked like her never came back. Her heart saddened from having hoped for something more. She was waiting for Virgil but knew he would be gone for a long time.

She never told anyone who Avonelle was, and their meeting became like a dream. Had it ever happened?

No matter, now she knew who she was. Because her father had come to her, she was no longer alone and without a beginning. Though they never again saw each other, he had given her the greatest gift. She knew from whom she came, who had given her life and that she had been created from love. Years later, when she had her own daughter, she gave his name to the newborn so he would never again be unknown or forgotten.

Chapter 11

America took its time entering the War.

Woodrow Wilson was re-elected in 1916 and tried as the Peace President, early in 1917, to negotiate a European Peace without Victory: all nations would be treated as equals. His approach resonated with both peace-favoring Americans and the war-weary European masses. March saw two significant events. First, Tsar Nicholas' Russian regime was overthrown by the unknown and "liberal" revolutionary government, and secondly, German attacks sank four American merchant ships. On April 6, the Congress officially declared war on Germany, in order to make "the world safe for democracy."

Most of the country entered a pro-war mood. Joining the complicated foreign war required the United States to assemble a modern fully-manned army and required support from every economic sector. Conscription began with a goal of a five-million-man fighting force: a total of twenty-four million men were registered, from whom three million were drafted and two million volunteered.

After proclaiming his age to be eighteen, Virgil Lee Medling enlisted in the army in April 1917, as soon as the United States joined the war. He arrived in the real world, and in short order was disabused of any notion that his charm and earnest manner would pave his way. His initial self-confidence, that life in the military would unfold like his childhood with his indulgent aunts and uncles, quickly faltered. For a rural youth, he was reasonably well-read and knowledgeable about politics, world affairs and the Scriptures. He left home an inexperienced country boy, to go live and work with men. He soon learned how untried he was.

He had never learned to follow orders. One day, during his first weeks, his sergeant assigned him to scrub and mop the barracks floor. He had missed dinner by hours when Sergeant Jakes came to inspect. The sergeant glanced around, shook his head, and ordered the new enlistee to scrub the floors again. Incredulous, hungry and furious, Virgil grabbed his mop and hit Jakes over the head with the handle, knocking him unconscious. Sent to the brig, the new soldier would be court-martialed and deemed an Undesirable. But manpower for the war was desperately needed, so the Army transferred him to the Princess Patricia Light Brigade in Canada. There many unruly, misfit American enlistees landed instead of being dishonorably discharged.

The transfer to Canada gave Virgil another chance. His new platoon trained men in rugged terrain warfare and hand-to-hand combat. His newfound awareness, that he had come very close to sabotaging his plans before he even got started, helped him keep his head down and nose clean. The Canadians found his performance acceptable, and he was sent to France, and later to Belgium, as a combat infantryman. His discharge papers noted that he had suffered war wounds in his left arm and right leg during the autumn of 1917.

Shortly after he joined the Army, the Bolshevik Revolution overthrew the provisional Russian government, which was an ally to the Americans, British and French. When the war ended in 1918, the western Allies tried to stabilize the beleaguered royalist White Russian faction by deploying support troops, including Virgil's Canadian unit, to Siberia. Unlike most American soldiers,

Virgil's military service continued after the war with Germany ended in November. He re-enlisted to serve in Siberia. The mission for the American and Canadian forces was chiefly to guard American armaments stockpiled in the port city of Vladivostok and to support the White Russians' anti-Bolshevik garrison there.

His platoon fought only in skirmishes, when small groups of Bolsheviks appeared. The Expeditionary Forces began their tour in late autumn, and quickly learned that the weather was the real enemy. Guns froze up, supply lines were unpredictable, and horses brought from the more temperate European climate succumbed to the bitter cold. Getting warm was impossible, no matter what shelter was erected or found. All agreed they had never, in their short lifetimes, felt such brutal cold. After a year in Siberia, Virgil was wounded for the third time since seeing combat. This ultimately sent him back home to the States.

His platoon was stationed at a garrison outpost near a tract of woods. During his European Western Front tour, Virgil had been promoted to second lieutenant and was now the platoon leader. One day in the summer of 1919 he led three other infantrymen pursuing a single Bolshevik. Tracking him through the trees, Virgil spotted the fugitive's footprints in the temporarily thawed summer permafrost. Looking up, he saw a dark form moving deeper into the woods. Virgil ran, calling out to his men, figuring he would tackle and hold the enemy while his men caught up to them. When he got closer, the Bolshevik suddenly stopped and whirled around, waving a knife. Virgil crouched, looking into the man's bearded face and large, brown, frightened eyes. The two were about the same age. The flashing knife blade brought back memories of the bayonet that had ripped into his upper right arm in Mons, Belgium. His adrenaline spiked even higher and the same right shoulder felt the heft of his heavy rifle.

Throwing off the cumbersome gun, he leapt forward and pushed his opponent onto the ground. They wrestled and his quarry's strength rolled them over, leaving Virgil trying to keep the stiletto in the man's right hand as far from him as possible. Pounding boots and his men's answering calls rang through the silent woods. On his back, he braced his arms and pushed both hands against the Bolshevik's right wrist, trying to keep the stiletto from plunging into his throat. His adversary's deep, jagged breaths misted in the frigid Siberian air. Time seemed to stop. The spell was broken when both men registered a break in the sound of running steps. Someone had tripped, fell and groaned. In that instant, Virgil's resisting arms weakened and the knife came down, below his eyes, into his nose. His whole body jolted when the blade plunged into his face; blood started pouring everywhere, partially blinding him. He screamed when his assailant pulled out the knife. Later, he vaguely remembered the other body rising and then hearing steps running away. One of his men, Gene, kneeled next to him as Virgil lost consciousness. He was told later that his other two men pursued the Russian while Gene stanched the bleeding by packing the gaping wound with icy mud. After they apprehended the fleeing man, the men claimed his stiletto. They made sure the weapon accompanied Virgil when he was transported to the field hospital. He kept the knife for many years.

While he did not bleed to death, his sinus cavities became so infected that field surgeons had to operate. When he was recovered, Virgil was shipped back to the States. His discharge papers listed his condition as Poor when he was honorably discharged in the autumn of 1919. His sinus condition was severe enough that he was awarded a permanent disability pension.

From April 25, 1917, to the last day of September 1919, Virgil's childish rebellion and overconfidence had been transformed into adult ambition. His military experiences had shown him a much greater world. He saw how men working together could make big things happen. His initial impulse to leave the countryside and see the world had grown into a determination to become someone. His promotion to a ranking officer had whetted his appetite to live well and be known. By late 1919, he had clear ideas about how to begin.

Chapter 12

During his time in the service, Ethel Willard had kept Virgil informed about her whereabouts. He knew she was in Saint Louis, working in sewing factories and boarding with the folks who had brought her from Malden. They arranged to meet soon after his discharge.

They reunited in the city park overlooking the river on a warm afternoon in early October 1919. Virgil arrived first, dressed in his uniform. As he looked for Ethel, his eyes swept over the young women strolling by. After a few moments he turned towards the river, hands in his pockets. He looked at the sky and breathed in the warm moist air. Autumn in Missouri! A slight layer of sweat broke out on his brow and he smiled, relishing the sensation of warmth. He was still mentally adjusting from the frigid Siberian seasons.

He heard his name from behind, and turned towards the soft, calm voice.

"Virgil Medling, is that you?" There she was, Ethel and yet not Ethel. Gone were the flimsy, shapeless cotton shifts she had always worn in the fields, no matter the season. Now, Miss Ethel wore a stylish black dress with puffed sleeves that tapered from her shoulders and closely fitted her lower arms. A wide lace-trimmed bib studded with buttons down the center covered the upper front part of her dress, and the full skirt was short enough to show her bare calves just above her ankles and elegant black heeled shoes. No trace of the country girl remained.

Three years older, her swarthy skin appeared exotic. When she smiled, her slightly crooked teeth startled him with their pearly whiteness. Her manner was as restrained as ever, but she had become a young woman. Her dark penetrating eyes, however, could not hide her feelings. She was entrancing.

"Lord have mercy, Ethel, is it you?" he said. She smiled.

"You aren't the girl I remember when I said good bye to you. You were in the field and . . ."

She broke in with, "Yes, I was pulling ears of corn, and you came at me like a streak of fire . . ."

"You were wearing that thin cotton dress . . ."

Ethel's face softened, especially about her eyes, as she took in his amazed admiration. "Oh, I hate to think how I looked then. But I don't work the fields here. I work . . ." Ethel turned from the park and pointed to a group of buildings west of them ". . . at the Mayline shirt factory."

He looked where she pointed. "Do you like it?"

"Yes. Yes, I do." Her voice was firm. "To work with my hands and with fine detail. I sew the shirt collars, the hardest part. They fetch the best pay." Ethel's voice softened to almost a purr. He had never seen her proud before. Her dark eyes pulled him in.

"You make your own money now. You wanted to leave the farm and make your way, and by your dress, you're doing good."

She shook her head slowly as he spoke.

"What?"

"The people who brought me up here, the McFarlands . . . I stay with them."

He nodded. He knew this.

"They take my pay. They give me some car money and a bit more, 'specially if I need something for clothes. They claim it's right for them to have the rest because I stay there and I eat. I can't save because I can't keep any of what I make."

"That's not right, Ethel. Did you sign anything, or is there any legal power they have over you? No adoption or such?"

She shook her head again. "How do I get ahead? I make the most money of any worker in the factory."

"Truly?"

She nodded, quietly laughing, a couple of her teeth flashing at him. "The shirt collars get the best pay and I stitch so many that I get the biggest pay. I didn't say a word, but when I changed to collars, one of the McFarland girls, Carrie, grabbed my envelope. After she looked, she called it out to the whole group, 'Ethel Mae has more'n any of us!' I was rattled by her knowin' and tellin'. I learned some time ago not to say much about how you do. It's no one's business." She looked sad for a moment, and then her happier look returned. She pulled his arm, and they sat down on a nearby bench where they held hands.

"I'm so glad you're back, Virgil. And you: you look so handsome in your uniform. How're you?" She emphasized "you."

He didn't want to talk about the Army, not right then. He was swept up in seeing her after such a long separation. "That's for another time. I am back, a little worse for wear, but ready to get started."

She looked at him knowingly. "Got to get those plans of yours goin'? I thought of you so often, how you'd find me in the fields. Finally someone's here that comes from where I do, where both of us come from. I've a new life in the city but I've yet to find my own self here."

"I promised to come back t'ya. It's so good to be with you. And yes, good to be here, knowing how we got to this place and this time." Ethel shyly laid her head on his shoulder.

"Ethel Mae, when can you come back to meet?"

She thought for a moment, then said, "Three days from now, same time in the afternoon. The McFarlands will be off to visit for the evening."

He put his arm around her and pulled her close. "Let me think this through, and when I see you next, I'll have a way to get you all your pay and some other lodgings."

She tilted her head and looked at him with soft and tender eyes. "You always come up with plans, Virgil. I know we'll work this out, together." Lifting her head from his shoulder, she glanced over to the nearest large tree and pointed. "See the robins about the nest? They work together for their hatchlings, their little ones. What did you say to me years ago, that day—about our mutuality? I didn't know that word, but I asked and learned it means giving and getting from one another."

"That's right, and together we can be better than we'd be without each other."

They stood up and embraced. He leaned over and looked into his dark-skinned girl's eyes, and they kissed.

"Three days from now, Virgil. May they be good days!" Ethel turned towards the city streets. He stood watching her, while his mind spun with thoughts on how to get her away from the McFarlands.

Chapter 13

Virgil left St. Louis and returned home to Cotton Hill after
he helped Ethel settle into the Clay Street boarding house.
The Dunns joyously greeted his return after two years.
Mary still kept all the men fed and in clean clothes and minded
the house. During his absence, Bardie had married a farmer from
Wayne County. No one knew where the youngest Dunn, Fred,
had gone. He had deserted because he found barracks life too confining. His attempt to return home failed. Edley loved his son but
would not risk the wrath of the law. After two weeks of Mary
secretly feeding the young man at nightfall, Edley met with him,
instead, and told him to either turn himself in and face the consequences or leave for good. The family never saw Fred again.

Virgil's return lifted their sadness about Fred. His military
success as a second lieutenant both pleased and surprised everyone. No longer little, bookish Virgil in their eyes, they marveled
when he spoke of places they had never heard of, let alone seen.
The names France and Belgium sparked a glint of recognition
in their faces but Russia, Poland and Vladivostok left the Dunns
mystified. That he spent a year somewhere that never got warm
was beyond their comprehension. How could a place not have hot
summers?

Despite the plainness of her cooking, Virgil's first taste of

Mary's food made his eyes sting from tears. Being home, with his blood kin, filled his chest with strong feelings. Years earlier he had desperately wanted to get away. Then the house and farm had seemed so limited. Months in Canada followed by months in Europe and finally almost a year in Siberia had transformed what had once felt confining and removed into intimate, safe and warm. His new perspective comforted him through his recovery from his sinus surgery. Being home with the Dunns was exactly what he needed.

Headaches had begun to plague him and he often remained in the house with Mary and his grandfather while Jim and Will tended the farm. Edley had been retired for many years, no longer up to daily farm labor, especially during the winters. On Virgil's worst days, when a headache persisted, he sat with his aunt and grandfather in the kitchen and listened to stories of earlier times in Missouri. Mary added other stories she had heard from her quilting circle. Much of what they spoke about concerned the hardships settler families had endured before the Little River Ditch project began.

The old man would sit at the kitchen table; his long white beard flowed beneath the table's edge, down to his belt. His grandfather never had talked much and had to be drawn out question by question. Virgil knew he had lived an unsettled childhood, partly because the father had moved the family from Tennessee to Mississippi. Edley had left when he was twenty years old and worked for hire or farmed in Missouri. The only ease he would know in his old age would be if he had sons who lived long enough to help him. He was fortunate, because that had happened.

The three were sitting at the kitchen table after lunch, drinking coffee, on a cold blustery November day. "Tell me, Grandpa, about the swamps," Virgil prompted. He loved hearing about the first settlers who came after the Civil War.

Edley looked up from his half-full cup of coffee. The thinning hair on his head was as white as his curly, thick beard. His dark eyes came into focus. "What do you want to know?"

"Something. I never get tired of hearing your stories, if I can get you to talk."

The old man sat quietly for several moments. Then, he began his words in a slow even cadence. "Getting about was always a problem. You would not think so if you are in town or living on the higher, drier prairie parts." He stopped, closed his eyes and leaned back in his chair, raising its front legs off the floor. Virgil sat across the table from him and Mary. If he kept his mind on the story, perhaps the potential fury of his dull headache would not explode above his upper nose and forehead.

"This farm never flooded that I can recall," he prompted.

"Oh, but it did. Only few times, but when it did, only the high hills of the Ridges escaped. Towns got drenched by the spring rains but houses stayed dry." Edley always kept his eyes shut when talking about the past. It seemed he watched inside for the memories to materialize.

"And what were the Ridges?"

"You know Malden?" The old man paused, waiting for a verbal response, but his eyes remained closed.

"Yessir."

"And then there's Kennett, Four Mile, and then Dexter and Bloomfield in Stoddard."

"Yessir."

"All these were built on the Ridge, the first towns. Because they are on the highest ground. There's Big Ridge, where those towns are, and there's Sikeston Ridge up north in Stoddard. All on the highest ground."

"But what about the plank roads?"

His grandfather chuckled. "They started building those when the railroads was built for crops and the logging." He paused again. "Once, logs were floated to a rail track or carried by oxen. The plank roads allowed carrying logs on land. The spring rains flooded everywhere and the plank roads kept the mules, oxen and horses from belly-deep mud. They worked pretty well but needed rework a lot." His words stopped. He reached for a plug of tobacco in his shirt pocket and tucked it under his lower right lip and sucked. Mary and Virgil waited. "I worked in some of the logging camps before I married the first time. As much as farm work can tear a man up, between plowing with mules and clearing the acres, the logging is even harder. Men died."

"I never heard about you and logging, Grandpa," Virgil commented.

Edley slowly nodded and shifted in his chair. His eyes opened, and he leaned forward for his cup. Mary looked up, glanced over, took the empty cup to the stove and filled it with warm coffee. She set the cup before her father, who drank several gulps as if fueling up. His leaning position resumed, he closed his eyes once more.

"Not the most exciting talk, but you seem to want to know. You ever been in a swamp?"

"I've wandered through some marshes when I've been hunting but I've never seen the old swamps from a boat or canoe."

"Years and years before you came along, before your mother left to marry, most of the land in this Bootheel was swamp. Some of it was swamp grasses, marsh you name it, but there were runs of cypress and tupelo mixed in with old oak and sycamore so thick, and the water so high, that boats was the only way to get about. The worst swamps are nearest the St. Francis to the west and those next to the Little River eastward, along the Mississippi. Next county over, Pemiscot is among the worst but west Stoddard, close to where your father came from, next to the St. Francis, had terrible swamps, too.

"I've heard such."

"The swamps went on for miles and miles. I hired onto a logging crew down in Pemiscot. We lived there, sleeping, eating and working." Edley stopped for another swallow. "Never seen trees that big before or since. There was a fellow who gone ahead and marked the trees by thickness and the color of his marks told the boss which size trees to cut first. We had to have a place for each'un to fall right. When a tree was down, then we took it apart so we could get it carried to the closest mill. We stacked the cleaned logs on skids and oxen pulled these to carts that rode the plank roads. Either oxen or mules pulled the carts."

"You said men died?"

"Many got hurt bad and some was left crippled. Downing a tree on hard ground is tricky but doing it in the marshes and swamps is ten times worse. There's no solid ground. Winter, when the mess iced over, we could cut more. On the coldest days at the shallowest places, a felled tree didn't sink much and was readied quick for pulling to the carts. Unless 'twere one of the granddaddy cypress. Those monsters were so thick, I heard some were greater than twenty foot across. Tryin' to fell a tree that great was most dangerous. Yeah, uh-huh, men died." Edley halted. He gnawed a bit on the tobacco plug.

"You saw it, grandpa?"

"During the felling of the biggest one I ever seen. You ever see a tree, a big one taken down when more than one man cuts?"

"Will and Jim cut a big tree when I was maybe eight."

"The tree I'm talking about was bigger than twenty trees that size all together. You can't cut it down with axes alone, 'cause it has to fall right, clear of the men and other trees. If you cut from one side alone, the tree will fall on the cutters. A wedge cut is started that is so big four or five men could lie in it. Standing boards are spiked into each side of the cut so a two-man saw can be used. Usually the standing boards are many feet off the ground or above the swamp water. They called the two-man saw a misery whip. Men sawed in twos and stopped when they got tired or the blade went dull. Then two more men took their place and started sawing. The blades dulled so fast for a granddaddy tree, it could take maybe five saws and many, many hours to get the slice deep enough, right for felling. But the fall of such a big tree can have a mind of its own."

"How do you control the fall?"

"The cutting is across from the fall direction. When the wedge cut is sawed to its deepest, steel pole wedges get hammered in. Depending on the span of the tree, might take six, seven or more men to place the pole wedges and the tree should fall in that line. But that granddaddy tree had its own mind. 'Twas a mighty windy day. The cold should have cut through to our bones but we had worked up such a sweat and we had been at that cuss of a tree since dawn." His voice stopped once more. He'd spoken as much as he would on a typical day. They all sat and waited. Mary reached into her apron pocket, pulled out some mending and started stitching.

The old man swallowed and began again. "Some new young-uns, maybe fourteen or fifteen years, came into the camp the day before. You had to work on smaller trees before the boss let you work on big ones. But there were chores the green fellas could work, like carrying water out to crews. Cutting was terrible thirsty work. The young-un assigned to our granddaddy crew, his name was Hank. I was mebbe twenty-two and showed him around. I did such with the new men.

"He'd come to the camp for money to send back to his mother and the other children. His daddy had died the spring before. The hiring for harvest had ended and he heard about logging, so he came to our camp. In the winter, only weather could slow us down. Hank left a couple of buckets of water and was on his way back to the cook's tent. We'd angled the fall away from the path he took through the woods back to camp. After we drank our fill of water, the boss chose who was to man the pole wedges to start the tree tipping. The men, I think there was maybe ten, stood in a line, each behind a pole wedge. They each hit their pole with a sledge hammer, again and again after a fresh push. At last we heard a huge crack ring through the woods as Granddaddy started to tip. But a gust of wind came at us from the side, not behind us. That tree was so tall, we couldn't see its top. The boss figured the wind must have caught the highest branches and gave enough of a nudge to push the tree more towards camp. Not straight across from us. Trees that big take a time to reach the ground, many counts, maybe a count of eight, even ten. But when it cleared the tree line and hit the frozen swamp ground, we heard a scream." Once more Edley paused. Sadness crossed his face and he shook his head.

"Grandpa, was it?" Virgil was on tenterhooks to hear what he sensed would come. He had to hear the words.

"I liked Hank. I was the youngest, until he came. I ran as fast as I could and was first to reach where the tree top landed. An upper limb had pinned him below, to another tree felled the day before but hadn't been pulled yet. He was crushed but still breathing. Blood was coming from his mouth. He was in terrible pain. I stayed with him while others cut away the upper branch. We carried him back to camp. I stayed with him through the night, and slept next to him in his tent. He was dead by morning. Yeah, men got hurt and a few died. Uh-huh." Edley's slow words hung in the air.

Mary shifted in her chair, looked at her silent father and then into Virgil's eyes. "I never been to swamp camps, loggin' or ditch diggin' but I heard some 'bout what life was like for any wives and children there. Some men brought wives, not having any kin to leave them with. Life outside town is hard when the land has to be cleared but life in a work camp is the worst because there's no cabins. Only tents. Everything's done outdoors except sleeping." Edley nodded at her words.

Virgil felt his headache lifting, almost like hearing these stories took him outside of his body. Edley rarely talked this much and hearing his stories about how the area was before his own birth was a peek into Before Now. Virgil stood up to refill his empty cup. Standing next to the woodstove, he asked, "Mary, if wives were with husbands, then I suppose babies . . ." Mary nodded. Virgil shook his head at the thought. She then pointed to the stove's firebox. He pulled a short piece of wood from the neat pile next to the stove, lifted up one of the stove-top pot rounds and dropped it through the hole onto the fading coals below. He returned to his chair.

She smiled wryly. "Babies do come and birthin' is never easy. Out in a camp it's worse. No bed. There might be another woman about or not. Babies come regardless. The one I heard about, the birthing went well. But she'd had the baby in a tent and her husband was fortunate enough to get some tenting cloth that shielded her even more. The loggers shared big tents and married couples slept with all the rest. But there was no bed. She and the women that helped, everyone was on covered ground. There the baby was born. God must have been looking because mother and baby did fine. But it took some weeks before she could leave and stay with friends in a cabin, some miles away. Leaving out from a camp, weather permitting, took days to get anywhere, to dry land."

Virgil shook his head. "Makes me wonder why any tried with so much swampland all about."

Edley's eyes flew open. "Heaven's sake, boy, you know why! The hope of owning land. Some'll do anything for their own piece. 'Twasn't my lot in life or my sons', neither. But even if I did rent from another, I made enough for me and my own. It's always about the hope and chance it might happen. Some land is easier to come by for farming than other. This ditch digging in all these counties is changing everything. Land is finally becomin' its full worth. Too late for me, but who knows, for you, maybe?"

Virgil looked askance at Edley's words and shook his head. "I love you all dearly. You took me in and raised me. But Grandpa, working the land, my heart's not in it. But your stories have me thinking about what owning land means for some. For my uncles. But for me, going to college is about finding work apart from the land."

He looked at the two sitting across from him. His heart swelled in his chest. "Aunt Mary, you remember the girl at the orphan farm? Ethel Mae?" Mary nodded, her eyebrows raised. "Before I left for the army, she promised to wait for me. I saw her in St. Louis when I returned from Russia, before I came back here. We're to marry sometime this next year."

Both Edley's and Mary's mouths opened and surprise flooded their faces. He was relieved to see no signs of disapproval or alarm.

Mary spoke first. "Virgil, how? You're sickish from the surgery. Right now, adding a young wife, how?" Edley's eyes were alert as he waited for his grandson's answer.

Virgil smiled. "Mary, when she agreed to wait, we talked about working and building our life together. She's a hard worker and makes the most money of all the ladies at the factory. When the time's right, we'll take her savings and set out for the Teachers' School in Cape Girardeau. She'll work while I study and when I'm graduated, I'll support our family. I have no stake as some first born sons do. Where there's a will, there is a way."

Mary reached across the table and touched his hand. Her once black hair was now streaked with gray; she still wore it pulled up and back in a bun. "You do come from different stock, what with William Marion being your father. The Medlings did own

their land. Maybe you wanting to do else other'n farm is different but it's right for you. If you and Ethel Mae can do otherwise
and thrive, you should. If people always did just as their elders,
nothin' would change. 'Sides, I hear with the price of cotton so
low, farming such crops makes nothing."

Edley nodded. "At your age, you've time. Don't be in such
a hurry to start a family until you know what can happen. You
seem to have the luck, though. Having a woman keep things going while you study. You and books, ever since you first learned
to read."

Virgil felt warm and tended by these two. Never harsh, demanding or critical, the Dunns were his emotional home, where
he was always enough. The start of his life after the army, when he
got stronger, filled him with anticipation. Especially starting life
as Ethel's husband. But his return to Cotton Hill, and his mother's
people, made him recognize that they alone held his heart.

Chapter 14

About a year after his return, Ethel married Virgil in the First Baptist Church in St. Louis. A few days after she had told him about her indentured state with the McFarlands, he unexpectedly came to their apartment. Once Ethel joined him in the parlor, he announced to everyone that she was leaving that night. When the elder McFarlands protested, Virgil informed them they had no legal standing: Ethel was eighteen years old. Furthermore, he was going to marry her. She then packed her clothes and left with him. Due to her sweetheart's intervention, she began a new life as his fiancée and lived in the Clay Street boarding house.

The week before their wedding ceremony was as rushed as everything seemed to be in Virgil's life. Ten days before the wedding, the couple traveled south two hundred miles to get their marriage license in Kennett, the county seat of Dunklin. Thirty miles north of Kennett, Virgil brought Ethel to meet the Dunns in Cotton Hill. Their next stop was forty miles farther north, in Cape Girardeau. Virgil would attend the Teachers' College there. They stayed for two days, looking for a place to live after their marriage. After returning to St. Louis, they were married on December 29, 1920.

Ethel quickly noticed how restless her new husband was. He moved forward to the next step in his plans, to become a certified school teacher. Though he spent hours at a time studying the Bible, he seemed to have little peace or calm. Despite always being busy, whether working or taking care of them both, crocheting or tatting lace, she knew moments of stillness and tranquility. She missed her former days working outside. When she'd been alone in the fields, early in the morning or late in the afternoon, if a birdcall sounded, or hawks flew overhead or suddenly a gentle breeze arose, she felt opened up to something greater. Fishing could be the best. With her pole in the water, she felt her breath joined all creatures' breath. In these fleeting moments she was no longer separate but felt part of a larger order. These differences between them prompted her to wonder how she fit into Virgil's plans, what years before he had called their mutuality.

A year after their marriage, when the couple lived in Cape Girardeau, Ethel became pregnant. The town had little factory work and she returned to fieldwork. Her wages were lower, but her pregnancy made her feel fulfilled. When they had stood in front of the minister, in the church sanctuary, she had felt a promise, a possibility. That the losses of their mothers, their families refusing them, and growing up without their parents, could all be set right when he and she brought their children into the world. She believed that raising their own children could restore what had been lost to them when their mothers died. That giving their own children what neither of them had ever had could heal each of them.

While she carried her baby, Ethel felt a reaching back towards her forefathers. She knew little about her parents, but as the baby grew in her womb, inklings of those who had come before her started to gather in her awareness. Like grains of sand flowing through an hourglass, she felt her connection to previous generations, flowing through her to her unborn child, the next descendant.

Her pregnancy was not difficult, but as her delivery drew closer, Ethel's inexperience with childbirth and newborns made her nervous. Clottie, one of Virgil's Dunn cousins, had often helped with babies being born and caring for newborns. Clottie arrived in late August, and her presence soothed Ethel's nerves. On September 5, 1922, Nova Dunn Medling, a boy, was born.

The baby cried endlessly and would not nurse. Nothing the women tried could calm him. Clottie saw the child was sickly but none of her country remedies helped. Six days later, their infant son stopped crying, stopped moving and stopped breathing. Now his still little body lay peacefully in Ethel's arms. She sighed and tears streamed from her eyes. Her swollen, milk-filled breasts ached while she rocked him. He seemed smaller than when he was born. *I have milk for you,* she thought, *but you can't take it.* Her baby's struggle had ended but her own to keep going had begun. On the death certificate, the doctor wrote the cause of death was hemorrhagic colitis. His little bowels did not work right. *Why,* she thought over and over, *why did this happen?*

She resumed working—anywhere possible—late harvest field work, or laundry, or sewing. She felt dazed, half-dead, and spoke little to Virgil. He came home only for meals and sleep. Neither comforted the other. They didn't know how. Their bond frayed and weakened.

During their visits to the Dunns, the sisters tried to comfort them; Bardie had lost a baby a few years earlier. Losing babies was not uncommon, they said, but attempts to explain didn't help the young couple.

That winter seemed longer, colder, darker to her. Gray skies reflected Ethel's inside dullness. When short jobs ended, she became frantic to find new ones. She needed to get away from the apartment where their boy had died. The couple slept with their backs to each other. Mornings Virgil rushed out of the house and continued with school but said nothing about how things were going, good or bad.

Spring's arrival began to lighten the winter's bleakness. The slightest glimmerings of feeling broke through her numbness. She started to sense her body, her breath, her heartbeat. The sunlight and increasing warmth of the longer days heralded a season of new life. An awakening, a growing vibrancy began to stir within her. The silence between the young couple remained, but her hope reappeared. The doctor said she could have another child; they could try again. Virgil, however, was deeply absorbed in school and in his ideas about becoming someone. Ethel's old self was re-emerging but she said nothing. Almost a year after Nova's death, she knew she was ready to begin their family again.

Thunderstorms had cooled the mid-August evening when Virgil came in for supper. She cleared the table after they finished eating, and he opened a book while she washed the dishes. Then she stood next to him where he sat at the table, and waited for him to look at her. When he raised his face questioningly, she held out her hand.

He protested, "Ethel, can't you see I am studying? We have an oral presentation in two days."

She shook her head and smiled. "Come."

Virgil irritably narrowed his eyes. "Come where?"

"Take my hand." She smiled, pressing him for what she wanted and needed. *Truth be told,* she thought, *what we both need.* He put his hand in hers, pulled him out of the chair and led him to the small bedroom.

"It's been a long time, Ethel."

She nodded and sat on the bedside and unbuttoned the front of her dress, staring into his eyes. She pulled open her dress, showing him her breasts, and lay down. "Come."

Her husband lay beside her. They looked into each other's eyes, as they had when newly married. Unspoken grief had raised this wall of silence between them. *Now,* Ethel thought, *we need to tear this down and begin again.*

Despite the death of their first baby, their first son, Ethel believed they could resume their partnership, their mutuality. Virgil reached for her breasts with a shaking, tremulous hand as he searched her face. His eyes swept over her dark skin, hair and mouth. For the first time in a year she felt seen as a woman. He kissed her. She opened her mouth below his lips and, hesitantly, his tongue entered. Her body started to move, her arms reaching towards her husband as her womb throbbed, hoping to be filled. The promise of another chance, another beginning set her on fire.

"It's been a long, long time," Virgil repeated, in a husky whisper. She nodded and smiled, and felt the power she held. She knew he would not refuse. She un-hooked his belt and he pushed her hand away as he finished releasing the buckle and unbuttoned his pants. She reached for his swollen penis as his tongue delicately traveled over her teeth, and traced her tongue. She lifted her skirt. Virgil rolled away as he clutched her hips and lifted her off the bed to straddle him. Shifting her weight onto her knees, she eagerly lowered her moist, parted lips onto his erect member. Both gasped, and she felt once again as she had on her wedding night. Little by little, slowly his tip opened her more and he pushed deeper. She rocked gently, praying that she could stretch wider, and he entered further. Both were tense and breathing hard. Looking down into his face was new: never before had she been this bold, and deliberate: the taker. Before, she'd been the one lying on her back, and he had looked down into her eyes, always the one knowing what their next steps would be. Then, it had seemed proper that he took the lead. Her urgency now disregarded marital propriety. Her body was ready for conception and their next child.

His fullness reached her deepest womb, and they started moving in rhythm. She felt him deeper than ever before because she was on top! Her movements controlled their speed. Virgil's hands held her hips, while they gazed into each other's eyes. Lost in sensation, she lifted and lowered herself again and again. His face tensed and his eyes closed as she felt his penis start to spasm. She met each thrust as he moved faster and faster until he emptied all his seed. Neither moved for many moments and then she slowly rolled off him and slipped onto the bed. Neither spoke.

The following days she reached for her husband frequently, after his dinner or when he awoke, or during his study time. Her craving for sex was new but her hope for a healthy child was more important. Virgil obliged her, for he loved the sex, even though he was no longer an eager bridegroom. The easy, tender days of their courtship and marriage were past. He commented coolly on her increased appetite. *As long as he satisfies me,* she thought, *I do not care.*

For four months they continued in this manner, until she was sure she was pregnant. Then their physical intimacy diminished as her pregnancy progressed. This time she was nervous, even skittish. Her first pregnancy had been normal but the baby had died after a few days. Only when her next child thrived would she be able to relax.

She kept working in the fields while Virgil moved closer to completing his schooling. Her grief receded and she attuned herself to her husband's moods. He became increasingly distant when he was home studying. He seemed to be mulling something over. During her later months, several times each week he did not come home for supper, telling her he had late study meetings. She accepted his absences because her mind was focused on the baby.

Outside Cape Girardeau the spring of 1924 brought the delicate yellow-green of emerging field grasses. Ethel was six months into her pregnancy. Watching spring's fecund transition from winter's dormancy temporarily lifted her spirits. The late spring heat began when she was in her eighth month. Fieldwork became impossible; she took in whatever laundry and sewing she could bring to their apartment, so she could rest as needed. Virgil was looking for his first teaching job. The timing was good because once the baby arrived, she would not be able to work outdoors.

On June fifteenth, Ethel's labor started in the earliest morning hours. Virgil borrowed a friend's car and drove her to the hospital. About twelve hours later, her second child and first daughter was born: Silva Avonelle. The doctor's assurances that the baby was healthy could not calm Ethel's fears. Clottie came back to help for a few days, and the two women anxiously watched the infant, but nothing went wrong. The baby girl nursed and slept, and when she cried, they could hold and soothe her. She was beautiful. Her big blue eyes were Virgil's but her skin, even though lighter like her father's, felt more like Ethel's. As Ethel calmed, she looked to Virgil to see how he felt, for he also had lost a first child. Silva's birth seemed to please him, but his continued detachment troubled Ethel. As she healed from the birth, ever watchful of the baby, she sensed something was amiss. About six weeks later, Virgil came to her.

"Ethel, I know you're happy with the baby and her good health. This is the beginning of the family you wanted for so long." She nodded, with a look at Silva sleeping in the cradle borrowed from Mrs. Hokey, a laundry customer. The baby quilt she had fashioned before Silva's birth covered the infant.

"We're so lucky, Virgil. We had a difficult start when we lost Nova. But Silva got us over that. She's a good baby, and I'm going to expand the laundry and sewing as much as I can. You've one more term in school and then your first job . . ."

"We had a tough break losing our first. This past year I plunged into my studies more deeply and got to know my classmates better. Few of them are married."

When Virgil paused, she tensed up. A shock of alarm coursed through her.

"It's a big load to have a wife and baby when trying to do any kind of degree," Virgil went on. "We've managed so far."

She nodded. Her hand stroked the worn wooden edge of the cradle's headboard, as she asked, "Are you leading up to something, Virgil? Because I don't know what . . ."

"To be blunt, Ethel, we got married too early. I shouldn't have asked you. I didn't see the complications of having a family and setting my ideas and plans into action. There are many unmarried women in my class and the class behind us. I haven't had the chance to know other women. These girls are doing what I am doing. They can understand and talk about what I study and think about."

"How nice for you, Virgil. Yes, you should take this time now to talk with these girls. When we leave for your first job, you won't be surrounded by so many young unmarried women." Her voice remained calm, but her fingers squeezed the cradle's edge, and she shook with fury. What she had been sensing these past months, what Virgil had kept hidden from her, was very close to breaking through to the light.

"Ethel, I wasn't finished. What I'm telling you is I want a divorce. I need to change how I'm living now, so I'm better prepared for later on."

Ah, there it was! Completely visible, fully expressed: they had a brand new baby, and Virgil wanted a divorce. *You think you would cast me and your child off so easily.* The thought raced through her mind. As his father had cast him off and as her widowed stepfather and her mother's family had cast her off.

"I see. Yes, you're being clear. I don't have the book learning and education that you have, Virgil. I'm a country girl. I've worked all my life in the fields, in sewing factories or doing household chores like laundry and sewing. Two children I've given you, which we both wanted." Her words hung in the air between them. Her voice remained steady because what her husband demanded was out of the question. He could not control her part in staying married. He stood very quietly, waiting.

"There'll be no divorce. Never. We have a baby girl who needs us both. We will not do what was done to us. We will stay with her and raise her because we are both healthy and can support her. You will graduate soon. Your plan will be as you said before. Silva will have both her parents in the same house." Ethel finished speaking softly, kindly even, because she knew he had no choice. Virgil usually got his own way. But not this time. She turned on her heel, went into the bedroom and closed the door.

She stood at the door, listening. For several minutes there were no sounds: no footsteps or papers rustling, nothing. All of a sudden, she heard him stomp across the kitchen to the front door. The door creaked open and then loudly slammed closed. The baby began to whimper. Ethel returned to the front room and rocked the cradle, gazing at their baby girl, murmuring to calm her cries.

She was relieved that her husband had left. As her anger eased, a queasy feeling cramped her stomach. What would come next? Virgil would have to live with not getting his way. What would her refusal bring her and her baby? What would be Virgil's next step?

Chapter 15

The drive to Kennett from Doniphan would take another
hour. Grabbing the steering wheel more firmly, Virgil
abruptly shook his head about this second visit. Next
to him, Ethel looked up questioningly from her crocheting. He
glanced over at her, curtly shook his head and turned his eyes
back to the crude country road. Harvested cotton fields lined both
sides of the road, appearing to ripple as they reached away from
the car. His eyes swept across the monotonous stretch of desic-
cated brown sticks this dreary mid-November afternoon.

Autumnal gusts buffeted the occasional clusters of oaks and
poplars near the edges of distant flood ditches. The trees' few remaining leaves provided the fall's last bright colors. The foothills
of Ripley County were behind them and now the eastbound road
cut through the flatter lowland fields. In the rear-view mirror he
looked at the children in the back; his oldest, now usually called
Sissie, was absorbed in her book and four-year-old Bud was napping in the seat's corner with his round blond head thrown back,
eyes shut and rosy lips parted. His snap decision to leave early
had come when he saw the futility of any more effort.

Whatever had been the point? He mused. Contacting his absent
father had always seemed like something he eventually would do.
Especially now, when he had his own family and a solid means

of supporting them. His childhood has been spent as his father's castoff. He never heard his aunts or uncles say it out loud, but he sensed that they felt Will Medling didn't consider any of them to be good enough. Why else had he never returned for his firstborn son? Virgil reached into his coat pocket for the Beech-Nut tobacco packet. He saw Ethel look over and raise her eyebrows when he pulled out a pinch and tucked it under his upper lip. Now, his unsettled nerves would calm.

His newspaper job had made locating his father possible. Virgil had determined that his grandfather, John Alexander, had died eight years earlier, in 1923. But not before both he and William Marion had left Stoddard County and relocated in the Varner township of Ripley County. Their new homes lay among in the lower foothills of the Ozark Mountains, away from the sunken lowlands of Stoddard and Dunklin counties. Months before their first meeting, he had written a letter to William Marion. His father's response had been grudging and questioning but he agreed to a visit. Virgil had disregarded the letter's tone and had come fully prepared, or so he had thought.

The first time they saw one another, the past August, was at his father's house. Virgil and his family had arrived in the late morning and stood in awkward silence after his father's wife, Ada, asked them into the front room. After Ada had given each visitor their own glass of cold tea, William Marion gestured to him and he followed his father out a back door, onto a generous porch. It faced a sweeping stretch of wooded hills that sloped down towards the house. A couple of rockers, with a small table between them, faced the hills. Ethel and the children remained inside.

"This is where I prepare my Sunday sermons," the elder Medling declared and motioned to him to sit down.

"Really. I've been teaching Sunday school since I was fifteen," Virgil offered. He waited for a reaction.

"Care of a congregation requires great diligence and humility. How else can the Spirit of the Lord be heard?" The older man rocked and looked out at the hills.

Virgil felt he hadn't been heard and tried again. "It's true that teaching classes of young children would not require the depth of preparation that a preaching minister needs, especially for Sunday morning services. I'm a working man, with a family to support. But participating in the Church of Christ, in the fullest measure I can, and have all these years, to help build and support the faith and religious education of the young is something we share . . ."

"Preaching the Word has a long tradition in the Medling line. My daddy, your grandfather, preached. His brother, on the other hand, was a doctor. Out here," William Marion pointed at the hills, "in the early morning, when I seek, God speaks." He nodded his head, gazing out, and did not look at his son.

Virgil sat, nonplussed. How could he engage this man? He changed the subject. "I know a little bit about you and my mother. I want to know more. About you and your kinfolk. The Dunns raised me the best they could. I learned self-reliance, how to make my way. Because of my time in the army. When I finished the Teachers' College, I taught grade school." The older man kept rocking and offered no response. Virgil plunged ahead. "I had the good fortune to be hired as a journalist. That's how I found out where you and my grandfather had moved to and . . ."

Virgil stopped speaking when William Marion raised his hand. "You said all this in your letter. I felt you had a right to come and that we should see each other. It's incomplete business. Yes, that's true. Incomplete. And now we should bring some resolution, some clarity, to this, to our situation."

Virgil waited. This stranger who had given him life kept rocking and looking ahead, as if he were alone. He looked at the older man. The additional pounds he himself now carried revealed how similar their faces were. The older man, in his fifties, was gray with remnants of a fair complexion. His round face was bordered by a wide chin and jowls; spectacles shielded his cold blue eyes. None of the Dunns had had blue eyes.

"You, son, have no idea what it was like growing up in Tennessee, especially during those years. The closest town was Dyersburg in Gibson County. Getting there took a half day's buggy ride. My father, John Alexander, was born to a doctor, Francis Marion. The Medlings have been in this country since the 1600s.

We're English stock and helped build this country. We've always been Southerners." William Marion's eyes turned towards him.

He felt like a small boy in the presence of this humorless preacher. The last time he had felt so inconsequential was when he'd left the St Louis barracks in disgrace. He had come to see who this man was, no matter what he did or did not say.

"Tell me what it was like, in Tennessee," he prompted.

He felt the older man assessing him. "Children died. A lot of them. My father, your grandfather, was only one of two sons that lived old enough to have their own children. There had been five sons in all, among many girls. Families were very large. We had to keep having children. With God's blessing, enough would survive."

I, too, lost a child, firstborn and son, Virgil thought. Yes, babies and their mothers died. But he didn't mention the similarity. "Tell me about my mother."

The older Medling swallowed and turned his head back towards the hills. "It was a different time. We'd been in Duck Creek for a few years. After Daddy set up his farm, he gave me a stake, the wherewithal to mortgage some land and buy some animals and plows. I even had enough to hire some men and set in some crops the first spring. When we needed farm goods, we went to Malden, for hardware and such. A couple of the Dunns were doing business in one of the stores and Nettie was with them. Very few young women were in our area and she caught my eye. We went back to our farms and she stayed in my mind." William Marion paused. He turned to face his son. "A few weeks later I returned to Malden and asked about her, where she lived. I rode out to their farm, where you grew up. She answered the door. I asked to speak with her father. I told Edley Dunn I owned my own land and needed a wife. She would come to live in my—our home. Did he agree to my marrying his daughter?"

At these words, a pressure started to build in Virgil's chest. His breathing became tight, as if his chest were bound. His not-knowing of his beginning was disappearing, word by word. Shadowy images started to fill this void: how these two people had come together, how William Marion had entered the Dunns' world, and how his own life had been created.

"And?" he prompted. *Don't stop now. You owe me this, at least.*

"She stood apart from us. I turned and looked into her eyes. She seemed surprised but I saw no repugnance, no abhorrence in her face. She said nothing. Edley said, 'Daughter, we'll be hard pressed without you but you're eighteen. The law says you may marry without my signing. What do you want to do?'" His father's words stopped.

Virgil took his first sip from his glass of tea, no longer chilled. The porch was warm and a breeze had started blowing.

"And?" *Clearly she had said yes.*

"She looked me in my eyes for some moments and asked, 'Where will you take me? I'm my father's oldest. I know mostly Cotton Hill. How far away is your farm?' I told her it was a day's ride to Duck Creek, in Stoddard County. If she needed to come back to visit her kin, that was acceptable to me. But I needed a mate, a wife, to bear me children and sons. Would she come now and marry me?" William Marion raised his glass of tea and his body softened as if a stiffness had released.

Virgil pressed on. "She said yes. And you married."

William Marion paused. "The Dunns, you know this, never owned their land. But I did. My father did. She knew if she came with me, her life would be easier because there would be just the two of us, until children started coming. She had carried the load of doing what her dead mother had, for many years. Edley offered me the hospitality of staying the night. We left at dawn the next morning and just before nightfall, we got our marriage license in Bloomfield. We married on October 16, 1898. Ten months later you were born. Nettie had given me a son. She couldn't have done better."

"Why was I born in Malden and not Duck Creek?"

"I left the birthing business to Nettie. She wanted her sisters and folk in Cotton Hill. My mother was not up to helping her and we Medlings kept to ourselves. I carried her back to Cotton Hill in her last month and the birth went well. You were healthy and a crier. Once I brought the both of you back, she suffered many sleepless nights tending to your colicky ways. After a couple of months, my parents came to visit. You were the first grandchild of John Alexander."

"You brought me to the Dunns just after my mother and your second died. They said I was about eighteen months old." *Now we are at the crux of the matter. How does he justify what he did?*

"When she died, I'd no means, no person to care for you. I was running my own farm and sometimes helped my father. Maybe if her family had been farther away, maybe if more of my brothers and sisters were older, with their own families. None of that was true and taking you to your mother's family was most reasonable."

"But you never came back. You never visited or wrote." His voice choked and emotion rushed through him. *Why now?*

The older man looked back coolly. "You think I abandoned you. Many might see it that way, I'm sure. My father was a more fortunate man than his father. Maybe it was the times or where he lived. Certainly it's why our family moved to Missouri in the early 1890s. None of his children died as young or often as his father's had. It's a terrible thing to lose babies when they are born or die within the first years of life. But as bad as losing babies can be, it's even worse when they die as young boys or girls or young men. All that happened to Francis Marion, a doctor. This was during the bad years of yellow fever and malaria and people of all ages died in Tennessee, many in the river lowlands. Land prices in Missouri had fallen, especially in Stoddard County where much of the cleared land needed draining. So my father decided to move his family there. The youngest, my sister Grace, was just seven."

Impatience surged through Virgil. He'd been waiting for these answers all his life. "You still haven't answered the question," he insisted.

William Marion nodded. "I'm getting to it. You've come for your answers and you'll get them, though I'm not sure they will bring you any comfort." He took another drink from his near empty tea glass. "The Medlings in Tennessee, especially my grandfather Francis Marion, were fairly prosperous. Despite the war, he sent his second son, William T., to medical school. My father was schooled in his letters but chose farming. My grandfather agreed to settle a comparable stake on him, for his start. Father was successful enough that when we moved to Stoddard, he settled a small stake on me, as his first born son. And when I brought your mother to her new home, she had security she'd never known as a tenant farmer's daughter."

Thoughts surfaced about what the Dunns had never voiced. "Did you feel we were less than those you came from?"

"You, of course not. You've my blood running in your veins. My branch of the Tennessee Medlings had proven themselves some time ago. We became, especially my grandfather, prominent members of our communities. He was the doctor for the whole of Gibson County. And his son, William T., too, became Gibson's doctor. I've heard that William T's son, William Linn, the third generation, my cousin and yours, also continues as the county's doctor. We were property owners and had influence, well before the Civil War. But the Dunns, at least Edley's line, had limited means. He told me his family had moved through many southern states, Tennessee, Mississippi, then Arkansas, and finally settled into Cotton Hill. I heard of his death a few years ago. My understanding's that none of his sons own their own land."

Virgil nodded. No one moved off the farm unless they worked for another landowner. Working the soil was all the Dunn boys knew. He had escaped their fate only because he had run off and pursued a different path.

William Marion continued. "It is like the parable our Lord told of the talents one is given. Does one bury what one has, hoping to keep them safe, or does one take what they are given and grow them into something greater? My father and I chose to invest in the land and become self-sufficient. If your mother had lived, she and you would have shared the fruits with me. Regrettably, she died. When I returned from leaving you with the Dunns, I had to sort out what had gone wrong. I concluded that some of what my grandfather suffered had fallen upon me. This time, though, I also had lost a wife. Had I made a wrong choice? Had I displeased God and been marked? Was losing both my wife and child a sign of my own pride and willfulness? If I surrendered the fruit of this first union, the one that I had not prayed about, could I move forward with God's favor? I couldn't forget Nettie after I saw her that once, but rather than seeking God's will, I went ahead on my counsel alone. I cost my wife her life, our baby's life. Surrendering you and leaving my failure in the past was the right thing to do."

Virgil was stunned. Failure? Grandfather's suffering or curse? Surrender? Wasted talents? "You remarried," he commented. He sensed no remorse or regret in anything his father spoke.

William Marion nodded. "After a time. My life as a married man had been ripped apart. I was able to make my mortgage payments; the crops sold well enough. My heart was broken, and my overriding sense was that I had lost my way with God. It was best for me to ask for forgiveness and wait before I tried to start a family again. Also, my father told me I had married too quickly. We'd always been close as both of us are first sons. His favor was important and I leaned on his advice."

William Marion tapped the arm of his rocker and leaned his head against the chair's back. "This was a powerful period of reflection. I felt my patience grow and many blessings flowed from God. I felt called to preach part-time. And started, during the cold months. Three years passed and Ada came to a preaching I gave in Duck Creek. We prayed together and waited on the Lord. She was a widow with a daughter, Opal. After a year, we married in 1905 and within a year, she gave me Clarence, our first son."

Virgil's memory of Mary and Jim talking in the kitchen, when he was seven or eight, suddenly erupted. They'd been talking about Clarence.

His father continued. "I felt blessed once more as a father. Three years later she had a baby girl. At least we had many months with her, before God called her home. We had Goldie a couple of years after that. I felt whatever had marked Francis Marion had been lifted from me." Once more his father looked him the eyes. "I never returned to see you or wrote you, because I was afraid."

"Of what?"

"I knew you were safe and had enough. I'm not a man of intense emotions. I missed your mother; she was a good mate. Our life together was very simple and centered about the farm and raising a family. She went to church with me but never understood my love for God. I would talk to her about the Word. I'd read passages to her and tried to explain them to her. She let me but her heart wasn't in it. After I gave you to the Dunns I felt it best to stay away. None of the Dunns were strongly committed to the Word. Their life was the farm. I was afraid that if I had any connection with you, perhaps the suffering of my grandfather would return. It could have been dangerous for you and for my other children. It was for the protection of everyone."

He considered his father's reasoning. Had the loss of Nova Dunn been part of Virgil's great-grandfather's curse? It too much to sort through now. "I felt it was important to bring you your grandchildren, Silva Avonelle and Virgil Lee. It seemed silly for you never to meet them. We're close enough to visit."

"It's good to see the new generation. Clearly you have succeeded in your life. They are my first grandchildren, thank you." His father spoke factually but without strong feeling.

The back door opened, and a vibrant young woman, in her early twenties, burst onto the porch. "Daddy, aren't you finished yet with my half-brother?" She turned to Virgil, who rose to his feet at the sound of her voice. She thrust her right hand towards him, "Virgil, I am Golda, but everyone calls me Goldie." They shook hands as she spoke. She tilted her head, with its stylishly short hair, and looked over at her father. She wore a simple light-colored short-sleeved blouse with an open collar over a flowered mid-calf pleated skirt. "We've been waiting ever so long. It's rude to keep him all to yourself."

She hooked her right arm through Virgil's left and slowly led him toward the door. "Virgil, I hope you and Daddy have finished, because Mother can entertain your lovely Ethel, Sissie and young man Bud only so long by herself. Daddy, are you going to join us? Or would you rather ponder those hills a bit longer?"

Virgil stopped and looked back at William Marion. His humorless father kept rocking and looking out at the hills. His lively, light-hearted sister's sudden intrusion, with her take-charge manner, dispersed his intensity. For the first time since he arrived, Virgil relaxed and smiled. He instantly liked her.

He turned to William Marion. "Thank you for your time and

explaining what happened. I'm sure this won't be the last time we see each other." The older man looked at the both of them, nodded and then turned his eyes back to the hills.

Goldie led him back to the parlor where Ada, Ethel and the children sat. The room was furnished with overstuffed loveseats covered in subdued flowery upholstery and a few hand-crafted curio cabinets. Dressed in a darker day dress, Ada wore a delicate white sweater. Her grey hair, too, was stylishly coiffed. He guessed her to be the same age as his father, in her fifties.

As soon as he entered the parlor, young Bud jumped off the sofa and ran to him. Both his small hands clutched his father's left hand. "How much longer are we going stay, Daddy?"

He knelt down to look the boy in his eyes. "We'll be leaving in a little while. Have you been minding your mother?" The little boy quivered with pent-up energy. Virgil knew he could be quite rambunctious when surrounded by neighbor boys. Ethel caught Virgil's eye and shifted her gaze to the boy. She mouthed, "He's hungry."

"Ada, do you mind terribly if young Bud got a little treat, an apple or some bread and butter? Sorry to impose . . ."

"Nonsense, Virgil, you're Will's son and Bud, here, his grandson. Let me fix him a little bit and you all spend some time with Goldie before you leave." The older woman took Bud's hand and led him to the kitchen.

"I'm so glad you wrote our father, Virgil. He never would have written you." Goldie's outspokenness charmed him. Her verbal fluency appealed to him in the same way as the more educated women he had met at the Teachers' College, and others from his work life. He almost wished she wasn't his sister, he felt so comfortable with her. *Watch it, boy! She really is off-limits.*

"Well, sister mine, how about that? Not only did I meet my father but I found a sister, too!"

"Sorry Clarence isn't here, but he has some other family things going on. So, I have you all to myself." She glanced at Ethel and Sissie. "I love your wife and little girl. Promise me, brother mine"—she smiled winningly and fluttered her eyelashes—"no matter what happens with you and Daddy, we'll stay in touch.

I think we'll get along just fine!" Goldie really had been the high point of this first visit, he thought.

Despite the strangeness of that first meeting with William Marion, Virgil had found a connection to the Medlings: his own generation of them. Goldie made sure he knew where his cousin Steve, a lawyer, lived in Caruthersville. Her flirtatious enthusiasm overrode any hesitation he'd felt after hearing William Marion's story.

His father—they had the closest blood connection. But the older man's revelations had left him cold. He bestowed only facts. There were few people Virgil could not charm, Ethel being one of them. Now he could add his father to that short list. Another meeting should clarify which Medlings would want to be part of his life.

Several weeks after that August visit, he had written to ask William Marion if they could meet at the Baptist church in Doniphan for the Sunday morning service. The eventual reply suggested a Sunday in November: his father would not be preaching that day. Virgil confirmed that date and offered to take everyone out for a midday dinner afterwards.

Attendance was very high that November day. The church was large and imposing; the community could support a full-time minister. Harvesting was complete, Thanksgiving and Christmas holidays were coming, and people came from the entire township. When Virgil's family arrived, Ada and Goldie stood outside and greeted them warmly before they all entered the church.

As Virgil entered the pew where William Marion and his family were seated, his father nodded to him and said nothing, not even to his grandchildren. Ethel had dressed Sissie and Bud in their best clothes and the little girl was ready with a Bible quotation Virgil had her memorize. She never had the chance and his stomach tightened with dismay. His father's somber and taciturn demeanor remained unchanged. Virgil decided to expect little.

After the assistant minister completed his sermon and the offering plate had traveled through all the pews, Virgil chose his opening. After finding the verse from the sermon, he asked, "With your years of studying the Word and preaching, what other insights have you about this verse?" How to address this man? "Father" hardly felt appropriate, neither did "William Marion," and "Mr. Medling" was even more absurd.

He waited for his father's response, while Ada, Ethel, his children and all the other members of his father's group stood and made their way from the pew to the front door. Ada bent to his father and murmured, "We'll wait for you two outside." She smiled at Virgil and entered the center aisle.

When they were alone, William Marion turned to him. "He spent a lot of time speaking of forgiveness. We do need to forgive, as our Lord counseled . . ." Virgil found himself listening for what his father did not say. ". . . But how do we distinguish what we think is our heart and love, from willfulness cloaked as the right thing to do? We should forgive and embrace what was lost to us, but when? And under what circumstances? Even if we are the ones to be forgiven, is this the right time to embrace and reincorporate what or who was lost? Forgive, yes, as our Lord exhorted, but to bring back into the fold what was left behind so long ago? Out of necessity, perhaps, the circumstance calls for a different resolution." *A continuation of what he started in our first encounter*, Virgil thought. *But what do I really know of his life, since he gave me away?*

The older man's words continued. "To address our—your and my—situation: I've told you what happened and what I chose to do. I see you, now, as a grown man, able to stand on your own, beholden to no one. That is good, good indeed. You're mannerly and respectful but I don't know you. How could I? Such has been the decree of fate, the Lord's will. You were the sacrifice I made, to find my way back to God. As Abraham obeyed the Lord and prepared to offer his only son, Isaac, as a sacrifice, so I felt that letting you continue your life with the Dunns, without interference, was what was required of me. Both of us, you and I, have lived what was required from each of us." The older man turned his face to the altar.

Abraham and Isaac, what an imperfect analogy and faulty justification! Anger started to rise and then resignation damped it down. William Marion looked into his eyes, again. "But there's a singular difference between you and me, and our lives. I've lived most of my time and you've most of yours left, God willing. I pray you make the right choices and lean on the wisdom of the Lord."

Virgil stood up and looked down at his father. "Sir, thank you for this opportunity to spend time with you. Perhaps a meal together is too much to ask. But before we leave, I want to take some pictures of the whole group." He held out his hand and William Marion awkwardly took it. They shook briefly. His father's handshake was soft, almost flabby. After they released hands, Virgil left the pew. He strode quickly towards the front doors, craving the cool fresh air that would meet him. Ahead, congregation members were still gathered, waiting their turn to speak to the minister. Slower footsteps sounded behind him. When he reached the church's open double doors, he waited for the older man to exit first. Outside, Virgil searched the milling parishioners for the Medlings and his own family.

Ethel, the children, Ada and Goldie stood near the bottom stone steps. A few of the other Medlings were couples, in smart city clothes. The women wore heavier calf-length coats that covered their skirts and small beret-like hats capped the short hair styles that exposed the napes of their necks. Only Goldie stood bareheaded, without a coat or scarf. She stepped towards him.

She took his right hand, "What's next, brother mine?" Her eyes sparkled, and he knew he would disappoint her.

"We need to leave, Goldie. I think it's best. I'd rather not tire our father. But here," he reached into his front pocket and pulled out a wad of cash, "I promised a midday dinner. Please be sure that you all go ahead and have the meal on us."

As he anticipated, her face fell. "Say it's not so, Virgil! I have been looking forward to this for days . . ." He pressed the money into her right hand and closed her fingers over it.

"Goldie, before we go, we need some pictures of everyone, together." He looked over at Ethel. "Ethel Mae?" She smiled, nodded and pulled a camera out of her large satchel. Stepping closer to Goldie he said in a low voice, "Finding you has been the best part. I'll be in touch. No way we won't be, I promise." He saw her dejected look, took her hand, raised his voice to the group, and called out, "We gotta take some shots. I'm a newspaperman: we can't go anywhere without a camera!"

The group formed two lines on the two stone steps. William Marion chose to remain by himself at ground level, and faced right, near the group's right side. He kept his hat on and carried an air of resigned toleration. Goldie, Clarence, two of his friends and their wives joined the group picture. Ada and the children waited to one side while Ethel snapped the family pictures. On the top step, Virgil stood on the group's left end. The group picture couldn't serve as an expression of family unity and possibility. Instead, it was a record only. Afterwards, he took separate pictures of Goldie, Clarence and a couple of male cousins from Ada's side of the family.

After thanking Ada, and saying goodbye to his half-siblings, Virgil spoke last to William Marion. "You said we had an incomplete situation between us. Please consider it completed. Thank you again, sir."

Ethel stood waiting with Sissie and young Bud. As they parted from the group, he knew he had made the best choice. Returning to what was familiar and known would be a relief.

Halfway back to Kennett, the tobacco plug had smoothed his edginess. He thought about his father's last observation. What Virgil could do with his life very much lay ahead. He'd always gone after what he wanted. He'd had his rough moments and setbacks but somehow he always got back on course. Rumors had surfaced about a job opening on the Poplar Bluff paper. He would keep pushing ahead. Who knew what the limits could be? He always had believed that God was on his side. Even staying married to Ethel, no true stumbling blocks had appeared in the offing.

"Do you want to stop somewhere and eat?"

Ethel looked up from her needlework. "Do you have any money left?"

He chuckled. "You know I always keep something squirreled away, just in case. There's a little filling station about five miles up the road, with sandwiches and sodas. We'll stop there. That'll wake Bud up. Sissie, you're awfully quiet back there. Something got your tongue, Princess?"

Her perpetual frown smoothed from her brow and she looked up from her book. "No, Daddy. You were so quiet and I wanted to stay the same."

He chuckled again. "Okay, Princess. Now recite for your Dad the Scripture you were going to say to your grandfather. Don't rush and speak clearly."

The girl drew in a deep breath and spoke her first words haltingly, "And, lo, the angel of the Lord came upon them and the glory of the Lord shone round about them and they were sore afraid . . ." His mind drifted back: *Yes, all's right: I have the majority of my life ahead of me. I grew up without a father and that never stopped me. Why he left me, those are his reasons, his justifications. They have nothing to do with me. He answered my questions and I know more about the Medlings than before, but the Dunns are my true family. Full steam ahead!*

Chapter 16

T he period in the Medlings' lives from 1920 to 1938 was documented through my mother's childhood memories, marriage licenses, birth and death certificates, family photographs, a family bible, censuses, newspaper articles, insurance maps, Jefferson City street directories, archived court proceedings and prison documentation. The following unfolds chronologically from 1924 to 1938. Through this period, outwardly, my grandfather, Virgil Lee Medling, led an increasingly successful life.

Ethel stood in her garden in the little Bootheel railroad town of Campbell on a sunny summer day. Fourteen years had passed since she had worked in the farm fields outside Cape Girardeau. Well into her thirties now, she was stocky and thick-waisted and her hair was snow white. For years, she had dyed her early greying hair. When they fled Jefferson City just months before, though, she stopped. The longer the family lived in the capital, the more hidden she had become from Virgil's public life. There, she rarely joined him at public functions, but he frequently brought people to the house for dinner. Then she cooked, served and cleaned up after her husband's guests. Keeping her hair dark seemed necessary and reasonable.

When Virgil began teaching in Hornersville in 1924, their

family life's new tenor persuaded her to dress more simply. Her husband either worked long days or came home only on the weekends. Simple dresses and heavy black heeled shoes were practical and required minimal upkeep. They were cheaper, too. It hadn't helped that he never gave her enough cash to run the household. Between their underlying tensions and keeping home life as normal as possible for the children, her health suffered. She had aged quickly. Now, fallout from his scandal forced their retreat to Campbell and threatened their survival. She planted the garden as soon as spring's warmth had arrived.

Weeks later, the rows of string beans were bearing well; she would pick some for supper. Corn would be ready in about a week. She inspected the row of potatoes. The vines were healthy and she saw only a few potato beetles. Maybe in a couple of weeks she could start digging the larger young potatoes. She bent over and quickly plucked off the pests. Not enough to share: away with you! Behind her, the clucking young hens scratched for worms; they were beginning to lay. One less thing to buy; how to stretch what little money remained? Sissie and Virgil had left earlier that morning for some filling station in Tennessee they would run for the summer, while he—no, make that all of them—waited.

Making things work, and working, seemed to be what she always did. What to do, or in which direction to swing, whenever Virgil pulled a new plan—or a new mess—out of his hat. Living with his whims, would she have chosen differently if she could have seen into the future, that day long ago in the cornfield? What good did it do now to question her ancient choices? Nothing past could be changed. She needed to make work what was here, today, now. Virgil had offered no explanation when he suddenly announced that they were leaving Jeff City, but she had known whatever had happened must have been very, very bad.

Her thoughts drifted to the day fourteen years before, when he came running into their Cape Girardeau apartment. Weeks after she'd refused him a divorce, the front door had suddenly swung open, slamming the inside doorknob into the wall, as he entered, triumphantly waving a torn envelope. Excitement flushed his pale cheeks; his blond hair was windswept.

"Ethel Mae, it's done! I found my first teaching assignment! Hornersville."

"When do we need to leave, Virgil?" Her quiet voice had been tight with strain. They had talked very little since she had refused him a divorce. When he was home, most of what she said in his presence was to young Silva. Today's news had thawed Virgil. He was effusive.

"We're paid up through the month. I can go down to Hornersville and find a place while you pack up. When I get back, we'll load the car and be on our way." The next step in Virgil's plan had begun to unfold.

Life in Hornersville began uneventfully. The change in towns and apartments seemed to dissolve their marital distance. Virgil threw himself into his new job. His many years teaching Sunday school had primed his innate teaching ability. He loved to tell stories, making social connections and relationships with his students, co-workers or superiors. After settling into his new job, he resumed Sunday school classes at the town's Baptist church. Had his interest in other women waned? She wondered.

For the first time in her life, Ethel was able to stay at home with Silva and not work for pay. Never idle, she continued to quilt, crochet, and tat, and kept their home immaculate as she tended their infant daughter. Sitting with her needlework, however, she was not at peace. Her husband did support his family. They did have a healthy, vibrant child. But being a housewife and mother was not relaxing or soothing, with Virgil whirling through her life like a small twister. She felt out of place. Tension and edginess were her daily companions.

Unconsciously she became attuned to every nuance of his demeanor. Her shattered trust had made her vigilant. At the same time, his current satisfaction with his new position and associates dissolved his tension towards her. His affection for Silva showed that he accepted being her father. Much of his time outside of work he was gone. He explained only when she asked. His increasingly busy life was absorbed by work, church, meetings and cultivating connections. His home filled in the few remaining hours. She sensed that he had not changed his mind about other women.

It would be a relief to know, once and for all.

Their first Christmas season in Hornersville brought the sound of the second shoe dropping. A knock sounded at the apartment's front door while she washed the baby's clothes. A young woman stood in the doorway, nervously holding a wrapped present.

The stranger hesitantly stammered, "Is this where Mr. Medling lives?" Her dress was simple. A heavy, dark woolen coat shielded her from the biting mid-December wind. Her left hand clutched the crown of a hand-knit hat as another gust blew about her.

Ethel looked into her pretty, flushed face and big blue eyes. "Yes, it is. Can I help you?"

The woman thrust the package towards Ethel. "Mr. Medling has been so helpful and kind. I wanted to leave a token—my appreciation—what with it being the Christmas season . . ." her voice halted. She looked questioningly at Ethel. "And you are?"

Ethel's jaw tightened. "I'm his wife and the mother of his baby girl. I'll take your present and be sure he gets it." She took the gift, which was tied with a generous red bow. "Goodbye." She closed the door in the girl's shocked face.

Her back against the door, she began to shake from surging adrenaline. Her heart pounded. What to do? She tore at the ribbon and ripped open the box. Wrapped in plain tissue paper lay a knit blue scarf. Its color would make Virgil's eyes stand out. She felt the yarn's texture; it was good quality wool although the stitches showed a novice's skill. The costly material further substantiated the girl's infatuation with Virgil. Had she known he was married and a father? Now she did.

Ethel had been right all along. Yes, Virgil had stayed with her and their baby. At the same time he was not denying himself the companionship of those other educated, like-minded women who—as he had phrased it that day—could truly understand and talk about the things he studied and did daily. Silva started whimpering. Ethel sighed. She left the open box and scarf on the kitchen table to go to the crib.

Confirmation of her suspicions brought no relief. Each subsequent gift increased her rage and humiliation. Sometimes it was a pair of gloves, or maybe a book of poetry by some long-dead writer she'd never heard of. Or another scarf. While no woman ever again came to the apartment to deliver a gift for him, gifts had continued to arrive during Christmas seasons or around his birthday for the next few years.

Her feet still planted in the dirt, Ethel shook her head and the row of peas came into focus. She knelt down and started to pick some plump pods; she could shell enough for their supper tonight. That had been the real beginning of the next fourteen years, hadn't it? *Always I knew there was — or would be — a woman, or more, wherever he worked. Never did I think, though, that he could go as far as he had in Jefferson City.*

Silva was about two years old when, one afternoon, Virgil came home unexpectedly. He was in a serious but expansive mood. In the small parlor, Ethel sat quilting and Silva played on the floor with cut pieces that would later be sewed into the quilt top. The toddler was singing a song, of a sort, as she picked up and laid down the shapes into her own patterns. Mother and daughter made a pretty domestic picture. Ethel looked up from her stitching, surprised by Virgil's untimely appearance before dark.

He knelt by the little girl and looked at her trail of cut pieces. "Sissie, darling, that looks so pretty. One day, though, you'll go to school like your Dad and do great things." He picked her up in his arms and gazed down at Ethel. "Ethel, I think we need another child. You're able to stay home and look after Sissie. Another child would be perfect. Maybe we might have the son we both want."

She looked hard at him and said softly, "Are you sure about this, Virgil?"

"As sure as you were, Ethel Mae, before we had Sissie. There was no stopping you until you were sure you'd conceived. Don't you want another? Wasn't having a family, our own children, something that you saw as completing you? To be a mother, to be a parent, as a way of leaving behind what you yourself never had?" His eyes were steady and she saw how much he wanted her to want this. She sensed, though, that something else lay beyond his words. What now? He was promoting another child because somehow it would be to his advantage. Her own course was set and another child did make sense. Ethel dropped her eyes to her quilt and slowly took another stitch. As she pulled her needle up from the underside, she looked into his eyes and nodded.

"Then we start tonight, after my little Sissie, my princess, goes to sleep." Virgil left the parlor, carrying their prattling blond, blue-eyed daughter. She heard the front door open and he took Silva outside. Ethel sat very still and thought about how this pregnancy would be not be driven by her need to bear new life, but instead was another link in the chain of Virgil's plans.

In June 1927, Virgil Lee Medling Jr. was born. Ethel's second son and third child was not named in honor of previous generations. Instead he was his father's namesake. The usually absent father and his son were not close. Ethel raised the boy as best she could. Virgil was too busy living his outside life to be very involved.

Peas and snap beans sat in her harvest bowl; a few eggs were left in the icebox. Boiled store-bought potatoes would complete supper. Now eleven years old, Buddy had a large appetite. She had just enough milk and bread for breakfast. She would have to shop afterwards and the grocery tab was getting high. Virgil said there was enough money to keep them in food for several months. Thank goodness for the Singer sewing machine he had bought her several years ago. Once back in Campbell, she immediately put out the word that she was available for any type of sewing. He had bought her the Singer in 1930 when he landed his first journalist job in Kennett, Dunklin's county seat.

Wherever they lived, Virgil routinely joined the local organizations and connected with that town's leaders. The local church was another place he forged connections. Virgil made sure that friends and associates knew of growing connections he was making, as a newspaperman, throughout the Bootheel. Another opportunity arose within a year and he was reporting for the *American Republic* newspaper in Poplar Bluff. Early in 1932, he bought the house in Campbell. Its location ensured the perfect arrangement in his home and work lives: he came home on the weekends and stayed elsewhere during the weekdays. At home and in town, he was the proper, upright Sunday school teacher, and an established journalist. During the weekdays, he went where he needed for his journalistic work and politicking, and met his women in the evenings. Gifts no longer came to their house.

She didn't know much about Virgil's political connections but his years at the *American Republic* proved lucrative in his continued search for success. His stories about life and doings in the Bootheel attracted the attention of influential people throughout the state; none the least was that up-and-coming politician from Independence, Harry Truman. The Truman and Medling families socialized occasionally and Sissie had been dandled on the future President's knee. The dealings of influential men, in their meetings and critical conversations, however, were conducted apart from the womenfolk and children. These were the times of backroom political deals accompanied by cigar smoke, shots of whiskey and sometimes cash.

The Pendergast machine, operating out of Kansas City, was at the height of its power and corruption. Tom Pendergast's influence was so pervasive he was able to "help" Harry Truman become a state judge from the four-county area around Kansas City. Later on, Pendergast helped Truman become the junior senator from Missouri. In 1932, Pendergast's machine delivered the Missouri Democrat vote, which helped elect Franklin D. Roosevelt to his first presidential term. Virgil circulated in the outer orbits of corrupt state politics but no one close to him knew the details. Ethel certainly didn't. But she did know his infidelities continued.

As she bent over to pick up the bowl of freshly picked vegetables, she felt a sharp twinge. It was under her right ribcage, at her gall bladder scar. The surgery had been performed two years before in Jefferson City, when things with Virgil were at their worst. *Well, their worst except for now,* she thought, as she waited for the twinge to ease. Her health had been deteriorating for a number of years: she had been hemorrhaging heavily and a Jefferson City doctor had treated the recurrent bleeding. Most likely no one in Campbell would know what to do if it started again. *An old familiar song,* she thought. *We do what we can and pray for the best; it is all that we have.* Fourteen years of struggling with Virgil's schemes had worn her, but with two children to raise, she had little recourse but to get up each day and get through. Protecting her children and herself, honestly, was uppermost.

Late in 1932, after Roosevelt's victory, Virgil had come home and announced he had been hired to work in the State Auditor's office in Jefferson City. He would be starting in the new year. Initially he commuted while settling into his job. His monthly salary was $200, huge for the Depression years. His boss was State Auditor Forrest Smith and Virgil worked as the managing clerk for the Blind Pensioners' Fund. Working in the state Capitol put him in the center of state government politics. He had arrived!

The next year, 1934, the family moved from Campbell and joined him on Moreau Street, just across from the Moreau Elementary school. Sissie literally just walked across the street to school. Buddy would begin first grade and for the first time in her life, Ethel had many hours free each day. Jefferson City was a much smaller, a more intimate city than St. Louis and her return to city life was gentler. Life in the capital city did bring significant changes to all of them.

Now they all lived together. The Capitol building was downtown and Virgil traveled out of town infrequently. His habit of chewing tobacco daily invaded her life. It required spittoons throughout the house, which she emptied and cleaned. He claimed a skin sensitivity to water and would only sponge-bathe. Accordingly, he liked to change his shirt several times daily, so she routinely laundered and ironed enough shirts for a week's worth of three daily changes. On the other hand, she encouraged the children to take daily baths and their once-used towels and washcloths went into the laundry hamper. She kept the house pristine.

She and Virgil had separate bedrooms. He kept his room unheated, with the windows cracked open during the winters. In there, his "reading" wall was lined with stacks of racy detective story magazines, the contemporary version of tame pornography. Now physically united, the family became overtly divided in its loyalties. Ethel tolerated and coped with the range of Virgil's idiosyncrasies, all of which their daughter noted. Sissie uneasily straddled the chasm between her parents.

The young girl loved her father but never hesitated to say what she thought. She was quick-witted and often sarcastic, but never with Ethel. Her father loved her spunk but would deal with her unwanted impertinence. He never struck either of his children. Instead, he adopted the military approach of physically demanding tasks such as carrying in heavy pieces of firewood. In the end, his ill-humor never lasted. Father and daughter always made up and their temporary strains dissolved. The girl, however, knew too much about her parents' marriage.

Occasionally traveling baseball teams came through Jefferson City and Virgil loved baseball. One time he got free tickets and took eleven-year-old Silva with him. It was an early June Saturday afternoon. Both had been excited when they left the house and Silva was bubbling about seeing her first live game. When father and daughter returned that evening, each was quiet and not looking at the other. Both disappeared into their respective bedrooms. Ethel went to Silva's room.

"What happened, Sissie?"

The young girl's downcast, bespectacled face was streaked with tears. She shook her head slowly as she sat on the side of her bed, swinging her feet. Ethel's heart ached for the girl. "We had a good time at the park. And the teams were pretty good for minor leagues. But on the way back, Daddy started to talk about you. And I stopped him, right there, right then. 'You stop it!' I said, 'Stop it! Don't you say anything about my mother . . .'" Silva started to sob.

Ethel sat down and gently hugged her. "Now, Sissie, it's all right. We're getting used to being together again. It's been a few years since your father and us lived in the same house, all the time. Virgil loves you. You're his pride and joy. It'll smooth out. It always does, between you two. Let it go, right?" Ethel pulled a handkerchief out of her dress pocket and handed it to Silva. In a soft, low voice, she said, "You're a good girl, to both of us. We're lucky you came to us," and gently rocked the girl as she blew her nose. Silva sniffed and nodded quietly. "Come help me with dinner. It's almost ready."

Recalling that moment, Ethel felt the twinge let go. She picked up the bowl and walked into the kitchen. She learned that day how protective her oldest was. For the first time since Avonelle had come to her that Sunday afternoon, one of her own cared for and even defended her. She was no longer alone. Her daughter would not tolerate anyone, not even her father, saying something unkind or untrue about her mother. As Ethel watched the peas popping out of their pods, her heart pained at memories of her own harshness towards the little girl.

Through all those years, Ethel remembered too well, worry and rage over Virgil's girlfriends would boil over. Several times, when little Silva was out playing and wandered near the Hornersville railroad tracks, Ethel panicked. She would rush out, hustle her daughter back into the house, pull down all the window shades, and whip her. She would flail her daughter's thin little legs with a switch she made specially. Like they had made at the orphan farm, before Auntie Grace. She didn't stop the whippings until, one day, Silva pleaded with her. That day, she looked into Sissie's sad, tear-filled blue eyes and they struck a bargain: Ethel never hit the girl again, and Sissie never wandered again. Ever. Shame flushed through Ethel at the memory. Her throat tightened. She'd treated her own blood the way she'd been treated during her early years at the orphan farm. The girl amazed her: she'd had the courage to ask for better. *She* is *something,* Ethel thought.

Then Lillian Wadlow entered their lives. Virgil had hired her as his secretary. The two of them were as thick as thieves from the beginning. Ethel shook her head as she started snapping the beans. Lillian was an imposing woman. She had been in her late twenties, full figured, top and bottom, almost a little heavy. She was a blonde, with sharp grey eyes and a hearty, loud laugh. She was an accomplished pianist and gave lessons. The other part of her spare time was spent as Virgil's lover. They never touched in front of anyone but their affair was obvious. Ethel heard the rumors that Virgil had given Lillian a baby grand piano and a full-length fur coat.

Virgil no longer saw a need to divide the private and illicit from the public and family in his life. He decided it would be wonderful for Sissie to take piano lessons, and Lillian would be the perfect teacher! Never again would they find such a capable teacher. Silva's piano lessons were given in the evenings, and Lillian always came to dinner beforehand. Ethel cooked and served dinner to her husband's mistress. On cold winter evenings, Lillian wore her fur coat.

Over the snap beans, Ethel wondered, *What will become of Lillian now?* Her boss had been fired. Even though she had helped put together the evidence for Virgil's indictment, would the State Auditor keep her on? If not, perhaps selling the baby grand and fur coat could help pay her bills for a bit. Ethel smiled bitterly. Sissie had mastered Stravinsky's *Rite of Spring* (Ethel never liked the piece, a bunch of crashing, ugly notes) through Lillian's tutelage; the entire time she knew how appalling her father's behavior was. But the girl kept her head through the Jefferson City years.

Ethel had fallen terribly sick and suddenly became bedridden. Twelve-year-old Sissie kept checking on her before and after school. One morning, Ethel was in such pain that she could barely maintain consciousness. Weeks later, in the hospital, her doctor told her what happened next.

"Mrs. Medling, that daughter of yours is one impressive little girl. She called my office and insisted she speak with the doctor, that her mother was very, very ill, she no longer could speak when spoken to. And that her father forbade calling a doctor. Apparently, as soon as Mr. Medling left the house, your daughter did call and I came on the phone line. She told me your symptoms and I immediately came to the house. When I saw you, I knew you had very little time left. Your gall bladder had ruptured and you would have died that day or the next. Your daughter's disobedience saved your life."

The doctor also told her he had called Virgil up and torn into him. He told him he should be grateful for his daughter's interference, because otherwise his wife would have been dead in a few hours.

It took almost a year for Ethel to recover, much of the time spent in bed. Sissie interviewed women for maid and housekeeper work and found Christina. A college-educated colored woman,

Christina couldn't find work as a teacher and settled for domestic work. She kept the Medling house running and stayed on after Ethel recovered.

In 1938, two years later, on a cold, blustery February day, Sissie came from school to see all their furniture being loaded onto a moving truck. Without warning, Virgil had hired the truck and movers the previous day. He fired Christina the next day.

Ethel had been washing breakfast dishes when Virgil walked into the kitchen and broke his news. He was tense but very businesslike.

He refused to look her in the eyes. "Ethel, Steve Forrest fired me yesterday. We're moving back to Campbell today. A truck will be here in an hour. Don't ask me what went wrong. I don't know but I suspect it's politics and I'm a scapegoat. Thank God I never rented out the house in Campbell. We have a place to go." He turned on his heel and walked out of the kitchen.

She stood at the sink for several minutes before starting to pack up the dishes, flatware, pots and pans. *Well, it had all come crashing down, hadn't it?* So much had been bought over the years, but he gave her money to pay overdue bills only when grocery credit was stopped and the power shut off. He controlled all the money and told her only after his latest purchase or acquisition. How he could afford the club house on the Osage River, the cabin cruiser boat, a new car every year? How had he bought close to a thousand acres of farm land for the Dunn aunts and uncles, all on a state clerk's salary? Where had he gotten that much money? It was all gone now, except for the Veterans' Bonus he received in 1937. That was Sissie's, for her future college. Still Virgil would not say anything that made any sense.

Several weeks after the family returned to Campbell, three men dressed in black suits came to the front door. They needed to speak with Virgil. When he came to the front door, his face turned white. He walked the men to a back bedroom, out of earshot. Silva was reading a book in the front room.

Ethel leaned over the absorbed teenager and whispered, "Sissie, those men are talking to your father about his situation. Something about the grand jury investigation. He took them to the back bedroom. I know the windows are open. Go listen to what they are saying." Crouched between the bushes and house below the window, Sissie listened.

The girl returned with her eyes flashing and cheeks flushed. Her voice shook. "Mom, Dad confessed. He confessed to every-thing. He took checks of dead people and cashed them." Ethel's stomach dropped and she grabbed the love seat's arm, feeling almost nauseous. Stolen money! Worse than anything she had thought. But now things started to make sense. Virgil never talk-ed about the men's visit, and never knew his wife and daughter knew he had confessed.

They had been in Campbell about two weeks when the first newspaper articles started coming out. Virgil returned to Jeffer-son City for his arrest on March 20. Both he and his accomplice were arraigned on March 22. The next many months would be spent waiting for his rescheduled court date in October. No more the upstanding Campbell citizen, he hid out in the house. As sum-mer approached, he asked young Silva how much money she had. The total sum of all her birthday gifts and money from odd jobs was enough to finance his temporary escape out of town during the summer: a friend knew of a filling station with upstairs living quarters for lease in Tennessee. Virgil asked the girl if she wanted to come, and Ethel raised no objections. Let father and daughter spend some time together, because his confession guaranteed a prison sentence.

Ethel put on the shelled peas to boil, then the snapped beans and chopped potatoes. These, with scrambled eggs and toast, would be enough for Buddy. It had felt good to be out in the gar-den, despite her twinges and aches. She still knew how to grow food. Virgil's fall from grace had not cowed her: she talked to any neighbors she saw at the store. Her soft directness, when she looked into their eyes, signaled her refusal to be lumped in with her husband's doings. Her unapologetic manner generated re-spect and the townsfolk offered her information and advice about where, and with whom, she could barter for food. She made sure she and the children attended every church service offered, in-cluding Sunday and Friday evenings. Young Silva hated going but Ethel knew that steady, consistent attendance gave them a cloak of protection.

Having Virgil out of the house for the summer would be a relief, but she already missed Sissie. Young Bud was oblivious to the whole mess. Neither she nor Sissie had talked with the boy and he didn't ask. He found other boys to pal with and outside of running his daily newspaper route and the few chores she assigned him, he was scarce, unless it was mealtime.

Life without Virgil. What would that be like? She wondered. Certainly more peaceful. Being in Campbell was a relief. The years of her battling with Virgil and the constant uproar over his exorbitant expenditures had exhausted her. In Jefferson City, it was only during the summers when she and the children were exiled to the club house on the Osage that she had been able to let go. Then, Virgil stayed in town mostly, carrying on with whomever in the city house. On the river, she was freed from knowing what he was doing or with whom. On the river, she fished and that kept them fed when the money ran out. She let the kids sleep late and mosey about through the days. Virgil sometimes came with some of his Medling kin, but usually stayed away. The river house had no indoor plumbing and, so close to the dam, the river would flood. She never minded. The place was a respite and a return to the simplicity of her orphan farm years. Sissy would complain about having to get water and using the outhouse and Ethel just nodded and smiled. The extra work hadn't hurt the children.

Life without Virgil would be different because he would not be able to stop by whenever it suited him. She would change how money was managed. If they didn't have it to spend, then they would barter or do without. When he could no longer interfere, then their lives could be calm. They didn't have much but she had always lived honestly. Somehow she would make it work. Because that's what she had always been good at.

My grandfather's court date for sentencing was October 5, 1938. His sentence was three to five years for check forgery. He surrendered himself

to the Cole County jail on Saturday, December 10, 1938. He was transferred to the Missouri State Penitentiary on the following Monday, and
processed on December 13, 1938. As inmate 51730, he received an FBI
criminal number with a correlating fingerprint identification. He served
approximately thirty months and was released with conditional commu-
tation on May 23, 1941.

Chapter 17

E thel gazed through the window of her room in Mercy Hospital. It was a sunny late afternoon and she was exhausted. The fading Southern California sunlight fell across her bed, silhouetting the palm trees across the street. Palm trees, what strange shapes, like up-ended feather dusters! Not at all like the oaks, cypress, tupelos and maples in Missouri. Despite soft pillows, her neck and back ached. Because no energy remained for crocheting, she pulled a long loop to secure her current medallion and dropped her hands to the beige blanket. She wearily closed her eyes and slowly released her thin body into the mattress.

At forty-one years, now Ethel looked younger. She had lost a lot of weight since arriving in San Diego. Her days of being an exotic dark-haired girl were long past, although sometimes, when she and Sissie walked along the beach front, strangers had asked if they were sisters! But her continuing poor health had become a crisis. When Sissie first left for San Diego in the summer of 1942, Ethel and Buddy had adjusted. But the hemorrhaging returned, and her Campbell doctor could not manage it. Perhaps a specialist might have a solution. Sissie came back to Missouri, closed the Campbell house and brought both her brother and her mother to

San Diego. Once more the Medlings were together in the same city.

Ethel's longtime bleeding condition was diagnosed as cervical cancer. After Virgil lost his job, regular medical care was too expensive. Only emergencies were addressed. After Virgil left for prison, the little extra money that remained was spent on twelve-year-old Buddy. He had hurt himself falling from a tire swing. After his broken leg was set, the doctor discovered an intestinal blockage, operated, and saved the boy's life.

Ethel's current treatment was possible because Sissie paid the medical bills. Today had been her first radioactive cobalt treatment. The young nurse vaginally inserted a shielded plug of cobalt and timed the exposure. The doctor said the treatments would kill off the cancer cells but was not specific about the therapy's effectiveness.

Sissie had told her, in Missouri, that Virgil had found the best cancer specialist in southern California, a Dr. Sherman. *Virgil in the middle of it once more,* she thought. Deep irritation began to rise and then ebbed: she was too tired. When she had thrown her lot in with him, her life had taken such queer turns. Their "mutuality" had dissolved twenty years before when he brought up divorce. Old images of baby Silva in her cradle, hearing him slam the door as he left the apartment and her sense of dread floated through her mind. She started to drift and was almost asleep when a masculine voice softly pronounced her name, rousing her. Slowly, she opened her eyes. The sight of her estranged husband rendered her speechless. It had been two years since she had seen him.

His eyes wary, Virgil said, "I came by to see how you are. Sissie told me today was your first radiation treatment."

Each word jolted her. "What are you doing here, Virgil?" Flabbergasted, she narrowed her dark eyes. "I never thought I would have to see you. Again. Or hear you. Again. But here you are." She took a deep breath. "So much damage, so much—Why are you here, Virgil?"

His face drained of color as she spoke and his eyes opened wide. "I wanted to check on you and be sure you are being treated well. Sissie has . . ."

Rage tore through her body. She sat up and held up her shaking right palm to stop his voice. Her voice started to rise. "You want to make sure? Then listen to our daughter and get out, now! Don't you understand? You tore it all to pieces back in Missouri. I never asked for myself. I made my bed and accepted the senseless, shameful things you did. But when I tried to protect Sissie, her future, what was promised to her by us, by you, you would not listen to me. All you could think about was your future, what you needed and wanted and to hell with us!" She was almost screaming at this point.

His mouth agape, his face was ashen. "Ethel, I didn't come to upset you. I'm concerned, and there's no need for . . ."

When is he going to go away? He just won't listen, she thought. "No more . . . I don't want you here, I don't want to see you ever again. Never, nev-ver, never again."

A couple of nurses walked through the door, both with questioning looks. One stepped to the foot of her bed. "Is anything wrong here? We heard your voice all the way to the nurses' station." Her eyes shifted from Ethel to Virgil and back to Ethel. The smoldering look on Ethel's face showed her agitation and fury.

Ethel's voice dropped to a conversational level. "I do not want Mr. Medling here. I don't want him to visit me again." Her eyes held his for several seconds, then she turned her face away from his.

The nurse closest to Ethel laid her hand on Virgil's shoulder. "Mr. Medling, please come with us. Mrs. Medling's very upset. The treatments are very tiring and she needs her rest." He nodded and left with the nurses.

She slumped down when the door closed and turned her face to the ceiling. She was so tired. The sight of him was like setting a match to kindling. Not since their fight over his Veteran's Bonus money, before he left for San Diego, had she felt such anger. Life with the children had been peaceful with no big uproars. Seeing him now, with his need to make an appearance, to ask *Was everything going well?* As if he'd arranged it all. It instantly sparked her old rage. This time she held nothing back. Her adrenaline slowly drained away, and her exhaustion seemed deeper. Lifting her smallest finger would be impossible. She sighed and felt every muscle collapse. Her breathing slowed and deepened and sleep returned.

On the ocean shoreline, looking out to the horizon. My, what a view! It goes on and on—the Mississippi is big and wide but the ocean dwarfs it—then she was swimming in the salty water. A large rowboat headed towards her, filled with people waving to her, calling her to come join them. How inviting! But she would have to swim some distance to get to them and she raised her right arm to take a stroke . . . Ethel woke with a start. A dream. She didn't remember dreams very often. Avonelle came to her mind. *Where did you go, my father? You never came back to me but in those few dreams.*

Suddenly a nurse briskly entered the room with her meal tray. "Time for dinner, Mrs. Medling."

Ethel stretched her legs under her covers and raised her arms a bit. "I'm not hungry. Not doing anything to get hungry."

The nurse smiled. "Your radiation treatments dampen your appetite, but try to eat something. You need to keep your strength up. Is your daughter coming by?"

Ethel smiled back. "Silva will be by soon. She hardly ever misses a day. Don't know how she does it, working the night shift, seeing me almost each day and she has a handsome young husband, too. I stay with them when I'm not here."

The nurse nodded and started towards the door. "Have a good visit with her and I'll check in later." Ethel nodded.

She looked at the tray: this evening's offerings were unappealing, as usual. She missed getting fresh home-cooked food. Wartime shortages didn't help what with sugar and butter being rationed. And Sissie was always complaining about gasoline coupons. Ration coupons were bartered for this and that; she was always bargaining for gas, as much as she drove to the hospital.

Sounds of evening meal carts, rolling from one patient room to the next, echoed through the hall. A few moments later, she heard high heels clopping and knew Silva had arrived.

The door slowly swung open and her blond head appeared. "Are you awake, Mom?"

She waved to her nineteen-year-old daughter to come in. "You're early, Sissie. Something going on?"

Silva pulled a chair to the bedside and sat down. Ethel watched her with concealed astonishment. The girl took her breath away, how her beauty, grace and poise radiated. Slim and small-boned with curled shoulder-length hair, she dressed smartly. Today, she wore a gray suit. The skirt had a central single pleat and grazed her knees. The matching jacket with high lapels covered her simple high-necked white blouse. Beneath her glasses, her heart-shaped face still had a little baby fat, which didn't detract from her pleasing features. When she arrived in San Diego, she started wearing makeup. Her smiles lit up her face and revealed beautiful white teeth. How did she and Virgil produce such a child? He had been handsome but . . .

"Nothing special, I just wanted to spend a bit more time visiting you." Silva leaned closer to her mother and touched her closest hand. "I know today was the first treatment. How'd it go?"

Ethel smiled wearily. "Easy as pie. All I had to do was lie there. The nurse did all the work. Then she brought me back here. And I've been resting ever since."

Silva looked concerned. "So, you've just been resting? That's not what the nurses told me when I stopped by the station. They said they could hear yelling coming from your room." Ethel nodded. "Mr. Medling, they said, came to visit you and . . ."

"Yes, yes. I hoped Virgil knew how I felt about him. I, well . . . I just let him have it! Told him to get out of here and never come back. Told him he had finished it off before he came out here." She chuckled softly. "He was speechless, like a cat got his tongue. The nurses showed him out." Silva dropped her eyes to the bed and Ethel patted her hand. "Sissie, worry none about it. He got the message. Your father'll stay away, now. That's all I want. I'm tired, don't feel good and the past stayed right where it's been until his visit today."

"You've got to get well, Mom. You're right, what happened in Missouri needs to stay there. Once you're better, then we can think about a new place to live. I'll keep an ear out . . ." Ethel shook her head and pressed Silva's hand to stop her.

"Sissie, don't be makin' any long-term plans where I'm concerned. When I get better, I'll go back to Campbell. My friends and neighbors are all there. And when I get my energy back I want to spend some time in the country. Around Malden there were some good fishing holes. Oh, the best was on the Osage, at the club house. But getting out of town and sinking a hook into the water and just waiting, that's what will bring me all the way back."

Silva listened, skeptically. "Back to Missouri? Mom, it's so beautiful out here. The weather is perfect. No tornados or muggy summer afternoons or snow."

Ethel nodded. "You're happy here, Sissie. Stop worrying. I'll go back because that's where my home, my life is. I'll be fine. You're all grown up and goin' your own way. Buddy likes being here with Virgil. It's the right time for a son and father to be together. Lord knows I haven't done what he needs. Young men at his age don't need their mothers. And your father always pulls somethin' or someone out of his hat. You have Blaine, so you're taken care of. Though seems like you run the show and he obliges." Ethel sighed. "I'm looking forward to returning." All this talking, was the radiation tiring her this quickly?

Silva nodded. "All right, Mom, whatever you want. Now, let me catch you up on the latest goings-on at the Night Flight group." The young woman launched into a tale of her co-workers and the one-upmanship ploys the competitive stenographers resorted to.

Ethel smiled, laughed and commented as she listened to this confident young woman. She had Virgil's way with words and her stories were always catchy, amusing and dramatic. Not many of her co-workers met with her approval: Silva always figured she knew a better way to get the work done. Just like me, Ethel thought. Friends didn't come easily for this young-un.

The years in Jefferson City and Campbell had been mixed for the girl. Despite Virgil's doings and prison term being known everywhere, she had excelled in school and resisted having boyfriends. Ethel and the children kept to themselves, and worked any job possible to bring in cash. Sissie had combed hair for a dime a session and at one point worked at the funeral home applying makeup to corpses for open casket viewings. Ethel

shouldered all the housework so the girl could study all she needed. She just missed being her class's valedictorian. Yes, Sissie understood work and never complained about what had to be done.

Silva changed topics. "Mom, Blaine and I are working like
dogs. It's six days a week, week after week. We're thinking of going out of town for a couple of nights, just to blow off some steam
and dance! Seems like forever since we've danced." She looked
questioningly at Ethel.

"Sissie, you're doing everything. You work all the time, come
by to see me when you should be spending time with Blaine. Of
course you both should go. Don't worry. Where am I going to go?
And Buddy comes to see me a couple times each week. Just let me
know when so I won't look for you."

Silva looked deep into her eyes. "You're sure? Because I can
put it off . . ."

She shook her head, "How many times have you been putting
it off? No, go when you can. You have a wonderful man. He's
given up a lot because of me."

"He's the best, Mom. I never planned to marry when I came
out here. Blaine's really something, and what a dancer! All right,
I'll tell him to see when he can get away from the base and as soon
as we can work it out in the next several weekends, I'll let you
know."

She stood up. Ethel narrowed her eyes and ordered, "Stand
over there. I want to see how that suit fits you." Silva walked several steps from the bed towards the door. "Slowly turn around."
Ethel watched carefully. "You know, the back of that suit needs a
couple of darts in the back. It'd shape to you a bit better . . ."

Silva started to laugh, "Mom, let's face it. If you haven't sewn
it, nothing I wear fits right for you."

Ethel chuckled. "True enough. But you have the shape you do
and store-bought never catches the slimness of your hips. Wish
we had my sewing machine at the cottage."

Silva walked back over to the bed, leaned over Ethel's face and
kissed her forehead. "I love you, Mom. I need to get going. Rest
well and I'll be by tomorrow evening."

"I'll be here. Travel carefully in the dark, Sissie." Ethel raised her arm and waved as Silva turned to face her at the door, and then she was gone.

Avonelle entered her mind again. Oh, yes, just before the nurse brought dinner. She hadn't thought of him for a long time, now twice in the same day. Maybe, because of Virgil's visit and then Sissie? *My father, you came back only in my dreams.* Her heart clutched as old feelings flooded back. Standing in his arms, heart against heart and then he let her go, walked out the door and that was it. She never saw him again. He said he would come back, how did he put it? God willing. He had, but only in her dreams. Now, for the first time in twenty years he slipped back into her thoughts. Why now?

Chapter 18

By the end of 1943, Silva was no longer able to keep the hospital bills paid. Ethel was released from the hospital and returned to the beach cottage. In January, a few weeks later, her condition took a turn for the worse and this time Silva took her to the county hospital, next door to Mercy Hospital. The patient rooms were more cramped and most were shared by two or even four people. As before, Silva visited her almost every day. Now, Ethel was even thinner and frequently in pain. Her doctor continued to visit weekly but all cancer treatments had been discontinued. Her condition was terminal but no one told her. She continued thinking she would return to Missouri.

On the afternoon of January 30, she was resting in her bed. She shared the room with another woman, Mrs. McEvoy. Just after the supper trays were distributed, Silva came in and sat by her bed. She looked a little tense but smiled cheerfully.

"How're you doing today, Mom?" Ethel had pushed away the remains of her dinner and was crocheting another medallion for the white cotton bedspread.

Looking up, she nodded. "I feel tired and was hurting some. But the nurses gave me something and the pain's eased considerably. I think this medallion is coming along. I pieced a lot of them together but there are about sixteen I need to join. See if my count is right."

Silva reached down into the paper sack on the floor that held all the medallions. She pulled out the loose ones and laid them on the hospital bed and counted. "You never lose count, do you? Yes, fifteen in the bag and you have the sixteenth on your hook."

Ethel smiled. "Not much to keep track of around here. At least I'm getting something going. I've been thinkin' a lot about fishing the last couple of days. Even been dreamin' about it. I don't remember dreams very often."

After gathering the medallions into the sack, Silva crossed her legs and leaned back in the visitor chair. "You have always known your counts, your numbers, money, how much time. And no one ever worked harder. If things had been a little different, you could've done anything you put your mind to, Mom."

Ethel paused looping her needle and looked Silva in her eyes. "If wishes were horses, then beggars could ride . . . I heard that said once. What's done is done and there's no point chewing on the past. It's like poundin' sand down a rat hole. We, you, me, and Buddy, we did the best we could. Despite Virgil's blessed plans, you turned out just fine." She reached out a hand to Silva. "Sissie, you've always been at my back, at too young an age. At times, more a sister than a daughter. You grew up too fast. But we come from families that had no mothers. Their youngsters, your father and me, grew up different than a lot of children. Our losing our mothers shaped us. We'd no say in the matter." She shook her head as if to shake off these memories. Silva looked at her questioningly.

Ethel continued, "What I'm saying is that you turned out just fine. You know what you want and you'll get it, one way or the other. And you get that from both Virgil and me." She pressed Silva's hand affectionately and her eyes glowed with pride. *What a joy to behold this young woman.*

Silva's eyes started to tear and she smiled back. "Mom, do you remember when I said Blaine and I wanted to go off for a couple of nights out of town and dance?" Ethel nodded. "Both our schedules have cleared at the same time and we leave this evening."

"Good! It's been too long since you two spent private time away from all this."

Relief crossed Silva's face. "You're sure my missing a couple of visits will be all right?"

Ethel shook her head impatiently. "Go on. You need to go. I'll be fine. And I know Buddy'll be by tomorrow. I'll continue to rest and work on the bedspread. Mrs. McEvoy and I chat some, so I'm hardly without company. In a hospital, you never can be alone, not for long. So when're you two leaving?"

"After I get back to the cottage and pack a few things. We're going to Palm Springs, a couple of hours from here, in the desert. The desert is lovely in the winter and the days are very comfortable. There's a nightclub Blaine heard about from one of his Air Corps buddies. They have some great bands come through and a good dance floor."

Ethel nodded and took a deep breath. "Just what you've been lookin' forward to. While you're gone, I'll think 'bout fishin'. Bein' in the skiff and sinkin' a line into the Osage—my favorite times of those years. The Osage took me back to when I fished as a girl. Probably'll dream about it."

Silva stood up and Ethel gazed at her. "Are those your travel clothes for today?" Her daughter nodded and then spun around in her blue two-piece suit. The stylish knife-pleated skirt was A-lined and just covered her knees. The jacket had wide black leather lapels, and her lacy blouse cuffs peeked out from its shorter sleeves. Its nipped-in waist emphasized her slimness.

"Seems well tailored," Ethel commented.

Silva's face lit up. "Got it on sale! 'Twas sized wrong, and said size ten. I tried it on and think it's the best suit I've found since moving out here. Blaine loves it!"

Deep fatigue swept through Ethel. "You best be on your way. Sounds like a long ride before you get to your hotel." Silva leaned over and kissed her forehead; Ethel reached up and touched her daughter's face. "Travel safe, Sissie." Silva nodded, flashed a dazzling smile and walked to the door. Ethel waved before she disappeared.

She gathered up her crochet thread, hooked and secured the

unfinished medallion and put everything into the paper sack. The pain was back. She pressed the nurses' call button. She glanced over at Mrs. McEvoy, still napping from an earlier afternoon procedure.

A nurse entered and came to Ethel's bed. "Mrs. Medling, I saw the call button at the station. What do you need?" Ethel told the nurse about her pain and the nurse returned a few minutes later with the medication. After swallowing the tablets, Ethel turned off her bed lamp and waited for the pain to subside.

It seemed all her time now was spent waiting. She remembered when all her time was spent doing. Footsteps sounded outside the door and echoed down the hall. Only late at night did the floor get really quiet. Sounds of the ocean surf at the front of Silva's cottage echoed in her mind. The endless, soothing rhythm of the waves that never stopped. They grew louder and her body, bit by bit, sank into the mattress as her pain lessened.

She was back in the water, her feet no longer touched the bottom and again she saw the boat filled with people waving and beckoning. She raised her arm to start swimming and the boat appeared closer. They were calling to her by name, "Ethel, over here. Ethel . . ." She wanted to get to them, but did she have the strength? As if they heard her thoughts, they called, "Wait, Ethel, just wait, we're almost there." She relaxed and kicked her legs and moved her arms in the salty water. The boat was almost to her.

The ocean became the Osage. The sun shone brilliantly; the boat was close enough that she could see faces. Ocean swells and waves became the river's smooth, flowing currents. Closest to her, a man stood with his back to her. He turned around and faced her, he reached out his hand. When she touched it, she found she was in the boat, facing him. It was Avonelle! He looked brighter, more vigorous and less worn.

Her heart swelled; tears filled her eyes and started flowing down her face. "Father, Avonelle, is it you?"

"Ethel Mae, we're here, together. Now."

Ease spread through her but thoughts of Silva and Buddy intruded. "Now?"

"Your body has given out. Your children, our children, will carry on."

She looked about her and saw many others surrounding them. She looked back into his eyes. "You never came back, only in my dreams." She looked down at her hands, and realized she was sixteen again.

He nodded. "I was killed after, in the city street. But I never left. My very last thoughts were of you and . . ." he gestured to a young woman standing next to Ethel, ". . . your mother, Maudie." Ethel turned and recognized her mother. Heavy braided blond hair crowned her fair-skinned face and her large blue eyes shone. She held out her arms and Ethel stepped into them. Wherever this was, she felt strong, vital and whole.

"What's happening? Where am I? I think I'm not ready."

Avonelle softly offered, "We're not in ordinary time and place. This is your time to leave. But it can be later. What do you want right now?"

"I want to feel it's my time. I feel full of life right now. How can I leave with such strength within me?"

"You can do anything you choose now. There are no limits in where you go or who or what you choose to see or do. You may spend as much time as you need. Everything is possible."

She found herself sitting in the old fishing boat on the Osage. Maude sat next to her, leaned and murmured in her ear, "Your father and I made you in a canoe, out in the swampland." Surprise and joy rose within her. Maudie smiled. "Why do you think you love fishing and being alone so much? Your father and I were swamp children. We loved the water, the trees, listening to and watching any and all creatures that appeared about us." Then her mother disappeared. Ethel grasped the oars and started to row. Each stroke increased her strength and agility. She tilted her head to look at the tree-lined river's edge and breathed in deeply. Radiant energy spread from her filled lungs. Her heart beat strongly. Her youthful potency and capability was back and her body was perfect. On her left, two hawks lifted up from a tree. They flew as a pair, one calling to the other with high-pitched cries. Rising high into the sky above, they flew in an arc and then swooped lower to hold a steady course down the middle of the river. Their cries called, as she watched. Then she was flying between them.

The three flew and flew and flew. The river below became huge tracts of woods, which eventually dropped away to grasslands. One of the birds asked, "Where? There are no limits."

"Everywhere, everything. I want to see it all." Their flight took Ethel to places she never had imagined or heard of. Endless oceans with small archipelagoes, then jungles with waterfalls followed by vast empty deserts. They rose and caught upper wind currents that propelled them over sparkling, snow-encrusted mountain ranges. The farther she went, the more she saw, increased her vibrancy as never before. Her sense of being separate blurred: she was no longer an observer. Her vitality mounted, while she sensed she was becoming less solid, nebulous, even amorphous. Then, she felt she was everything all at once.

In the distance ahead, an ethereal gathering appeared. Closer, it became clearer, more substantial: a tapestry of souls. They were interwoven like a swath of blooming flowers in a single sweep of color but composed from individual lives and experiences. What she had sensed as a young girl during her moments of peaceful solitude was now fully present. She, too, was another, in the greater order.

Silva entered her thoughts. They stood together on the ocean shore in front of the beach cottage. She put her arms around her daughter and they stood heart to heart. "You saved my life when you were born. My first baby was my hope of the family I never had before I married your father, but when he died, part of me died. You've been the best daughter. I'll be watching and wanting the best for you always. Take care of your brother for me." Her mind turned to Virgil.

Suddenly she was facing the sixteen-year-old youth in the cornfield. She reached out and touched his face. "Virgil, that day you changed my life. Some of it was very good, even wonderful. Much of it was terrible. My time is at hand and yours, one day, will come. Think on our time together and become who you could and should be." Her bitterness released.

It was enough. Back in the boat with Avonelle, Maudie and the others, the water glowed brilliantly. Bright colors and lights shone, wherever she looked.

"Who're all these beings?" she asked Avonelle.

"These are your and my and Maudie's families. These are the ones you felt around you when you carried your first child. We all have our own, those souls that brought us into this life; they gave us the gift of life. They welcome you as you join all of us, while we wait and hope for the next ones. Are you ready, Ethel Mae?" Avonelle and Maudie each extended their hands.

Their hands in hers, Ethel looked into her mother's and then her father's eyes and smiled. "I'm ready."

The night shift nurse came into the hospital room to check on Ethel and Mrs. McEvoy. When she touched Ethel, she felt for a pulse and found none. She checked her watch and noted the time was 12:30 a.m., January 31, 1944. She returned to the nurses' station and called the doctor to notify him of Ethel's death. She called Virgil next.

Chapter 19

My mother always referred to her father as "Med." Probably it was a nickname he adopted from buddies when he was a young man. My feeling is that she started using his nickname after he left for California: she distanced herself from thinking of him as her father.

At one o'clock in the morning, Med woke seventeen-year-old Buddy. "Your mother died a little bit ago." Med paused, scarcely looking at the boy. "The hospital called. I knew the doctors didn't give her long to live, but no one expected she would go right now. Sissie and Blaine just left for the weekend and I have no idea how to get a hold of her." He shook his head in bewilderment.

Buddy lay in his bed and nodded. Round-faced and very overweight, he had a placid temperament. Med walked out of the bedroom into the small sitting room. He pulled a bottle of Scotch and a glass from the cabinet and set them both on its surface. He debated as he stood looking at them. Ethel certainly wouldn't have approved. She hated his drinking. Now was her time. After how many years of trying, she finally had his attention. No, a glass of Scotch would signal more of his old disregard.

Where had the time gone? Pangs shot through him. Just before the phone rang, he had been thinking about that day in the cornfield when he marched over, told her about joining the army, asked her to be his girl, and kissed her! The first kiss, for each of them—he began pacing back and forth in front of the cabinet. How smitten he'd been when he saw her after Russia. She didn't look like all the other young St. Louis women. He loved that. She was ever a proper girl but when she smiled her crooked smile and her pearly white teeth flashed, he noticed other men looked at her, too. But Ethel was committed to him only and their mutuality.

In life, what seemed just right can later be seen as a limitation, even a liability. Going to the Teachers' College had been the right choice but when they had lost the baby everything changed. His first child and son perished, and Ethel became like a tomb, her eyes flat with grieving despair. Their mutuality and his commitment to their marriage faded.

Allowing her to get pregnant a second time had been thoughtless on his part. He asked for a divorce after Silva's birth: would it have been fairer not to have told her? Many men would have said nothing. Ethel's refusal brokered their remaining together but never constrained his dalliances. Unexpectedly, his daughter had proved to be both his heart's delight and a thorn in his side. No one else ever got to him like she did, because she said to him what Ethel never would.

Now Ethel was gone, forever. This wife hadn't fit into his life most of the years they were married. She became a hindrance and drag. When he had returned from prison, however, he had wanted his family. They had become precious. Suddenly, a new perspective burst into his awareness. She had been his bedrock, no matter how he had felt about her. She had come into and from his early life, when everything had seemed possible. Most particularly after she agreed to wait for him. Her death, now, brought another fundamental shifting of his life. He would never be able to see her again. Forever.

At 2:30 a.m., Buddy groggily appeared. "Can't sleep, Dad?" He stopped pacing and shook his head. "Do you want me to stay with you?" Virgil shook his head harder in refusal and turned away. When the boy left he sat in an armchair.

The air was heavy, hard to breathe. He felt closed in, almost claustrophobic and slightly nauseous. When was the last time he'd felt like this? Memories of the hole rushed back. No light, no clothes and no toilet. Just a slop bucket and the smell of his urine and feces. No mattress, blanket or anything soft that could ease his flesh against the rock floor. A slot in the wall next to the locked door was where plates or bowls of food appeared, accompanied by a momentary stream of dim light. His world was blackness and he had groped blindly. His senses became acute. Sounds, smells, touch, thoughts and the sliding of the wall slot marked time. It was winter and his nakedness kept him chilled during the days of darkness. He had always pushed, hadn't he? Never could accept rules until he was smacked down hard. He spent his time in the hole just once. No one outside ever knew; he never talked about his years in the State Pen.

Inmates were forbidden to speak. Ideally, prisoners were to spend their time turned inward, review their crimes, and assume a penitent demeanor. But being able to talk, to expound on his point of view about what he believed in, was how he'd gotten where he had. Telling stories—that's what he did! So he spoke, was warned twice, and the third time, two guards wordlessly grabbed each of his arms and almost dragged him to the lowest prison level. Down a narrow little hall, dimly lit by single bulbs along its ceiling, they stopped in front of a half-open door that swung into darkness.

Tersely, one guard said, "Strip." His heart pounding, Med took off his prison shirt, pants and shoes and dropped them to the floor. The other guard pointed to Med's underwear. Med pulled off his shorts and tossed them onto the pile. They grabbed his arms again and pushed him through the door into the dark. He fell, groaning when his knees crashed onto the stone floor. Boots kicked his feet, back and buttocks. Wands struck him until he was a quivering huddle. The light from the dim hall vanished when the door closed. The lock turned and footsteps faded away into silence. The ceiling was so low he couldn't stand upright.

After five days with no light or moving air, and only muffled sounds, the lock turned and the door opened. The faint light shocked his eyes. Something softly thudded next to him. A guard grunted, "Get dressed, 51730." His eyes tried to focus and his hand felt for and found a stack of wadded clothing and shoes. His eyes gradually made out the shape of the shirt he was shrugging on but he felt unsteady when he stood stooped to pull on underwear, pants and shoes. The guards' boots paced back and forth in front of his cell's open door. Finally dressed, he touched the ceiling with both hands to avoid hitting his skull, and thrust out his head while he held onto the door's jambs. One guard grabbed his right arm and the other his left. The dimly lit bulbs almost blinded him as they hustled him down the hallway and up three floors to the warden's office.

In his fifties, the warden had iron-colored graying hair, a generous mustache and steel-rimmed glasses. His appearance was fit, suggesting a military background. He'd been running the State Penitentiary since 1935, when his new administration embraced the Auburn philosophy of penology. He had no tolerance for inmates who violated the rules, particularly the rule forbidding speech. Inmates talking to one another, whether in conflict or colluding, created most of the Pen's troubles. He was sitting at his desk when the guards thrust Med through his office door. The warden continued to look at his paperwork while the inmate shakily stood before him. Med's face winced as his eyes blinked painfully from the office lights. After some minutes, the warden looked up and coldly stared into his watery, light-shocked eyes.

Warden Mendelsone nodded. "Prisoner 51730, you do understand that if you violate the no talking rule again, your time in the Hole will be doubled to ten days?" He started to open his mouth, and the warden held up his hand in warning. "Those ten days can begin right now. No talking, no speaking, no verbal expression at any time, unless you are directed to do so by a guard or prison administrator such as myself. I do *not* give you permission to speak." Med nodded and cast his eyes down to the carpeted floor. The dark color was soothing.

"Because this infraction occurred during the first three months of your time here, there will be no documentation of it in your records, providing there's no repeat offense. Understood?" Med kept his eyes on the floor and nodded. "I reviewed your file for the crimes you committed. You were a successful state employee and a newspaper columnist before that. Silence is just what you need. People who think they know how to speak their point of view, how to bend and twist words to get what they want, what they think others owe them, this is a good place for them. I also read that you were a Sunday school teacher."

The warden stood, walked over and faced Med, whose eyes remained on the carpet. The warden reached for his chin and raised it. Behind the steel-rimmed lenses, his eyes seemed much larger as they bored into Med's.

"And here you are. It seems that the good Lord has seen to your soul and its salvation. Make good use of your time here, and perhaps you'll not burn in eternal damnation." Disgust twisted the warden's face, "Blind pensioners' checks, indeed. Take him back to his cell."

Once more the guards half-dragged him through the long hallway and up two flights of steel stairs to the third floor, and half-hurled him into his cell. He faced the wall. When the large brass key was pulled out from his locked cell door's keyhole, and he heard the guards' boots walk away, he sat down on his bed. Never had his hanging cot with its bouncing springs felt better.

Five years later, in his room at the San Diego Hotel, he resumed pacing. When the repulsed warden had looked into his eyes, humiliation made him shrink and his face burned with shame. When Ethel had laid into him, that last time, his soul felt scoured. He never returned.

Never would he be able to tell her what he should have, that day. What he needed to say to her, now. How he remembered their beginning as a couple when he left home for the first time. How his knowing she was back home, waiting, had kept him strong all the years he was out of the country. That only the two of them knew from where and what their beginnings had come. How their mothers' deaths, and being left behind, connected them. Because she was gone, now, only he was left to remember.

She was gone. Forever. He felt closed in, clamped down, as if one of his limbs had been ripped away and a huge rock was crushing him.

Chapter 20

Silva organized the memorial service at Cypress View Mausoleum, four days after Ethel's death. She paid for the crypt, cremation and service. *The girl is in shock,* Med thought. He and Buddy, dressed in his military school uniform, sat in a separate pew. *Sissie has never been like this,* he mused. Before, when she became very quiet, he could feel her thinking or planning. Ethel's death, though, had knocked every bit of vibrancy and sassiness out of her. Dark circles ringed her eyes and her tears flowed continuously as she stoically sat through the service. Blaine supported her while her silent grief enfolded the proceedings. Before the service began, she had wordlessly nodded to Med and hugged Buddy.

The chapel was small and intimate for the casket service. A blanket of lavender flowers (Ethel's favorite color) covered the ceremonial coffin and a mausoleum pianist played several Baptist hymns Silva remembered from the Campbell church. The minister spoke briefly and then read what Silva had prepared. Despite her grief, the girl put quite a service together. Including himself, daughter and son, and Blaine, there were only four people. All of Ethel's friends were in Campbell and Med wasn't sure any of them knew. Even if they had, no one had the means to travel quickly, what with the war. With Blaine's arm around her, Silva sat tall and elegantly as her teardrops formed dark wet spots on her jacket's lapels. At the end, she walked woodenly out of the chapel, her arm in Blaine's. Med noted the time and nodded to Buddy that they, too, needed to leave.

After he dropped Bud at school, he returned to his desk. The rest of the day was consumed by two meetings and dictation of several production memos; all the while his mind struggled to focus. A good stiff drink, perhaps? That might shake off his gloom. He had no reason to feel this way. They had been on bad terms for so many years. He wrapped things up for the day. Once he arrived in the hotel lobby, he turned left towards the bar entrance.

Pushing through the black velvet curtains, he waited a few seconds for his eyes to adjust to the lounge's shadowy lighting. A catchy Glenn Miller tune was playing on the juke box and he made out a faint cluster of sailors drinking at the far end of the bar. He ordered a Scotch neat and turned his back to the bar while he waited. This bar was a favorite Consolidated Aircraft hangout after day shifts. At one of several scattered tables, he saw a group of women wearing Consolidated badges, as he did. Behind him, he heard the clink of a shot glass on the bar. He turned and pushed his cash towards the bartender. He looked hard at the golden fluid. Lifting the glass, he inhaled the fumes before he sipped. The Scotch's harshness stung his tongue and burned after he swallowed. His empty stomach felt the alcohol land. Booze never had tasted good to him, whether it was moonshine or legal, but taste was not the point. Glass in hand, he turned back to watch the women. A small-boned redhead sat in their midst. She was good looking and mature and wore a supervisor's badge. She looked up, lifted a glass towards him and nodded. He returned her gesture, but made no movement towards the women's table. Even if he was drinking, it was still Ethel's time.

He belted the rest of his Scotch and motioned for a second one. When it arrived, he took a deep breath and then threw it back. Time to go and see Buddy before turning in. Heading toward the curtained exit, he glanced back at the women and saw the redhead looking at him. He nodded to her and walked out. He suddenly felt drained; he hadn't slept much since the hospital called. The Scotch slowly crept through his body and mind, softening his focus. Things appeared a bit blurry in the elevator.

An hour later in bed, he drifted. The redhead appeared. He hadn't been with anyone steady since Lillian. *Lillian!* His groin stirred as images of her ample breasts, hips and velvety thighs brought back sensations of how luscious and juicy she'd been. Like biting into the ripest, sweetest peach. She never had put limits on their sex play. With her, he felt he was all he could be. She called him her Big Daddy. His right hand rested at the root of his erect penis and gripped firmly, imagining her hand and then her mouth taking him in as deeply as she could. No woman had ever tongued, nibbled and sucked him like Lillian. His hand tightened and he began stroking. A talented pianist, she played his body like she played her keyboard and took him to heights of release he'd never known with anyone else. He pumped harder as he rolled through his catalog of scenes and his hips began to rock. Whether she sucked or she straddled and rode him like her stallion or he pounded into her as she moaned louder and louder, she was gifted. Her secretarial skills had been merely adequate— urgency took over and his semen showered his groin and upper thighs. His arched back slowly flattened as he regretfully released memories of his perfect lover. His sated body and mind yielded to blackness and he slept.

Part III

Chapter 21

The redhead's name was Roselle Smith Rea. He'd asked around, knowing she would be easy to locate since she was a supervisor. The next time he saw her in the bar, he sent her favorite beer to her table. She came over to thank him and the rest flowed easily, if not smoothly. Roselle proved irresistible although quite prickly.

She was a west coast girl, from Washington State, born in 1905. Her father had moved the family several times, at one point living in Yuma, Arizona, where he ran a general store. In 1920, when the Torrance oil fields in California boomed, he moved them to Long Beach. She grew up in a working family and early on she recognized that getting a good education was her only hope for financial security. Although she married right out of high school, she and her husband moved to New York City where she trained and began working as a nurse. Something, she was never clear what, disrupted her nursing career and they returned to Southern California. She was a handsome woman with five children before her marriage blew up.

"It was messy. These kinda things usually are. I don't think I made the best choices, leaving the kids behind." They were sitting at a table. Despite the dim lighting, Med saw a teardrop sparkle as it rolled down her cheek. He took one of her hands. "Him and me were always squabbling. I was working and with five kids, it never seemed to get easier. As the years passed I spoke up more, what with him sitting around expectin' me to keep it all together. It was about four years ago when we got into it. He came home from a night shift and he smelled like he'd been with another woman. That was the last straw. I blew up and he came after me and started hitting me." Roselle looked down into her beer. Med kept quiet, sensing that she rarely spoke to anyone about her former husband.

"I knew he'd take care of the kids. He was fussy about how I kept the house and children. Also, my oldest was helping with the younger ones. I walked out after he stopped smacking me that night. It was the first time but never again did I give him another chance."

Med leaned back in his chair. "How'd the divorce happen?"

She smiled bitterly. "He told me he'd never let the children leave and come to live with me and he'd fight custody, despite my good pay. We went to court and his attorney attacked me for being a working woman, not interested in my children. The judge agreed and awarded custody to my ex. But there's a loophole. Custody could be revisited should I remarry. 'Course, I've had no prospects in that area."

He took one of her hands again. "But you never know what might be 'round the corner, do you, now?"

She looked at him warily. "I've dated a lot of fellows. San Diego is full of young fellas who don't think I'm too over the hill. But you aren't so young, you're the nicest and you listen. Most young men want to talk about themselves."

He smiled ruefully. "I did my own share of talking. All sorts of plans and dreams. Ethel had to listen to my yakking for hours at a time. I think you do outgrow that, if you can see beyond what you're aiming for. I was always aiming. Hit the bull's eye a couple of times, too. Ever heard of Icarus? We read some of the Greek stories when I studied Latin in the Teachers' College."

She looked at him, curiously. "Latin, huh? What's Icarus?"

Chuckling, he responded, "Who, not what. He was an ambitious youth, so the story went. He and his father were trapped on the Isle of Crete, in the Labyrinth built for the Minotaur monster." Roselle looked confused. "These are ancient times, thousands of years ago. The Minotaur was a half-bull, half-human monster born from the queen and a Cretan bull. Oh, I know, unseemly congress between human and animal, but these stories always had gods and humans and animals coupling in some fashion or another. Not at all like the Christian traditions."

His companion finished her beer and waved to the bartender. "Do continue, Mister Medling," she said, amused.

"Despite being trapped on the island, his father, I think his name was Daedalus, was a great craftsman, and fashioned two sets of wings. These were wooden frames covered with feathers that were held with wax. Father and son were going to fly together. Just as they got ready to leave, Icarus' dad warned the boy to follow him. How high or low they flew was critical to keeping their wings right. Too low to the water and the wings would clog with the damp. Too high, and the sun's heat would melt the wax and the feathers would fall off."

Roselle nodded. The bartender arrived with a fresh glass of beer with a nice foamy head. She held up her hand. Med waited, as he knew her beer-drinking routine. She picked up her glass, sniffed at the beer's yeastiness, drank a mouthful, swallowed while she held her hand on her upper chest and inhaled deeply. Her usual look of satisfaction registered and her body relaxed. Roselle loved her beer and especially the first swallow from each freshly poured glass.

"I'm ready."

"You're sure?" he asked before he continued, because she never hesitated to show irritation if she felt she was being rushed or pushed. She had a redhead's temper. She smiled, nodded and took another sip of her beer. She let him tell his stories but he never felt she could be dazzled or spellbound. Sometimes that frustrated him, but she was a worthy challenge.

"Father and son ascended and began flying like birds. In the beginning, Icarus listened to his father's advice and stayed with him. But the boy was astonished by the sea and the sky. He became giddy, loopy, and he started moving away from his father.

He looked at the sun and thought, 'If I can get off of the soil and fly above the water, why can't I fly higher and higher? And see if I can reach the sun.'"

She shook her head, "Not doing what he was *told* . . ."

He nodded in response. "And his dad called out to him, but the boy was entranced. He kept climbing higher and one by one feathers started shedding from his wings: the sun was melting the wax. Daedalus kept calling to Icarus, but the boy wasn't listening. Enough feathers fell off and the boy, despite flapping his wooden frames, started losing height. He fell into the sea and drowned. His stunned father wept as he crossed the sea and landed. The strait next to Crete bears Icarus' name to this day."

Roselle shook her head. "You studied stories like these in college?" Med nodded. "Not very practical. Sounds great but can't pay the bills. Unless you plan to be a writer or maybe actor?"

"As a matter of fact, I did make a living with some of it. I taught school for youngsters for a few years and then finagled a newspaper job for several years. Definitely kept us fed, in clothes and bought our house in Campbell."

Roselle considered his words and took another sip from her beer. "That's right, you're a newspaperman?" He nodded. "You told me this story for what reason?"

She never gave him an easy payoff, making him work for any approval she granted. He spent a lot of time these days working for things that, before, had flowed easily to him. Especially back in Missouri. She was a tough one. He persisted.

"The point I think we began with was the callowness of youth."

She sighed. "And fifty-dollar words, Mister."

"My apologies, ma'am. Inexperienced and self-absorbed young men. And how they didn't listen well."

"And you spend the past twenty minutes telling me a Greek story you learned in Latin twenty-five years ago?"

He chuckled again. "Come on, you know you enjoyed it. You needled me throughout it all. You feel better, now, don't you, Roz?"

For the first time this evening, she reached for his hand and squeezed it. "I do. My moods do take me over. Will be interesting to see if you stick around. Because, Mister, they are part of me. I say what I think. My kids know my nips. And I'm getting old enough to not care if a guy doesn't like it." Her wariness returned.

He wove his fingers between hers. "Nothing you've done or been can top my history. I've a far more difficult past than you. You know some of it but next time we get together, I'll tell you the rest. Then you can decide if you want to continue spending time with me. But I already know how I feel."

Chapter 22

The visits began the night when he and Roselle first made love. They'd been dating steadily for several weeks and one night they met in the hotel bar for drinks. Med did tell her about his past, as much as he was capable of. He never admitted the depth of his criminality to anyone, and Roselle knew everything he would admit because he still maintained he had been a political casualty who had taken the fall for irregularities with the Governor's campaign fund.

They drank a lot that evening. He'd looked deep into her blue eyes and asked her to come up to his hotel room. She made him wait for several moments.

"If I do, then we're committed. I'm too old for any trashy affair. I don't need to be with you. I want to be with you only if you want me, period." She looked provocatively into his eyes. He didn't want a way out. He'd been alone and on the outside for too long.

He nodded. "You make me not want to be alone any more. This isn't an affair for me, either. Come upstairs." She picked up her purse, stood, and looked down at him. He pulled out some cash, chose some bills, laid them on the table between their empty glasses and pushed back his chair. She walked over and separated his legs with her knee, and held his eyes. His groin pulsed. She was not a young one, no, she was mature and tested. His attraction for her was unfamiliar—an image of a girl leading a haltered animal down a path flashed through his mind. Lillian had been a sexual ringmaster but she always deferred to him. She'd known he held the ultimate power to fire her or leave her behind. Now, it was Roselle who called the shots.

"Are we waiting for something, Mister? Have you changed your mind?" Her right knee tapped against his sprawled left leg. "Maybe you're not up to it tonight?" Her taunting aroused him further. The bar's mirrored lights brought out the flame-colored highlights in her shoulder-length hair. Her bangs hung just above her thin eyebrows. *Not as thin as Harlow's,* he thought.

"Roz, my motor's running just fine. Let's be on our way." She stepped back and he rose from the chair.

He moved towards her and she stepped away. "No easy feels on the way up, Mister. I wouldn't want you to fire off too soon." She put her arm through his and they slowly walked from the dark bar into the brightly lit lobby. In front of the elevator, Med put his arm around her when the door opened. She leaned against him and he smelled scent in her hair as they rode up to the third floor.

She looked into his face and whispered, "We'll be alone? Your son's gone?" He nodded and the elevator door opened. The carpeted hall was softly lit by evenly spaced sconces. After unlocking his suite's door, he stepped to one side and followed her inside. After he closed the door, she faced him. Looking into his eyes, she dropped her purse to the floor, shrugged off her jacket and dropped it onto the purse. Still holding his eyes, she raised one leg, and pulled off her shoe by its heel and dropped it, and then her second shoe. She appeared completely at ease and confident, while his stomach was full of butterflies. He realized he was following her lead.

She unbuttoned her blouse. "We've been at this dance for a while, Mister. D'you have a radio? Some atmosphere, please." Her sureness, just like one of the guys, made him smile. He pulled her into his bedroom. He flipped the light switch and breathed a sigh of relief: he had requested service that morning and the bedroom was presentable. He strode to the chest of drawers and he turned the radio on. Big band dance music filled the quiet. "Not too loud, Mister, just a little background sound." He adjusted the volume and Roselle sat on the bed, leaning back on her arms. "D'you have any booze?"

"Scotch."

"Bring us a glass and we'll share." When he returned with a small glass three quarters full, he stood and took her in, lying on her side in her bra and skirt. When they had kissed before, he'd felt her full shape but now he saw that her full breasts sagged a bit. Four pregnancies and forty years of living will do that to a woman's form. She was not matronly or grandmother material, though, like Ethel had been when he returned from prison. He took a sip and offered her the glass. She sipped and set the glass on the bedside table. A Tommy Dorsey melody began and she nodded to the beat.

"Are you coming over here?"

"Just taking you in, ma'am."

She sighed, and patted the bed. "Come on, over here, Mister. I always figured you for an eager beaver."

When he sat next to her, she grabbed his neck and pulled him down to her face. Not since Lillian had he felt he was being swallowed by a sexual undertow. Her teeth nipped and held his bottom lip and they started to kiss. He shifted and she rolled beneath him. With his building arousal, he felt something else. While he wanted to plunge into her, her intensity and presence were bewitching him. His senses craved her flesh, but something, hidden and coiled, titillated his awareness. He ran his fingers over her back and shoulders and stroked her breasts, while increasing apprehension accompanied his desire. He pulled her skirt up and felt her stockings and girdle. He unbuckled his belt while she unzipped his trousers and his swollen member sprang free.

"Not so fast," and she wrapped her thumb and forefinger at the base of his penis. She squeezed and his urgency lessened. She looked at him teasingly. "It's been a while for both of us. Let's make it last. I know a few tricks. Are you game?" He nodded, acquiescing. He did not care; submitting to her was enticing and perilous. Her voice dropped to a sultry whisper. "I will bring you to the edge and pull back. But I want you to do the same for me. If we come close and then stop, the final release will blow your socks off. But I want mine blown off, too. Be my partner, all the way?" He smiled, letting her manage them both. "Do what I tell you."

She put his hand between her legs. "Feel how wet I am? Take your finger, wet it inside me and start rubbing where I show you." He slowly pushed two fingers inside her. She was juicy and slick. She guided his hand to her cleft mound and he felt her soft nub nestled where her outer lips began. He started to stroke the nub and she opened her legs wide and tilted her hips. She grabbed his neck, pulled him close and started kissing him again. He dipped his fingers inside her again and then ran them all the way from her wet opening to the nub. She moaned while kissing him and he felt her nub growing and becoming firmer. He kept stroking her rhythmically and steadily and he felt her tension grow as her hips moved faster. Suddenly she pulled back. "That's enough for a bit. Just think how ready I am going to be."

She wrapped her fingers around him again. "Unhook my girdle while I work you a bit." He reached for her front tabs as she began slowly pumping his penis. He started to unhook the front of her stockings but her touch excited him intensely and he stopped. "No, that's the trick," she instructed him. "Focus on the stockings and notice what happens." As he fumbled with each fastener, he felt his excitement stabilize. He found the girdle's back tabs and unhooked them. She then directed, "Take my girdle off, Mister."

He straddled her supine body and her eyes stayed on him as he pulled up her skirt to her waist and slipped his fingertips under the waist band of her girdle. "Kiss my belly," she demanded. She lifted her hips when he pulled the girdle over her pubis. Then he shifted to the foot of the bed and knelt to kiss her round belly. Her hands pushed his head lower and he brought his lips to her thick coiled hair and took some of it between his teeth and softly pulled. "Use your tongue like your fingers," she coaxed. After he spread her legs open and separated her hairy cleft, his tongue traced circles around her nub. She cried out and bucked her hips.

He smelled and tasted her juices. Never had he been this intimate with any of his lovers. He kept stroking her clitoris and her body rocked steadily as she inhaled deeply. He started to gently suck her button-hard pearl and suddenly she pulled away from him.

"Stop! I'm too close. You're good at this . . ." She took a slow breath. "I want you in me, now."

He pulled himself up next to her and she grabbed him firmly and brought him into her wetness. He looked into her eyes and forcefully entered, as deeply as possible. She gasped and shut her eyes, whispering, "That's right, lover." He felt her tightness but her juiciness made his entry smooth. "Not fast, slow and deep." Each stroke stopped in her deepest parts. She softly grunted each time he descended and claimed her unfamiliar territory. She looked between them and watched his penis, stroke after stroke. He loved her absorption and how she savored his invasion.

She looked into his eyes and smiled knowingly. "I got you, now, Mister, I got you," she said, and softly laughed. Her words were searing: he felt claimed as he plundered her hiddenness. Time slowed and he was lost in her depths. Delicate tendrils threaded their way into his fundamental awareness. She was, they were, spinning and weaving a connection he would never leave.

His thrusting quickened; her ankles gripped his hips and she began to moan. His back arched and her body began quivering all over. Her eyes fluttered and deep within her chest a sound started when he began his release. "Don't stop, don't stop . . ." her voice rose and she screamed. Her deepest muscles throbbed in spasms about him. Her eyes closed, her back bucked upward, her legs shook and then she collapsed. He sank onto her body for several seconds as their heads touched ear to ear, and gradually their breathing slowed. After he rolled to one side of her, he settled.

He felt exhausted, purged and yet cleansed: like his carburetor jets had been flushed out. He couldn't remember when he'd felt this calm. Opening his eyes, he saw her right arm over her eyes: she looked as spent as he felt. After several moments passed, her body stirred.

"Ever hear of petit mort?" She softly asked, her eyes remained closed. He shook his head. "It's French for the little death. If you make love right with a woman, she climaxes and will pass out. A release so strong I almost pass out." She stretched her arms hard, opened her eyes and yawned. She looked at him and smiled. "I have to get home so I can sleep and be fresh for work tomorrow." She grabbed his chin and wagged it playfully. "I thought we would be good. But not this good, not the first time. Feels like we were meant to be." She leaned over Med and kissed his lips tenderly. "Best be on my way, Mister."

"You're a lot of woman, Roz." He paused. "I'll walk you down and make sure you get home by taxi."

She shook her head. "A bus will be fine."

He shook his head and smiled. "I insist. And it's proper, given how we just spent the evening together." She shrugged, got up from the bed, and retrieved her castoff clothes. He heard the water running in the bathroom while he finished dressing. She emerged dressed and went out to the sitting room where she finished combing her hair and applied lipstick. They held hands as they left for the elevator.

On the sidewalk in front of the San Diego Hotel, the two middle-aged lovers stood silently as they waited for a taxi. After one stopped, Med gave the driver her address and enough money for the ride and tip. Roselle faced, hugged and pecked him on the cheek before getting into the automobile. When the taxi pulled out into the street, she waved from the back window and he watched it drive away, down Broadway.

Back in his suite, he finished off the Scotch, removed his trousers and shirt and pulled back the bedcovers. He was still enervated from their coupling. Felt like he had had a tigress by her tail. Somehow she had coaxed him into her lair—*do tigresses have lairs?* he wondered and he fell asleep with the lamp on.

A few hours later, his full bladder woke him. After he voided, he switched off the lamp. In the darkness, he closed his eyes.

"You slept well, Virgil, and not because of the Scotch." His eyes flew open; the words jolted him. He waited and nothing else came. Must be hearing things. He turned onto his right side and settled his head into the feather pillow.

"You did hear me, Virgil." He jerked up to sitting upright, and

leaned back on both arms. The bedroom window curtains were backlit by street lamps and he could dimly make out the dresser across the room. Who, what the hell?

"It's me, Virgil." He could hear her, but the words were inside his mind. The same soft cadence of her speech.

"Ethel? No, I know I am awake." He felt confused, irritated and incredulous. He did not believe in ghosts and voices beyond the grave.

"It is *me and I am not a ghost and you can hear me because I am part of you, your life and past. You let me in."* He shook his head. All he wanted was to go back to sleep. He had a long day at the plant starting in a few hours.

"If I let you in, then surely I can tell you to get the hell out. I am not nuts and talking to my dead wife is nuts!"

"Common wisdom about talking to the dead, or the dead talking to you, is wrong. Besides, no one else knows you better."

"You want to talk? My last memory of you . . ."

"I was within my rights. While I was still there, what I wanted when I was dying was my choice. I wanted peace and quiet. And you did *stay away."*

"I never said to you what I should have. When you sent me away, and then died unexpectedly, I lost any chance."

"That's probably what should have happened. You would have talked past your behavior during our years together. I can help you reflect on your life, now."

"We never talked like this before. We didn't talk at all. I'm not a contemplative man." He heard her laugh.

"That's not true. You thought a lot about everything when you were in the Pen."

"I never told you that. I don't talk about those years, ever, to anyone."

"And you still don't have to. I'm in your mind and see your memories and feel your feelings and your heart. I'm a sounding board of your choosing, responding to you, and I never played the piano, though Lord knows I heard Lillian talk enough about such at dinner! I'm watching, that's all. You're starting a new romance."

"Talking about Roselle makes me feel queer."

"You never hid any of your lovers when I was living."

"For the love of God, Ethel. This is crazy!"

"Virgil, you can block me from returning. But will you? We were each other's first love. We helped each other during the early years. We had three children together. When things went really wrong, I kept our children's lives going and their home running. I know you, like no one else, and feel your deepest yearnings. My dying brought you to a crossroad. You're free from your first life. You can begin another."

Her logic unnerved him but he didn't feel so alone, either. She said he could stop any future visits. Did he really want to? "Anything else?"

"You're sleeping the best you have since my leaving. No one knows the future. I certainly don't. Every choice you make brings new possibilities. Be aware." And she vanished.

Everything she said was true. Roselle was a new possibility. Not a bit like Ethel was, *or is,* his mind drily commented. Jeezus, what a handful. A new lover who ran the show, at least in bed, and then his dead wife appearing. Wasn't one woman at a time enough? *Not in the old days,* he admitted, abashed. He was too tired to sort it out now. He turned onto his side, punched his pillow and laid his head on it. He started counting backwards, one breath at a time. Blackness descended and he fell asleep once more.

Chapter 23

W e're spending so much time together, shouldn't we move in together?" Med asked Roselle hopefully. It was a beautiful September evening and they currently worked the same schedule. He was driving his green 1939 Studebaker down the palm-lined Pacific Coast Highway after their shift. Then, they usually spent dinner together, after which she frequently stayed at his hotel room. Because they weren't married, she never let him come to her house in eastern San Diego.

"Y'know how I feel about that, Virg. We've talked about this before. The hotel is one thing, but where I can be seen by neighbors . . ." Roselle looked annoyed. She didn't like revisiting issues if her answer or the solution remained the same. He glanced at her as he braked for a downtown stoplight. They both liked spicy Mexican food and he was heading south to a restaurant in National City. The food was authentic and he loved any dish cooked with lard.

"I have a proposal. Well, two proposals, if the first one is acceptable." Her expression softened with curiosity. "How about our getting married? We could get married this next Monday."

Her blue eyes widened as she absorbed his idea. "We'd have to get a marriage license and with our hours at the plant, one of us has to take time off to get to the bureau before it closes at five."

He shook his head and smiled. "Not if we get married in Mexico. We can go straight across the border and get married on any day except Sunday." She absorbed information piece by piece as she looked for possible flaws. She should have been an engineer. But none of the aircraft engineers he worked with could tantalize him like this redhead.

"I've heard about Mexican marriages. They *are* quick," she countered hesitantly.

"It's important to you that we aren't just an affair. I want to be with you and you want that, too, don't you?" She nodded her head, and wasn't digging in her heels. "Let's get married this next week and spend our wedding night there. I'll ask around about where we can stay overnight and not rush back." Med gently stroked her auburn hair and his hand trailed down her neck and rested on her left breast, which he softly squeezed.

"Already thinking about the wedding night, Mister?" she archly asked. "All right, let's make it a weekend. What's your second proposal?" She removed his hand but held it with their fingers interlaced. Med suddenly steered the car to the right curb and parked. He hoped no nails were lying in the gutter. A flat tire might show up when he pulled out into the road later.

He turned to her. "The most critical one: so I figure I better stop the car when I asked." He paused for a significant period, looking into her eyes. "Will you marry me, Roselle? I've lived a previous life and carry significant baggage. Knowing this, will you be mine? Forgive my not kneeling but these knees of mine . . ." She broke into a smile, her blue eyes danced and her face glowed. She *had* been waiting for his proposal.

"Took you long enough, Virg. Yes, of course I will marry you." She gasped suddenly. "That means I can petition to get my girls to live with us! You'll have little girls underfoot, you know." Bubbling and happy, she pulled his face to hers, kissed him hard and then gazed into his eyes, elated. He hadn't seen her this relaxed, and with her defenses down. She was a mother who could now bring her youngest children back into her life. She grabbed his other hand. "You can't know what having my youngest ones back with me means!"

"Roz, you're glowing. I remember what you told me about your divorce and custody arrangement. I think we're both ready for a home together. I need a home. I haven't had one for five years. You'll get your little ones back and I'll have a house full of women, big and small. I love little girls. Always have and always will."

"What about Buddy?" Her smile became a little tense.

"He can stay at the hotel. He'll be eighteen next June and will join the service then. I might stay with him occasionally. But I think he'll be fine. And once we're married, I want him to come regularly for dinner to your, our house."

Her face brightened as she nodded. "Sounds reasonable. I want a new life but simpler. Buddy's a nice kid and isn't pushy." Med sensed what she wasn't saying.

"You mean like Silva." His voice tightened.

Roselle looked defiant. "She's a big girl, Virg, and has a husband. I just . . ."

He shook his head. "She's my daughter, Roz. And always will be. This past year, what with Ethel's death, really affected her. She'll be back in San Diego, at some point, because Blaine's going to be shipped out. I'm her only parent, now."

Roselle ducked her head and swallowed. Her expression, when she looked up, was neutral and accommodating. "I know how you feel about her. And you should. She's your firstborn. As long as you give me warning she's coming, I'll work it out. But there's something about that girl I feel. All right, let's not let anything rain on our parade. I'm famished! Let's get to dinner."

His fiancée took his right arm with her left hand and settled back contentedly. Med smiled at her and started the car. On to dinner they went, hopefully with no flat tire. He knew they would be revisiting the subject of Silva. Today, though, Roselle was beaming. He enjoyed her momentary sunniness, with not a cloud in her sky. As long as they didn't broach the topic of Silva. Besides, they were getting married.

Chapter 24

It was a late November evening in the San Diego bus station, where Med and Buddy stood next to the arrivals door. Silva's bus from Colorado was due any moment. The day before, she'd cabled Med: Blaine had been sent to the Philippines and she was coming back. The war effort remained strong in the autumn of 1944, and trained people were always in demand at the aircraft plant. Ongoing battles in both the European and Pacific war theaters required planes, lots of planes. He reread the cable, while his secretary sent out memos asking for available stenographer openings. Father and daughter had an unspoken agreement that he would get her work at Consolidated whenever she was in town. He learned of two open positions Silva was qualified for and could start immediately.

He didn't know what to expect. Ten months before, Ethel's death had crushed the girl's world. After the memorial service, each time he saw her outside of work she exuded grief. Buddy had carried on, going to Brown's Military Academy as though nothing had happened. Father and son didn't discuss Ethel's passing. Med's lack of a father made his raising Buddy another rudderless, aimless circumstance. Their customary emotional distance was well established. Med treated his son more as a sidekick and never got too serious about much of anything. Any tensions between them never took hold. With Silva, however, their rapport always had been an emotional lightning rod with a turbulent history.

As a little girl, Sissie could twist him around her finger at one moment and the next, she would blurt out the things Ethel left unsaid. When he got riled by her directness and outspoken attitude, he loaded her up with back-breaking chores: she never cried or whined but looked at him defiantly all the while.

During the Jefferson City period, when he had just wanted Ethel gone, his daughter's defiance had saved her mother's life. When he started serving his prison sentence, his fourteen-year-old daughter became the true power in the family. Ethel acted accordingly. When he returned home thirty months later in 1941, his wife asked their seventeen-year-old daughter if they should join him in California. The girl emphatically said no.

Once in California, he made things work. In September he started his Consolidated Aircraft training in tool and die making and was hired at Consolidated that December. Government contracts made the plane manufacturer a major supplier in the military effort. Three daily shifts and employee work weeks overlapped and the plant was always open. Several thousand people worked there and outside of the Navy, Consolidated was the biggest employer in San Diego. Although he had never had any mechanical inclinations in Missouri, Med's prodigious memory made him a quick study for tool and die blueprints and he learned mechanical engineering as a journeyman. His previous military and political experience made him a natural leader; he was quickly promoted into management. He asked Silva to join him once she graduated from high school. California offered many more opportunities than Missouri. A week after graduating from Campbell High, Silva left for San Diego.

So their father-daughter connection resumed. They lived separately, worked in different departments and shifts at the plant but saw each other frequently. Even though his supervisor salary was far larger than hers, Med still asked her for money. The women in his life always had resources he could tap. Why would he expect any less from his teenage daughter?

While she settled into San Diego and her job, he introduced

her to young servicemen he knew from his veteran and USO groups. Blaine Hardy had been the one. She fell in love with and quickly married the Army Air Corps recruit who was seven years older. Med's daughter was making a new life in the same city that had given him a second chance. He was delighted.

A year later, when Ethel became seriously ill, Silva managed Ethel's illness and death with great aplomb and class. Afterwards, she functioned well at work, but privately she quietly wept most of the time. Med's talks with Blaine revealed that both were baffled by the unchanging depth of her grieving. Regardless of the disruption Ethel's arrival, illness and death had caused in his marriage, Blaine was clear that he stood by his young wife. Med's son-in-law's adoration of Silva was obvious. Three months after Ethel's death, the young officer was transferred to Butler Springs in Colorado for additional training and eventual deployment and Silva accompanied him. Both men hoped the change would help resolve her grief. After seven months, she was coming back.

The station door for arrivals opened and people streamed into the waiting room. Sailors wore heavy pea coats over their navy blue uniforms. Marines, stationed in Oceanside, arrived in their olive uniforms, and young women in knee-length skirts and high heels were crowned by little hats perched on their shoulder-length hairdos. All mixed into a bunch. Suddenly the terminal was full. Looking for Silva, Med craned his neck and leaned towards Buddy.

Buddy's face brightened and he pointed. "There she is. Sissie!" He called and waved. A transformed Silva walked through the terminal. Dressed sharply as ever, she now walked with an energy he hadn't seen since before Ethel's death. She saw Buddy waving, smiled, and waved back. They exchanged greetings, and she asked if someone could get her bag from the bus curb side. Buddy left and father and daughter looked into each other's eyes.

He held out his arms and she stepped into them. "We've been worried about you, Sissie, darling. It's good to see you back, even if Blaine's orders are the reason."

Silva nodded her head with a look of relief. "I needed to leave and be with Blaine since we didn't know when his orders would come through. But I missed San Diego so much. The weather in Colorado was all right when we arrived but at the elevation where we were, the cold comes in faster. Getting away from where Mom died, I needed that. For a while. But I missed here so much." Buddy came up to them with her large suitcase. Silva opened her arms and they hugged.

After they stood back from one another, Buddy looked mischievous. "Dad's got some news for you, Sis."

Med looked a bit annoyed. "All in good time, Bud. Let your sister get her legs before imparting any family news that's not yours to confide." Buddy continued his teasing look. Silva's jocular mood shifted and she looked at their father questioningly.

"Sissie, we'll talk about it once we drop Junior here off at the hotel. Let's get out of here and be on our way." He offered his arm and Silva linked hers in it and reached for Buddy's available arm as they made their way out of the noisy bus station to the parked Studebaker. After leaving Buddy at the San Diego Hotel, Med started driving from downtown towards East San Diego.

"Some things have changed since you left. I moved out of the Hotel but Buddy's staying in the suite." Silva shifted in her seat.

He felt her bracing herself for his news. "You know that gal I was seeing before you and Blaine left?"

"Roselle?"

He looked at Silva uncertainly "We got married in September and we're living in her house in the University area."

She exhaled sharply like she had been holding her breath. "Med, you've been alone for quite some time. Although not alone, alone. There's always been somebody. Look, Mom's gone. You were legally separated when you left Missouri. If Roselle makes you happy, then I'm happy."

He sighed with relief. "I'm glad you feel this way, Sissie. I was worried. And you have been so, so sad. Of course you'd grieve for your mother. She was too young. But I didn't want my new marriage to affect you and me, just when you came back."

"I'm not over Mom's death. Somehow I wonder if I'll ever be. But I'm better. Now, I have to figure out how to live alone. We've no idea how long Blaine will be gone, how long the war will go on." She reached over and touched his shoulder. "So what are the plans for this evening? And where will I stay until I get a paycheck? Assuming there are some openings."

He put his right hand on top of hers. "The good news, well, it's all good news." He told her about the open stenographer slots. "And I want you to stay with us until you get paid. We only have two bedrooms, so the couch will be your bed." She smiled and relaxed her posture. "And since you'll stay with us, let's have dinner at my—Roselle's—house and you can settle in. How's that sound?"

"You seem to have thought of everything. It's a relief, staying with family after Blaine leaving. Just for a little bit. As soon as I have some money, I'll be out of your hair. No way I want to intrude on newlyweds." He heard her chuckle. She'd taken the news well. He hoped their reception from Roselle would go as smoothly.

It was dusk as they drove from downtown. Small houses with small square patches of grass as yards lined both sides of the streets. They were driving inland, away from the water, and she enthusiastically repeated that being back felt good.

He turned off University Boulevard onto Wilson Street. He crossed two intersections and turned into the driveway of a modest white house with a flat roof. Annual rainfall in Southern California was low and flat roofs were common. Inland sections of the city had few trees and sunlight overheated rooms on the southern exposure. Striped awnings shielded those windows and a small square front yard bridged the driveway to the porch steps. The porch was spacious and wide enough for a divan and chairs. The temperate climate made sitting on the porch inviting year round, as many neighbors often did.

Med grabbed Silva's suitcase and they made their way to the front door. He knocked, opened the door and called, "We're here, Roz."

Roselle came into the front room. She was still wearing her street clothes from the day's shift and she looked tired. "So I see, Virgil. Silva, welcome."

Silva stepped forward and extended her hand towards Roselle.

"Thank you for letting me stay for a little bit. As soon as I get paid, I'll be out of here."

The older woman nodded and smiled coolly, "You are Virgil's daughter, and I understand. Well, Mister, I've a little something for supper. Come to the kitchen and Silva can freshen up from her trip." Things seem to be going smoothly. He relaxed and followed her into the kitchen.

Within a half hour, the three sat at the table in the small dining room off the kitchen. Everything in the house was small. For a woman living alone or a couple, it was modest and functional. They had finished dinner, the plates pushed to one side and he brought out a half-full bottle of Scotch and three small glasses.

Roselle looked surprised. "We've work tomorrow, Virg."

He nodded. "True enough, but I thought a shot for each of us, to celebrate Silva's return. She's my oldest and I've missed her." Roselle pursed her lips.

Silva held her right hand up, in warning. "You know I don't drink much, Med. Not even when Blaine and I went dancing. Maybe a little beer."

Smiling, he countered, "I'm sitting with my two favorite women . . ." He sat between them and took the closest hand from each. ". . . so, don't gulp it down. Sip it. Let's chat a bit and then we'll call it a night." Silva smiled and nodded and Roselle remained silent. He poured about an inch into each glass and distributed them.

Talk was sketchy with long silences. Silva complimented the house and its location in the city. She talked a bit about life in Colorado and how she missed Blaine. Med responded and Roselle still said nothing. He felt her watching. *This is my daughter, dammit. And if I want to talk with her, for a bit, I'm going to.* He launched into one of his fishing stories.

"And here we are. I've moved that blasted boat hither and yon, under the trees, out into the sun, moved across to the other side of the river. But no matter where we move, I can't get a bite. Nowhere!"

Silva chimed in, "That's right, you couldn't. But they sure bit for me. You even made us switch seats and that didn't work, either!" He sat in mock outrage because, together, they had told this story before. They both chuckled, took sips of their Scotch and Roselle quietly smiled.

Silva looked over at her. "Tell me, Roselle. Did you ever fish as a girl?"

"It's hard to fish out in Yuma." Silva looked at her questioningly. Roselle clarified. "Arizona? Lots of desert and dry country, not river country at all. Yuma does sit on the Colorado but we lived on the other side of town." Silva nodded with an understanding look. "Nope, my daddy ran a general store and my mother also worked there. We were open seven days a week excepting Sunday mornings. We didn't have a river house and a place in the city. We got by but there was no extra money lying around."

Silva looked at Med and he looked at Roselle. His stomach knotted. Maybe another approach? Silva took the lead. "Roselle, we did go through a period when Med wasn't working. In fact, one summer, he asked me, a fourteen-year-old, for my paltry savings, so we ran a gas station across the way, in Tennessee. What kind of sandwiches did we sell, Med?"

Feeling no better, he joined the attempted charade. "Pimento cheese. And we had no good way of keeping them cold. By the time folks bought them, they were a little on the warm side." Silva gamely smiled and Roselle continued to look dour.

"I never did like pimento cheese," Silva commented. "Give me a tomato and cheese sandwich with lots of lettuce and I'm all set. Bacon makes it even better!"

She stood up and waited until Roselle met her eyes, as she reached for Med's left hand. "I know my being here is an intrusion, Roselle. Thanks again for your hospitality. Time for me to turn in. I need to get to the plant early and talk to a future boss. Can I ride in with you, Med?" He agreed by nodding. "Great. Good night, both of you." She turned and left the kitchen.

Her footsteps, walking to the bathroom, sounded through the little house. Roselle rose from her chair, stacked the used dishes and glasses and carried them into the kitchen. She began washing and Med went out the kitchen door. *No sense in talking to her when she's like this. Let her work it through.* He walked around to the front porch and stood looking out, for a while. He pulled out his pack of Beech-Nut tobacco and slipped a pinch under his bottom front lip.

The houses sat right next to one another, like squares on graph paper, separated by fences and concrete driveways. Darkness had settled in an hour before and brought with it a coolness he always welcomed. He loved cold air and the mild San Diego winters made him miss Missouri's blustery cold winter nights. In Jefferson City, his partly open bedroom window kept him from overheating during the winters. Some plant production issues and a few calls to make the next day came to mind. Then he went back into their bedroom.

Roselle was in bed, her back to the door, but the bedside lamp was still on. He sat next to her. "It's just until her first paycheck, Roz. I know you feel . . ."

"You don't know how or what I feel! Why in hell is she here, for God's sake? You have the connections and power to find her a place somewhere else. Why here?" She whispered angrily.

Her intensity confused him. "Why're you so upset? If it were one of your older children, I could live with them staying here for a short time. Why can't Silva?" His logic did not calm her.

She jerked up to a sitting position, her eyes flashing. "She's a big girl. Yes, her husband has shipped out. But it's wartime. And her mother died several months ago. But it has nothing to do with our life together. Why did you bring her here?"

"It's her first night back in town and she's going to be working at the plant. I'm her father and I can help. Why shouldn't I?" His voice got louder.

She mirrored his volume and said loudly, "She's your past and I'm your now and future. Help her all you want but keep her out of our marriage. She knows you in a way I never can. Not because she's your daughter but because she knows how you were, what you did. Months ago, when I met her that once, when I asked her questions about Missouri, she was rude. She acted like I was prying. And her attitude about you. As if she knows better than you. And I know she reminds you of Ethel. It makes me crazy." The last words she almost yelled.

Furious, he did yell, "Silva's the only one who ever stood up to me." He stopped, swallowed and his voice returned to a quiet, conversational level. "When she was little, sometimes I punished her for it. But she's my little girl and a father . . ."

She clamped her eyes shut and framed her face with both thumbs below her ears and fingers at her brows, still loudly, "Daddy's little girl, huh?" Her eyes flew open and she pointed her finger accusingly at him and chided, "But she calls you Med. She doesn't even call you Dad or Pa or Father."

He knew Silva could hear everything they were saying. "For Christ's sake, keep it down," he whispered harshly. "She hears every word we're saying but we don't need the neighbors in on this, too. Fine, she stays here tonight and I'll make different arrangements tomorrow when I get to the plant. Please, let this be the end of it." He took off his trousers and shirt and slipped beneath the covers. Gradually his breathing slowed down and his tense muscles began to release. Roselle lay back down and seemed to have calmed. His anger dissipated and his mind began to drift. He was almost asleep when he felt her hand reach for his groin.

She turned on her side to face his profile and held the base of his limp penis. Reflexively, he responded. She whispered in his ear, "Just think about tomorrow night whenever you get to feeling sorry for her. We won't need to keep our voices down, then. You're mine, Mister. You like how I know you and how we take care of each other. Tomorrow night, Virg." She then released him and turned her back to him, her favorite sleeping position. He softly sighed, knowing she was right. He could make other arrangements. After this tiff, though, he had little hope the two women in his life would ever get along. After several minutes Roselle's breath got softer and very regular; she was asleep.

He awoke early and dressed immediately. When he came out into the front room, she was sitting, already dressed, with her suitcase packed. She said nothing when she saw him.

He leaned over her, took both hands and pulled her up to

standing. "I know you heard everything last night," he murmured.

She shook her head. "Let's talk in the car." He picked up her suitcase and carried it out.

After he backed out the car and retraced his way to the main boulevard, he spoke. "Look, Sissie, this was my mistake. She does have a temper but I had no idea bringing you here would set it off."

Silva looked at him, mystified. "So her temper is no news to you? What's going on? What have you gotten yourself into, Med?"

His look signaled that this was not a subject she could challenge. "You know we have dorms at the plant just for these types of situations."

Silva flashed, "You mean when fathers are forbidden to let their adult daughters stay with them for a week or two. We always did this for family in Missouri. You know that."

He shook his head and continued. "I'll be sure to find you a space in the dorm tonight and until you have money for rent. This isn't my first choice but it'll get you over the hump."

Silva looked out her window and said nothing more until they pulled into the Consolidated parking lot. She never entered Roselle's house again. Neither father nor daughter broached the possibility of another social occasion with Roselle. She did accept his life with Roselle. However, she was a person who never wanted to be where she was not wanted.

"Sometimes we make decisions not of our choosing." The words were startlingly clear. Med's shift had ended and he was walking to his car. Roz was working a different shift, so he would be driving home alone. Ethel!

"Sometimes it seems as if we didn't take a firm stand. But maybe by giving in, we've done what's needed although we don't understand." He shook his head in short little spurts. Maybe this was just his imagination. If it were, then she wouldn't answer. When he reached the Studebaker, he got in and sat.

"What are you referring to?" He asked, hoping for silence.

"*This situation between you and Roselle and Silva.*" Yes, she's back.

Med sighed and feelings of guilt and helplessness resurfaced. He rolled down the car window. "What am I supposed to do? She's my wife and she makes me happy. You know how I feel about Sissie . . ."

"*I do. Always did. Despite some of the storms between you two, I always knew she was special to you.*"

He continued, "Something about Sissie sets her off. It's more than being our daughter. She doesn't understand how Sissie and I are with one another. I have to accept . . ."

"*Yes. Accept, Virgil. You never could accept before. You stepped on, took from and took over, punished whomever when you didn't get your way. Now accepting things you did not choose or want has entered into your life. Sissie will be fine.*"

"I know she will but not being able to help her now, in all the ways I could . . ."

"*Not being able to steer the course for another just the way you want is part of accepting. Accept it gracefully. All of these changes, bit by bit, form new ways of you being different from what you were. Almost like harrowing a field.*"

"Farming words. What are you telling me, Ethel?" He heard her chuckle softly.

"*When we change, Virgil, it cuts both ways. Not only are we affected but we affect others. Perhaps Sissie needs to be turned away, but neither of you can know why. Now both of you will make new choices. Your new wife must come first because she is your wife. Honoring your marriage and your wife is new for you.*"

Med put his head in his hands. If anyone knew what was going on in his head — "It's bewildering to have my dead wife who I treated so, so . . ." — he couldn't choose a word, he groaned — ". . . talking to me about how to be with my new wife!"

"*How I come to you doesn't matter. Listen to what I am saying. Your reasoning keeps you from what your heart knows. Part of acceptance is that our hearts get hurt. My heart hurt lots when I was with you.*"

He took a breath and felt his heart ease. *Why?* "I know that."

"I'm fine. Sissie took very good care of me in ways I didn't under-stand. Religion and the Bible have always been very important to you. In prison you began to change. Not everything that happens is understand-able, but anyone who wants to know the deeper parts of life, of the heart and soul, they understand more the longer they live."

Philosophy! Ethel had never been one to speak of such mat-ters. She was, though, on the other side and seemed knowledge-able about these matters. At least she wasn't giving him hell about Silva. "All right. I will consider that there are no easy answers." He felt amusement emanating from her.

"Until our next visit, Virgil." And she was gone.

He started the car and slowly eased out of the parking lot. He did feel calmer about Roz pushing him to get Silva out of their home. He wanted his marriage to succeed and he craved a stable home. Keeping his relationship with his daughter separate was necessary.

Chapter 25

On August 6, the first atomic bomb was dropped on Hiroshima. Because the Japanese did not immediately respond, Truman authorized a second bomb to be dropped on Nagasaki on August 9. Upon verification of the Nagasaki bombing, they requested only that the Imperial Throne would remain. Although the official surrender occurred on September 2, the war ended in mid-August.

In late August, employee layoffs began. Silva lost her job in the first wave. She left for San Francisco to begin college at the University of California at Berkeley. The next month, Med was let go during one of the last layoffs.

It was late morning, the day after he received his own layoff slip. Roselle had been laid off the week before. As one of the last production managers to leave, he knew the company was regrouping to see what new direction manufacturing would pursue. Both the Depression and the wartime economy made it easy to save and both had ample savings. Now that the war was over and the economy had recovered, everyone throughout the country was waiting to see how their lives would change.

Lying in bed, he heard Roz in the bathroom. The bedroom window was open and a slight breeze blew in the morning's coolness. The prospect of no job and regular hours was unfamiliar but not disturbing. It was so unlike his memories of his public humiliation in Campbell, and the days awaiting trial and those he spent after his release from prison.

His idleness, then, was tinged by the shame that everyone knew what he had done. His shame was no less when he returned because everyone knew where he had been. His life in Missouri had become ashes. He left to begin again and reinvented himself in all the ways he had sought. On this idle morning, he saw God's forgiveness and blessings.

That last conversation, or was it a visitation? Whatever it was, Ethel had mentioned religion. Now he chose not to be public about his faith. His many years of lying, infidelities and emotional and financial abandonment of his family had not destroyed him at his core. Enough of him remained that could recognize the dissonance between what he professed and how he really had lived. A man of strong appetites, he needed to be visible, to be a major force, and to feel good. Feeling good included food, booze, and good-looking women who were good in bed. Feeling good was also Spirit, God, faith, the Word, the blessings from and being touched by God.

He had the blessing and curse of being able to convince almost anyone of anything. Once he overheard someone call him a silver-tongued devil. Once he adjusted to silence in prison, what he first thought was emasculation became a left-handed blessing from God. Over time his inward focus revealed what his past actions had inflicted upon the people around him. He grappled with his repeated denials of his wife's and children's needs while he took care of his Dunn and Medling relations. He could no longer defend his choices. Rather, he accepted that he had broken many of the Commandments.

The outbreak of war had provided him his opportunity. Although the family's refusal to join him had been wrenching, especially with Sissie, he hadn't lost his touch for recovery. His technical aptitude coupled with his rapid entry into management helped him once more acquire significant influence and power. Soon he was supervising eight hundred tool and die makers. His lapses into folky stories charmed his peers and subordinates. His mastery of quid pro quo built his reputation as someone who always came through in a pinch. Outside of work, he channeled his energies into the Veterans of Foreign Wars. He joined the Masonic Lodge. These organizations focused on helping veterans and social causes; he was active in their community functions but didn't seek to be a public front-liner.

Despite Ethel's death, and the sudden descent of Buddy coming to live with him, gradually he achieved everything he wanted. Silva's arrival, both of them working at Consolidated, and her marriage to Blaine, helped him feel anchored. Finding Roselle, though, was the beginning of a real personal life. Four years had passed since he came to California and he had thrived. What else would the future bring?

The bathroom door opened and she walked into the bedroom with a strange look on her face. She was still in her nightgown, her hair tousled from sleep.

"Something wrong, Roz?" he asked. She had been in a very good mood before she got out of bed.

"I missed my period last month. I'm pretty regular, with all the kids I've had. And I was counting in the bathroom. Today makes two months late. I'm starting to wonder . . ." she looked a little worriedly at him. He looked at her and suddenly felt a rush in his chest. No!

"Are you saying what I think you're saying?" His eyes opened wide as thoughts and feelings surged through his mind and body. "A baby . . . a baby . . . Roz, are you going to have a baby?"

"That's what missing periods usually means, Mister." She sounded less sure of herself than usual. She sighed. "I wasn't expecting this. We've been going at it pretty steadily since we got together. I guess since I still have periods, there's no reason it couldn't happen. So, here we are. Virg, I think we're having a baby."

He sat on the edge of the bed. "Come over here, woman." He suddenly felt like a young bull. A baby, at his age! She walked over to him. He ran his hands under her nightgown, cupped her hips and bottom. "Suddenly I am feeling in the mood, Roz. Don't remember wanting to take Ethel to bed when she told me she was expecting. Right now," he buried his head in her belly.

Her hands clutched his hair and she pulled his face away. "Are you all right about this? A baby at our ages and we're newlyweds, sort of . . ." her voice faltered.

He looked her in her eyes. "Roz, it's a shock, yes. Unexpected, yes. But a baby, our baby, makes a real home. I thought we had one before, but now. Our own little bear cub!" And he started to laugh softly. *Yes, blessed by God, indeed.*

"You're sounding pretty pleased with yourself, Mister," she chided him.

"Pleased with it all, the baby, and you and us. You've given me a whole new life, Roz. I love you, woman. I really do." His voice dropped to a whisper and tears sprang to his eyes. "I'm a fortunate man." He dropped his eyes.

He felt her shift and then her hand stroked his face and raised his chin. She had dropped her nightgown straps to reveal her full breasts. Her eyes watered with emotion. "Time to finish what you started, Mister. We got to make hay before I get too big. Don't make me wait any longer."

Roselle confirmed her pregnancy a couple of days later. With neither of them working, they spent their days together leisurely. As they prepared, the couple addressed several things. When they had married in Mexico the year before, he never thought about any legalities. In 1945, however, the legal standing of Mexican marriages could be disputed stateside. Roselle's pregnancy made him feel an unfamiliar sense of protectiveness and wanting his growing family secure in every way possible. This new awareness became fundamental in his life's second chapter.

Neither viewed their second marriage as a romantic occasion. Both wanted a civil ceremony. Because marriage in San Diego County was performed only by clergy, she suggested they go to

Yuma. A judge married them on October 5 in the Yuma court-house, almost a year to the day after their first ceremony. Med was forty-seven and Roselle was thirty-nine.

Although she had left her children with her first husband, Roselle was in frequent contact. Letters and visits were exchanged; either she went north or one of her children visited in San Diego. Except for the youngest, Med met everyone else. He enthusiastically embraced his role as both a new father and being her older children's stepfather. Their American marriage encouraged Roselle to pursue custody.

For the first time in his life, Med wanted to buy his own farm property for his home. Impending fatherhood brought back memories of growing up with the Dunns; raising his child in town had no appeal. Although he had never worked on the Missouri farm, he loved the countryside surrounding Malden. Thoughts of the open, spacious fields summoned a soft homesickness because he knew he would never see his kinfolk again.

San Diego County's outlying areas, in the north and east, held large tracts of farmland. The terrain was startlingly beautiful, with long sloping hills that stretched from one valley to the next. Some small stands of trees, like oaks and planted eucalyptus, could be found but mostly the vegetation was thick brush. The vistas included the sweep down into broad straw-colored valleys, spotted with small clusters of trees or expansive lowlands distantly condoned off by ascending hills. Occasionally, twenty or more miles outside the city, a few roads ran along edges of deep river gorges. Because of the low annual rainfall, the land appeared lush only during the spring season when the mustard grasses bloomed. Curvaceous hills, for a brief six weeks each year, were cloaked in brilliant light yellow blossoms that appeared velvety. In contrast, the westernmost valleys typically were saltwater marshes that ran down onto the ocean shoreline.

Citrus and avocados had been farmed for decades and fetched good prices; an established ranch could be lucrative. Their move to a rural area linked his childhood to his future. When they looked at properties, Roselle agreed to finance what property they chose.

The down payment for a lemon ranch outside of El Cajon

came from a second mortgage on Roselle's Wilson Street house. His relationship with Roselle was a partnership of equals but this time the balance of power tipped more towards her. In his middle years, Med was an influential person in his charitable brotherhood organizations and at work but at home he accommodated his family's needs at her behest. His years in California and life with Roselle slowly re-formed him into a stable, dependable husband and father.

Chapter 26

It was the first of May, 1946, and he looked down at the infant boy in his arms. He was a forty-six-year-old new father. Wonder coursed through him. His heart was full and thankful.

From her bed, Roselle looked at the two of them, her blue eyes twinkling, her red hair spread over her pillow. "Well, Mister, how does it feel? Holding your son, our son . . ."

Med nodded silently. All he wanted to do was look. He took her closest hand. "Good, really good. You've done it, Roz, you've been resurrecting my life." He paused thoughtfully. "So, what names do you think we might consider?"

"Goes without saying, no fancy Latin names. You are here with me, and our son. I've always like Scott. And I have an Edwin in my family on my mother's side."

"Edwin Scott Medling is a fitting name, I'm contributing the surname, ma'am, if you have no objections . . ."

"I'm counting on that, Mister." She yawned, released his hand and reached out for the baby. "Hand him back. You're not used to holding such a precious bundle."

He really didn't want to let the baby go. *What was happening?* Sissie and Buddy, when infants, had never affected him like this one. Yes, baby Scottie. The name felt right. He made a face as he laid the drowsy baby in her arms.

"All right, Roz. You going to rest for a bit? With the baby?" She nodded and yawned again. He walked to their bedroom window overlooking the acres of lemon trees and cranked it open a few inches. "It's a mild day and still cool. Just right for a late morning nap." He walked back to the bed, leaned over and kissed her on her forehead and then stroked the strands of her hair.

"Scat, Mister! I'm bushed." She wiggled under the sheets, adjusted the baby into the crook of her left arm and closed her eyes.

From the bedroom door, he turned back to look at mother and newborn together. His domestic life was now rooted in being a new father. He had never considered another child when dating Roselle. Two years later, he was amazed at where his life had landed. He lived on a working ranch, thirty years after he'd rejected farming. His scandal and imprisonment had cost him everything: reputation, friends and his only true family, the Dunns. Five years later, his newborn gave his second marriage weight and depth. He felt an overwhelming desire to nurture and protect his baby boy, no matter the cost. He walked out to the kitchen.

"A newborn son, Virgil. How differently you see your life now."

His stomach tightened. "You're back, Ethel Mae. I know you're not real, and just in my mind."

"Not that unreal, if you're talking to me. You do see your life differently, don't you?"

"I'm not a boy or the impudent young fool I was back then. I see how much of my past behavior was deplorable. Especially to you. I never admitted that to you."

"That's a lot to admit to someone not real. Even if I'm only in your mind, I can feel your heart. That's what I'm talking about. We never had your heart."

"He's so small and defenseless."

"So were Silva and Buddy, Virgil."

"I couldn't feel this much, then. I couldn't see."

She laughed softly. *"What men don't seem to know is that it's seldom that a woman won't feel this much when she has her children. Mothers are often puzzled that fathers aren't as overcome as they are. Children are everything. Everything flows from them."*

He sighed. "I understand that now."

"*You must need to acknowledge this, Virgil, or else I wouldn't have come. Your own father didn't raise you or even want to know you when you were grown. I saw my father Avonelle only once but that one time he let me know I was loved.*"

"Why do you come? We are not kin. I treated you and our children poorly and then went to prison. When I asked you all to come with me, after prison, you refused."

"*I come because you're finally becoming a man. This is a joyful day. Savor it.*" As suddenly as she had come, she was gone.

His stomach unknotted. *She's right,* he thought. *Today is a good day.*

Scottie's birth came while neither parent was working. Their life was simple, focused on ranch life, their newborn son, and getting ready for Roselle's girls' eventual arrival. The summer of 1946 brought unexpected news. Silva wrote from Reno saying she was divorcing Blaine and that she worried about how her father would react. He wrote back but she never got the letter. She wrote again and Med replied on October 20, 1946. Unknown to him when he wrote the second letter, she had remarried, six weeks earlier. She kept his letter the rest of her life.

> I was so sorry that you entertained for even one sec-
> ond the thought that your divorce action would create
> a barrier [within] the filial sentiment between you and
> me. That was and is so utterly silly. Of course I regret-
> ted it and as I told you in the letter you didn't get, kept
> hoping against hope that something might happen to
> bring you kiddies back together. It seemed to me that
> you really belonged together but on the other hand
> I realized that it was an individual problem and that
> our interference unsolicited in its solution, even from a
> father would be little short of unwarranted intrusion.
>
> . . . since I was not such a shining example of per-
> fection at the art of marriage preservation myself.

Anyway, to the bear situation, we are all bears in our
own way or another and of course cubs do leave the
parental home in order to become bears themselves.
But that does not mean the bears cease for that reason from being bears—unless it is to become wolves!
That's a joke, son; a joke, that is!!

You should see little Scottie. He is just tearing
around all over the place, on his part of it, at least
which is the 6'4" x 6'4" bed on the porch. He rears
up on his hind legs to announce his sentiments and
desires but cautiously keeping his fingertips in contact
with the bed—they and his toes—if you can picture
the position. Let us know what you are doing and how
you are getting along. The loneliness will pass away
of course as you make new acquaintances and new
horizons are opened.

The ranch is about the same—and to us at least it
is the finest place on earth. We have had an individu-
ally dry year but fortunately we have a splendid water
supply for all uses. You should see Roselle's garden:
she does everything but sleep out there. We had a nice
mess of green onions and greens out of it tonight . . . .

Well, Sissie, I do so sincerely hope you find happi-
ness if you have not already done so. I am not disappointed in you, I am just disappointed at what the
fates cast up for you. It of course comes as a shock but
I am sure you have everything under control—don't
even think your old Dad would turn his back to you—
you should know better than that.

Write us back real soon won't you please for we
will be anxiously waiting to hear from you.
With Much Love,
Dad and Roselle

The letter includes a message from Roselle:

Dear Sylva, you inquired as to the Mister's health, and he seems to have forgotten himself entirely. He looks and feels more fit than at any time since I've known him. Guess it is the hard work and the fresh air that gets the credit. Six o'clock in the morning milking the goats or irrigating. They say what one does after work counts a lot. We haven't seen a show since quite a while before Scottie's birth. We have nothing that resembles a car so we do little gadding about. For three or four months we depended on some good neighbor to loan us his car for our groceries. Well, let us hear often, I am at the bottom of the page.
Love, Roselle

The letter revealed not only Med's affection for Silva and his feelings about her first marriage, but glowing details about the ranch, their life there and his baby son. He would always care about his older children, but accepted that they were adults and their decisions were theirs alone.

Chapter 27

Three years passed and the correspondence between Med and Silva continued. Silva remained in San Francisco with her second husband, Arno Scheller. They, too, were thriving after the war, as so many Depression-weary Americans did. Then she wrote the surprising news that Arno wanted to leave the business world and become a dairyman. Given that he had grown up in New York City, this change was curious. His daughter's plans paralleled Med's own changing circumstances: a more lucrative lemon property in Potrero prompted their decision to move from the El Cajon ranch. Once the deal closed, their new home would be in southeastern San Diego County, a couple of miles from the US-Mexican border.

He came in through the kitchen door, walked over to the coffee pot and poured a hot cup. It was early morning and the goat feeding and milking was done. He would be off to the Convair plant in a half hour. Roz had left his sunny-side up eggs in the skillet and she had tossed in some cow brains; everything was still warm. His appetite whetted, he got two slices of bread toasting and assembled his breakfast on the plate waiting next to the stove. He heard Roselle in the living room, bundling up young Scottie for his ride to Mrs. Martinez, his babysitter.

He called out to her, "Got another letter from Sissie, Roz."

"And?" She appeared in the kitchen door, holding young Scott in her right arm.

Med finished chewing and swallowed. "Arno's started apprenticing with some dairy farmer and will be coming home only on the weekends."

"He really is serious." Sounding surprised, she put the boy onto one of the kitchen chairs and poured the three-year-old a small glass of goat milk. "Drink this, young Mister, this'll put hair on your chest!"

Med crinkled his face in dismay, "Not too soon, son, not toooooo soooooooon . . ." as he leaned in to the boy, almost touching noses. The young one ducked his head, giggling.

He looked up and nodded. "Quite a change from the fellow I knew when we both worked at the plant. You never know, do you? Sissie seems very happy about it all. We never lived on a farm but she has a feel for the land. But she also knows she'll miss the big city life of San Francisco."

Roz waited for their son to finish drinking, rinsed the empty juice tumbler and put it away. She picked Scott up. "They said he's thinking about Oregon?" He nodded. "Wonder if they have any idea how much it rains? The farther north you go, Washington, especially Seattle, it's cloudy at least half the year. Your son and me are off and I'll see you later for lunch."

He finished eating and changed his clothes. As he drove, thoughts of his little family summoned the realization about his first family, that he hadn't become decent marriage material until after prison and Ethel's death. He never would have guessed that at the old age of fifty, he could love family life so deeply. His wandering eye had gone blind. Not only would Roz probably kill him if he ever strayed, but once he fell in love with her, it was a done deal. He had finally become a man, in the fullest sense. Not that he ever regretted his first children. They were his flesh and blood. But he hadn't had the faintest clue how to be the father they deserved. Ethel and their children had paid dearly for his blindness to how precious family was. Yet Ethel, despite a much more limited childhood, had always known.

Sissie and Arno going into farming; how interesting that his oldest was now following the same inclination as him and Roz. His daughter had been married for three years and still no children, yet. Would that change? Farming and having babies seemed to go together for many couples. Since Scottie's birth, he and Roz had slowed down quite a bit in the romance department. They were older and their toddler son's presence had cooled their ardor considerably. But every once in a while, she reached for him and the magic came back. She was the only one since Lillian who could pull him into a sexual undertow that still could overwhelm him.

The suit for sole custody of her twin daughters dragged on. The details were tedious and the lack of resolution made her moody and testy. She always ended her latest story, about the last court session or discussion with her lawyer, with self-blame. Undoing her decision to relinquish the children was taking years but her lawyer was optimistic about her winning. Med looked forward to the girls coming. They would be a great addition since they were six years older than the boy.

When he arrived at his desk, he found a message to call Mr. Owens, the owner of the Potrero property. Their conversation gave him additional good news about the property. He could expect another ten years of commercial harvest from the lemons. The income should pay most of the mortgage, leaving only property taxes unfunded. Owens was ready to finalize the sale.

Roselle called him later. Could they go out to lunch? She had some news; her voice was controlled but he heard low-keyed excitement.

As he drove them to a nearby coffee shop, Med felt she was bursting, but she wouldn't say a word. When their waitress walked away, Roz leaned towards him and spoke in a very soft tone.

"Virg, it's happened! I got a call from the lawyer this morning. I got the girls! They'll be coming next month. I'm so excited and feel like it's going to land like a ton of bricks. There's so much to do and . . ."

He reached across the table, took one of her clenched hands and stroked it. "It's going to be fine, Roz. I got a call myself.

Owens has accepted our offer and wants to close in sixty days. The timing is good, isn't it? Well, we're already going to be in an uproar and discombobulated, so what's a little more commotion?"

"Mister, you've been with me through all of this since we got together. These won't be little girls, they're going to be ten in about five months. They need their own bedroom and they'll have to be enrolled in school and then I have to figure out how we do this in the mornings and . . ."

He nodded, and smiled calmly. He knew how worked up she could get. "And we'll get it all done. We knew they'd be coming eventually, just not when. Renovations on the new house will get us plenty of room for all three kids. I'm looking forward to it. I'm ready for a full, bustling house!"

She took a deep breath and slowly let it out. "I feel so mixed up right now. I'm so glad I—we—have the legal stuff resolved. But I start thinking back to when I created this whole mess."

He looked at her questioningly. "You've never said too much about leaving your first husband. I never probed because you'd say just so much and stop. Are you sure you want to talk about it here? How about at home, after we put Scottie to bed?"

She looked at him for a few moments, considering. "Tonight, let me tell you the whole story. I've never told anyone what happened. Now that my girls are finally coming to live with us, I need to set the record straight and make a clean breast of it all. Finally things'll be right." She playfully rocked his hand and then the waitress brought their plates.

At home, that evening, Roselle was withdrawn and said little from the time she brought young Scott home, cooked supper and fed the family. Med put the boy to bed and she went into their bedroom. When he came in she was lying in bed. She smiled uncertainly. He looked directly into her face and took her right hand. She swallowed hard.

"I told you that I went through a nasty divorce. I also said our marriage had been rocky for many, many years. We married young and I was twenty when I had Brownie. By the time I was twenty-five, we had two more. When my nursing job in New York fell through, we came back here and things started to go bad.

We were fighting one night and he'd been drinking quite a bit. One thing led to another and he got really rough with me. He forced himself on me even though I kept pushing him away." She stopped. Med deepened his pressure on her hand. She seemed so small and he felt her emotional deflation. So unlike the strong-minded and forceful woman who had usurped his heart and directed much of their life.

"I knew, when he was done, that I was pregnant. It was that time in my cycle. After three babies, and I was thirty-four, I made sure I wouldn't be. But this time he caught me off-guard. And in early 1940, I had the twins. About three months after their birth I left. I left everyone and everything behind. I went to work one day and never went back." Her lips quivered and she dropped her tear-filled eyes. "Do you know what that made me? I had to run away from everything I knew, for a while. Do you know what a bad mother I was?"

He put his arm around her. For the first time ever, she started crying and he felt her body shake with deep racking sobs. He pulled her into both arms. *Poor girl, no wonder she has such black moods.* He waited.

When her sobs subsided, she continued. "I was very unhappy during the pregnancy. I didn't want another baby. After how he treated me that night, I made sure he never touched me again. We'd had rough sex, but he never pushed me further if I really didn't want to. I knew I had to get out but with three kids, how? I'd put a little money aside but not enough to take them with me." She stopped again.

"We got all night, Roz, if that's what it takes. No matter what you say, I'm not going anywhere. I have my own ghosts I live with." He thought of Ethel's visitations. *Literally.*

"I delivered not one but two babies. I didn't bond with them, as they say in the medical world. Here I had these two perfect little babies and all I wanted to do was run away. Their births were normal and I was back home in four days. I had no help and had to take off from work for several weeks. I barely managed to bottle feed them enough because I didn't want to touch them or look at them. I was in deep and did as little as possible to take care of them because I didn't want to be in the same room. When they cried, I would run to the bedroom and put my hands over my ears. Their father seemed so pleased with himself. Like he had gotten the best of me and I was really under his thumb, now, with not one but two babies. It was a living hell. I'd never felt this way about my other children." Her voice faltered.

What could he say? What could anyone say? He steeled himself inside not to shrink from her. She needed him to hold steady as she opened up her shame and self-revulsion, without his judgment and condemnation. He nodded and squeezed her hand.

A minute passed. "On those really bad days, Brownie, who was fourteen, she'd come home from school and take over. No one in the family knew what I was doing and feeling during the day. And on weekends, I made the children all help. On a good day, I might manage to touch the babies only a couple of times. Their crying made me want to run. The thing I dreaded most was that I wanted to hit them then, and that's when I'd run into the bedroom and hide.

"I found someone I could leave the babies with during the week and went back to work. Being away from the house and the babies' schedule was freedom. I started to feel like I could breathe again. Weekends were difficult but my older ones pretty much took over their care. I was still thinking about leaving but not with the kids. I reached my breaking point one evening when he got drunk again, smelled of someone else's perfume and started coming at me. I was still dressed and ran out of the bedroom, grabbed my car keys and purse and ran out of the house. I had enough money for a hotel room. I went to work the next morning. He called but I wouldn't come to the phone. In the afternoon, Brownie called and I told her I was not coming back, ever. The next time I did go back was after I filed for divorce and got an order to let me see my children."

Med looked at her. "When did you want to see the children, how long after you left? Because you didn't want to be near the babies."

She searched his face, looking for disapproval. "What I had was a sickness, a madness of sorts. Some doctors say it's just baby blues. They call it postpartum depression. I found a room to rent and saved as much money as I could. When I started feeling like myself once more and started missing the children, *all of the children*, then I found a lawyer, to file for divorce. I went back to see the children six months after I left." She paused. "He told me it would get ugly, because I abandoned the family. Did I want custody? I decided to ask for only visitation. But we did ask for custody to be revisited if I should remarry."

He nodded, took her chin and kissed her lips. Slowly she opened her mouth and let his tongue inside. He lingered, his tongue softly and delicately tracing her teeth and inner cheeks. Suddenly she pulled back. "So, it's all right? That I told you what I did?"

He whispered back. "No matter how bad you feel about what you did, never question what I think. You gave me back my life. For years, I wandered alone, after I left the mess behind in Missouri. You gave me a son and I've been happy for the first time in my life. Right now, with you and our son. And I want your little girls finally to come home to their mother, who wants and loves them very, very much."

Tears started to stream from her closed eyes and she sighed with relief. Then she reached under the covers for his partially erect penis, smiled and whispered, "Come over here, Mister, and make me feel I am yours, the best way possible." They began kissing once more.

Chapter 28

He was at his desk, mid-morning in early June, when the phone rang.

"It's Silva, Med." Her voice was soft and a little muffled from the long-distance connection.

He smiled broadly. "Silva, darling, how are you? You've not written in a while. Catch me up on your doings."

"We've decided to come back to San Diego . . ."

He cut in excitedly, "Really? Why?"

". . . We miss it so badly. What pushed our decision is the kids' health. Both Nova and Nicholas are suffering from endless colds. She has gotten pneumonia a number of times. It has been so bad we had both kids' tonsils removed, but she missed so much school this past year in first grade, they almost held her back. Oregon is wet and rainy and it gets so cold in the winters. San Diego has the best year-round weather and we're hoping the kids will be healthier."

His "Hmmmm . . ." commiserated. "How can I help? What do you need?"

She sighed hesitantly. "Arno needs to get down there and get things set up while I hold things together up here and get the house on the market. He needs a job. Can you see what's available? So we can get things started?"

"You know I will. Things aren't what they were during the war years, but I'm sure something can be found. And he did work at the main plant as a supervisor during those years. Let me shake the bushes and rattle some cages. We'll find something for you."

"Thanks so much. If he can come down with a job in hand, then we have got the ball rolling." She paused. "So, how are you, Roselle and Scott?"

"We're all doing well. Still happy on the ranch. Roz is thinking about quitting General Dynamics . . ."

Silva broke in, "General Dynamics?"

"Oh, Convair was acquired in '53 or '54 by GD. She wants to leave in the next year or two. Fine by me; maybe she'll start feeling better. But GD is fine and the last Convair project, the Atlas rocket, is proceeding well. So I think finding Arno something will be fine. Tell me about those grandchildren of mine."

"Nova will be seven in a few days and Nicholas will be four in August. Funny, she was born close to Mom's birthday and Nick is born in your month. Grandchildren and grandparents, it'll be wonderful for them to see you. Mom died way too early. And you grew up with your grandfather Dunn. At least you had that connection."

"That I did, but Grandfather Dunn was older and I spent most my time with my aunts and uncles."

"I wish I could have met him." She sounded wistful.

"He went just after our first baby died, in '23. Having you back here with those little ones will be good. I relish the idea of having more little cubs around me."

She chuckled. "We're still going on about the bears, Dad?"

"Dad? It's been so long since I've heard you call me that, Sissie."

"Okay, let me get out of your hair. Here's my work number if you want to call during the day. Arno will be glad to hear we might get going sooner than we thought."

Their conversation raised his spirits. Sissie was coming back and with his two grandchildren! Fourteen years had passed since she had left for school in Berkeley and since they'd seen one another. All her fundamental changes, divorce, remarriage, working in San Francisco, moving to Oregon to run the dairy farm, having two children, selling the farm and moving into a new home, he knew from her letters. He picked up his phone and started making calls to other managers about his son-in-law.

Late afternoon, as he drove home, he pondered how to bring up the subject of Silva's return to Roselle. Her moodiness and ill-temper had grown stronger since one of her twins, Marilynn, had died. After high school, the girl had left the San Diego area and struck out on her own while her twin Rosalynn stayed behind. Her decision to go to New York City had startled Roselle. She tried to discourage the girl because of her own past professional difficulties many years before. Marilynn had carried her mother's moodiness. They never resolved their disagreement before Marilynn left. About a year later, a friend of Marilynn's, in New York, contacted them with the grim news. That was the second time he saw Roselle weep and then never again.

No matter how he tried to comfort his grieving wife, she refused to talk about her dead daughter. Even when Rosalynn had bad days and spoke of her sister, Roselle couldn't respond. She would walk out and leave Med with the grieving young woman. His sense was that Roz still blamed herself for the ten years of her girls' lives that she had lost. Any peace and comfort she'd gained from the eight years the twins spent under their roof had evaporated. After the girl's death, she seemed to have only two emotional speeds: neutrally civil and angry.

It seemed that aggressive surliness that lay at the root of her sexual expression had transformed into bitterness. *There's a plant that the Indians sometimes ate, called what? Bitterroot.* Bitterness wafted from her and contaminated their home atmosphere. In front of the boy, she was more restrained, but when they were alone, her mask fell. Now, they almost never touched.

When their marital intimacy dropped off even more after the twins joined the family, he had blamed it on Roz getting older and what was referred to as the Change. But after Marilynn's death, his wife shut off completely. He was slowing down, too. For Scott's sake, he'd managed to adjust and keep fighting to a minimum. When things got tense and she went on a tirade, he left the house and walked to the Silva Lane ridge. Weeding, digging in or reshaping the watering basins, and anything needed along the long row of boysenberries, the work restored his humor. When he returned, he'd find Scott. They chatted about school, Scouting, his ham radio and anything else the teenager was interested in or doing.

He turned off the four-lane highway onto Old Campo Road and glanced to the roadside. Something moved and he slowed to look back: a coyote was carrying something in its mouth, running alongside the road. Coyotes rarely surfaced during the day. *What do the Indians say about coyotes? Tricksters. Beware.* Med grunted and increased the car's speed. If he said anything about Silva at dinner, probably a ruckus would erupt. Better say something later and let young Scott have peace and quiet for any studying he needed to do. That would be best.

A couple of miles from the ranch, he started to really look about him. Clusters of old oaks were scattered throughout the valley on either side of the road. They often marked spots where the water table was nearer the soil's surface. The expanses of blue-toned hills that bordered and slid down into the lowland acreage were speckled and studded by deceptively small-looking rocks. A body couldn't walk in those hills, rather they would clamber from one boulder to another. The remaining soil was held in crevasses between boulders or cradled by clefts in the larger rocks. Tufts of sagebrush grew in these. Long ago, fierce rains had swept any commercially productive soil down from the rising hills onto the golden valley's undulating stretches. His heart swelled at the sight. For some, this terrain might be too sparse and arid. For him, this country had awakened a deep love of the soil and farming. He couldn't imagine living anywhere else.

Supper went uneventfully. Roselle was chatty at dinner, telling a story about one of the neighbor ladies who had come by selling raffle tickets. Young Scott was now thirteen, tall, slim and still blond. The height of his day had been when his science teacher complimented him, in class, on a project he was working on for year-end grades. Both parents expressed their delight and the shy, intense boy dropped his eyes and blushed. After supper, Med and

Roselle finished up any remaining chores for the day and finally settled into their bedroom.

"I got my first phone call from Sissie, let's see, must be at least two years since she last called." He lay in bed apprehensively.

"Really, what did she have to say?" Roselle's tone was non-committal. So far, so good.

"They are returning to the area. Oregon's worn out its charm. Once they sold the dairy, Arno going into accounting hasn't been too successful. Sissie's been commuting into Portland and is tired of the drive. The children are sick a lot." He related the health concerns about the children.

"Anything else?" She yawned and rubbed her eyes. He looked over at her and noticed how much more gray her red hair showed. Now fifty-four, her face showed the years. Her complexion wasn't deeply lined, rather it was like the crackling in the glaze of old china tea pots, very fine lines about her eyes and mouth. She had started to develop a wattle between her chin and throat. *We're all showing and feeling our age.*

"She asked me to look for a position for Arno, so he can come here first and get things going." He waited.

She looked into his eyes. "Of course she did. Didn't she always ask you for jobs? Well, none of my concern, unless she plans to move next door." She dropped her eyes and then curtly shook her head.

He persisted, "She's my daughter, Roz. I haven't seen her in fourteen years and she's bringing my first grandchildren here. I want to see her and them. They're part of my family, too. That also includes Scott, after all. He and she are half brother and sister." He spoke quietly and firmly.

"I can't stop you now, can I? You want to find a job for Arno, it's none of my concern. And if they visit, you're right, why shouldn't they?" Her voice lost its sarcastic edge and his stomach relaxed.

"I'm glad you understand. Well, lights out for me. Sleep well." He turned off the lamp on his side of the bed and took a deep breath. Maybe he'd get a good night's sleep, after all. Would she remain so calm once things get into gear?

Chapter 29

I t was six months later, on a cool autumn Saturday, and outside the rec room, Med paced around the swimming pool. It
was early afternoon, after lunch. Silva and her family were
due to arrive. The anticipation of seeing his daughter and his
grandchildren for the first time had rattled his nerves. They had
chatted by phone several times before she drove with the children
from Oregon. His heart panged at their fourteen-year separation.
How he had missed her!

Five months earlier, Arno had begun his new job. Finding him
a position had gone smoothly, although nothing in management
was available. His son-in-law was a practical man and both the
salary and the job duties were sufficient. Their rapport was ge-
nial but not close. If his daughter had not married Arno, the two
would have associated only at work. Arno's presence, however,
gave him the opportunity to catch up about Silva and the children.

After Sissie had left for school in Berkeley, Roselle became
much more tolerant of her absent stepdaughter. Her feelings
about Buddy were always softer; Med's older son was affable
and agreeable. When he visited, the men spent their time discussing military topics related either to Buddy's or Med's service. He
continued to treat his first son like a kid brother. In 1958, a year
before, Buddy had visited and brought gifts from Guam. Young

Scott received an ornately carved chess set from his half-brother and learned how to play during the visit. Buddy's manner and presence never raised Roselle's hackles.

Even though Silva was now in San Diego, Roselle's old hostility hadn't resurfaced. Silva's home in Pacific Beach, a couple miles from the ocean, was far enough away that a visit to the ranch required scheduling. Roz remained noncommittal about their impending visit. Young Scott was not aware the visitors were relatives.

Scott leaned his tousled blond head out the sliding glass door to announce, "Dad, they're here."

Med swallowed hard and followed his son to the front foyer. The small space was crowded as the visitors and Roz turned to look at Scott and him. Med couldn't see everyone clearly.

Roselle moved next to him. "Virgil, here's Silva and her whole family." She was civil, welcoming.

Med, his hands on Scott's shoulders, announced, "Welcome, you are so welcome here. This is Scott, our son."

Next to Arno, Silva said, "Med, these are our children." She put one hand on a young girl, with big blue eyes and blond hair pulled back into a ponytail. "This is Nova, who is seven years old." Then she bent over to touch the shoulder of a younger boy with a full head of brown hair. "And this is Nick, or Nicholas, who just turned four." As she stood straight, he could see her eyes glistening with tears.

Although he had known the little girl was his dead child's namesake, the sight of her jolted him. Hadn't Silva known the dead infant was a boy? No matter, a bit of Nova Dunn was now present and would move into the future.

His chest filled with pride, amazement and joy. His grandchildren, they were beautiful! How could they not be? They're Sissie's. And Arno was a good-looking fellow. He smiled and stood silently.

Roz broke the spell. "Well, come on in, please. I think the rec room is the best place for us all. What can I get you to drink?" She led the way as everyone slowly walked back to a big room next to the pool. Med felt a soft touch on the back of his shoulder and he stopped and turned to look at his thirty-five-year old daughter.

Her warm smile showed her pearly teeth. He thought of Ethel. "Med, you look well and Scott is a handsome, good-looking kid."

He whispered, "So do you, Sissie, so do you. The little ones are worthy cubs."

She chuckled. "They pass muster?" He nodded vigorously.

He ducked his head conspiratorially next to her and murmured, "We'll take a walk later so we can talk a bit?" Then he followed Roselle into the kitchen and Scott guided the visitors into the large rec room. The paneled space held a small organ, a formal gaming table, a couple of casual sofas and a small pool table. It was lit only by the fall afternoon sun.

After Roselle brought everyone their glasses and cups, she sat down on the organ bench. Med took his usual wingback armchair by the sliding glass door. The visitors were seated at the round table in the center of the room and Scott leaned against the edge of the pool table. Med moved his eyes from his daughter to her husband and to the little ones. Conversation began with their drive to the ranch, the ranch's location, General Dynamics and its transition from when it was Convair. The children were quiet and attentive. Finally, the focus turned to the children. Silva told the little girl to go to her grandfather.

He took one of her small hands and asked her how she liked San Diego. "Very well, thank you. It's a lot different from where we lived, you know, Oregon." He nodded. "It was a long drive to your house but I liked it." What poise and self-possession, just like Sissie. Silva then brought young Nick to him and guided Nova back to her chair.

He took the young boy's hand. "How are you, young one?"

The boy looked into his eyes and paused as if to decide the proper way to answer. "I am good, thank you for asking."

Med looked up, into Silva's eyes. "What do we have, here? A thinker, one who considers." She smiled delightedly.

They chatted a bit longer and then Med offered to walk them through the grove closest to the house. He turned to Scott. "Son, would you be our youngest guests' host? We'll be a little while. I want to show our guests around the ranch." The adults went outside to the pool and he led them towards the groves.

The closest trees were fifty yards from the house. Arno and Silva looked attentively to wherever he motioned as he explained the cultivation of lemon trees and the harvesting process. Once he'd guided them around the closest rows, he turned to Roselle.

"Roz, I'm going to take Sissie up to the farthest ridge where the avocados and berries are. Why don't you show Arno the lower areas and we'll be back in a bit." She flashed an annoyed glance at him and then gestured towards Arno.

"Arno, tell me about dairy farms. I'm a Seattle girl, so I know a bit about the Northwest and rain." She took him by his arm and they walked slowly, away from father and daughter.

When they were out of earshot, Med turned to Silva and smiled. Her middle thirties had brought a sculptured quality to her beauty; the baby fat from her early twenties had melted from her cheeks and chin. A stylish car coat hung to her hips with a tailored skirt that reached her mid-calves, and she wore loafers. "I see you have on shoes that can carry you for a bit of a walk. Let me show you the upper and outer stretches of the grove." She put her arm in his and they began the modest trek.

"They're beautiful, Sissie, just beautiful little tykes. I do see bits of Ethel in them, too."

"Nick has Mom's eyes." Her voice had become a bit huskier in its softness and still carried no accent. Shortly after she came to San Diego, at eighteen, she erased all traces of her childhood Midwestern pronunciation.

"Hers were blacker."

"Only because her skin was so dark."

"She had that, true. Made her teeth gleam like lit pearls. Your teeth look a lot like hers but you have the lighter Medling complexion."

"Do you ever think about her?"

"Yes, yes I do. A different time and a very different life. She and I struggled so."

She nodded. "Yes, a very different life." She paused. "I still miss her so. I think I always will."

They could see the ridge a few hundred yards away. They

made their way there silently. He no longer felt her old conflicted loyalties; ease flowed between them. When they walked through the last row of lemons, the trees on the ridge appeared. They stood taller, with thicker trunks and much larger leaves. At the eastern end, berry vines completed the cultivated area.

"We have a mish-mash of things up here. Most are avocados but I do have a pomegranate and an olive tree as well, at the very end. The berries are boysenberry. That's a cross between raspberries and blackberries. I put those in myself."

"Really?" Her tone was dubious.

He laughed. "Hard to believe, I know. Despite my earlier years, I got a yen to farm and like to dig a bit. There are days when things get a little rough and I come up here. It calms me and sets me right."

She looked worriedly into his eyes. "Are things OK, Med?"

He nodded. "Things are fine, Sissie, they are. She has her bad days but it always works out. We have the boy. He's doing well. I think he's a serious kid, makes good grades in school, like you and unlike Buddy. It always works out. It has to, because of him."

She nodded uncertainly. "If you say so . . ." He nodded firmly. ". . . then it is so." She looked back down where they had walked. "Tell me more about the farm and how's it doing." He told her the ranch had paid for itself, and its commercial life was ending. Now, agricultural real estate was gradually being converted into residential, since all parts of the county had grown since the war years. He even had built the swimming pool.

She raised her eyebrows at that. "And you were the fellow who stood outside our car with a flat tire, waiting for someone to stop so you could pay them to change it for you."

He laughed, "You do remember a lot of things, don't you? Not my finest hour, among many. Yes, I did lay out the pool and dig out some of it. We better start our way back." They began a leisurely descent back through the groves to the house.

After all the adults had gathered back in the rec room, the visit abruptly ended. The children were still outside, around the swimming pool. Nova suddenly appeared at the sliding glass door, yelling in a high-pitched voice something about Nick falling and the pool. He forcefully slid the door open. Silva and Arno rushed out behind the excited little girl.

Scott was leaning over at the pool's edge, attempting to fish the small boy out of the water, pulling at Nick's floating clothes. Just as the teenager caught a firm grip and lifted the little boy out of the water, Arno reached both of them. Silva stood next to her daughter and shook her head at the mishap. Roselle arrived last with several bath towels. Silva took them, knelt to remove the dripping clothes from her son and toweled him off. The boy hadn't cried out or wept, but stood stoically with wide eyes through it all. Silva kept shaking her head regretfully, occasionally murmuring to her son. Med tensed as he watched all the commotion, but smiled quietly when Silva's eyes met his. He knew she felt mortified. *Sissie hates awkward situations, especially if it reflects poorly on her and her own.*

Silva turned to Roselle. "I am so sorry, Roselle."

Roz shook her head and laughed. "I've had six, don't forget. These things happen. Don't think anything of it. Besides, it's just water." She bent over to the little boy. "Nice meeting you, Nick. You'll feel better once your mother has you in dry clothes."

Silva raised the volume of her voice. "This is our cue, time to get out of your hair and get home. Roselle, thank you for your gracious assistance. Scott, I am so glad you kept my son afloat and got him on dry land. He hasn't learned how to swim yet." She took her father's hand. "Med, what a great place you have." Turning slowly from him she looked at Roselle and Scott. "What a wonderful home and property to live and grow on. Thank you all for letting us come and visit."

With her usual poise she led her bedraggled but somewhat drier little boy to the front door and Arno and Nova followed. Med and Roselle trailed behind their guests to their car. Scott leaned against the front door jamb, watching. Once the children were seated in the back seat of the black Ford Fairlane, Silva raised her hand and flashed one of her brilliant smiles before sitting in the front. Arno started the car. Med's throat tightened as he waved back at her. *When will we be together like this, again?* The black sedan slowly followed the circular driveway and paused before turning onto the connecting road to Campo Road. He and Roselle stood for a few moments and silently walked back into the house.

Supper that evening was quiet. Roselle said very little; no one said anything about their visitors. Attentive to everything his wife did or didn't say, Med also noted that Scott was absorbed in his adolescent musings. He felt tired, very tired. He couldn't remember feeling so enervated. He decided to revisit the ridge while the fading daylight remained, and let his overloaded nerves ease.

Among the avocado trees, he examined the lower limbs where the past season's fruits had been harvested. *Sissie loves avocados. She missed them terribly in Oregon. Maybe next season I can send some home to her.*

"Quite a gathering today, Virgil," commented that voice—or that feeling.

"Ethel." It had been years since one of her visitations.

"*It's been a significant day.*" He was too tired to struggle with whether this was really happening.

"*Does it still matter whether I am real or not?*" He felt amusement in her question.

"Today it does not. You always have a message or observation. What is it, this time?"

"*You know what Sissie wants. She feels that her children will get a chance to know their grandfather. What do you want and what's the best thing for your current family?*"

"There's a lot to consider. The children are lovely. And to see how our family has flowed forward."

"*You wanted a divorce just after she was born.*"

He felt a surge of impatience. "Will that never be forgotten? I have changed, surely you see. You know that."

"*Because you have is why I keep returning. Now you see the preciousness and sanctity of family. Accordingly, you must weigh what's right, at this time. Because you have a second family and a second life that is separate from the first. What is the right thing, for the future?*"

His heart clutched sharply and he felt tears stinging. His tears had been joyful. Now they felt bitter and burned with . . .

"*It's your choice. Today you saw how Sissie's life has unfolded and saw your descendants. You've not been denied."*

"This is bitter medicine, Ethel."

"If you do choose this, and only you can, it'll be a measure of the man you've become. But you can also choose not to." She said these last words gently and kindly. Then she was gone.

About an hour later, both he and Roselle were in bed. She looked up from her novel as he read his Bible.

"Virg, what does all this mean for Scottie?" She called the boy Scottie when she was feeling threatened or protective. He closed the Bible.

"How do you mean, Roz?" *What is on her mind, exactly?*

"This was a big day for you, seeing your daughter and her children, your grandkids. What does their coming here mean for our family?" She paused. "Years ago you told me what happened in Missouri. Once I asked Silva. She wouldn't say anything; she told me to ask you. I never did. Now I am."

Chickens coming home to roost—they always do, don't they? Unless the fox gets them first, arose in his mind.

He shifted his weight. "Roz, I don't have anything different to say about the past. I felt you welcomed Silva and her family wonderfully. Too bad little Nick fell into the pool." He stopped. "I don't see anything changing for our family. Why would it?" He felt a knot in the pit of his stomach but his voice remained calm and steady.

Roselle opened her novel, found her place again and then glanced at him over the rim of her reading glasses. "Then you don't intend to invite them over or out for dinner, next? The holidays will be coming soon." The holidays! He needed to make his choice quickly. One way or the other.

"I really hadn't thought about it, one way or the other." She nodded and turned back to reading. The Bible rested on his belly, while a rush of uneasiness and foreboding coursed through him.

After fifteen or twenty minutes, Roselle closed her book and turned off her bedside lamp. "Night, Virg." He answered and put the Bible on his nightstand and turned out his light. Sleep would be a long time coming.

Two weeks later, Med called his son-in-law at work. This would be the easiest way.

"Arno, you need to tell Silva something for me." Forming words suddenly became very difficult. His son-in-law waited politely. "Please tell my daughter that you can't come back to the ranch." The other end of the line remained quiet as Arno absorbed his words.

"You don't want us, you don't want Silva, to come back to the ranch? Ever? What about coming to our place?" The sound of Arno's incredulous words pelted his nervous system.

His head started to swim and he felt faint. "No, Arno. It won't work, whether you come to our place or we come to yours or elsewhere. Tell Silva, for me. Please." He leaned towards his knees, almost doubled over. His stomach felt queasy and from his armpits cold sweat trickled past his ribs, down to the waistband of his trousers. His heart broke a little more with each word.

He heard Arno take a deep breath and then exhale loudly. The sounds of clucking disapproval and anger came into the phone's earpiece. "Will do, Med. Righto," and the phone line went dead. *It's done.* Slowly he hung up his receiver and straightened up. He waited for his pounding heart to calm and for his lightheadedness to lift. *I'm never going to see my princess again or those sweet little ones. It's for the best. It really is.* And tears streamed down his face.

Chapter 30

He awoke with a start. He'd never seen them before in the dream. He shifted his weight as much as he was able and reached for the call button: his bladder was full. Because of the stroke, all he did now was lie in bed. Had Ethel felt as tired of not moving as he did? When the doctors told him and Roz there was nothing more they could do, the Linda Vista Convalescence Hospital became his next "home." He shared a room with another patient, sometimes. It was much quieter than the naval hospital ward had been. There, the forty beds were always full and he'd learned to sleep with a constant background sounds of coughs, snoring and staff walking about all hours of the day and night. When he was seventeen, sleep had come much more easily despite the noisy St. Louis army barracks. He heard the door creak open and a young orderly appeared by his bed.

"What do you need, Mr. Medling?" Jerry was his name. Med motioned with his arm towards the bathroom door. The orderly nodded, pulled back his blanket and helped him to stand. Between the stroke and lying in bed for three months, he couldn't walk without assistance. Now going to the toilet, eating and dressing, all required help. The cruelest blow of all, he had lost his ability to speak clearly. So he stopped. The breadth and vitality of his life had shrunk to a hospital bed. To an observer it might seem waiting was how he passed the time. It was August and he knew the month because Roz had reminded him the day before that his birthday, on the eighteenth, was fast approaching.

After Jerry helped him back to bed and he was once more under the smoothed-out sheets and blanket, the dream fragment returned. He had dreamt it many times before. It started shortly after his heart attack in May. He stood facing the back of an older man who stood facing the back of another older man who likewise stood facing the back of another older man. The line of men facing the backs of others stretched out before him into the distance. This time, though, he had decided to look behind him and there stood Silva! She was in her car coat, calf-length skirt and loafers, as she'd appeared that last time. She looked into his eyes. Behind her he saw the little ones looking up at him, the little girl and boy. His grandchildren! He had suddenly jerked awake. How long had it been since that one meeting? That had been in '59, he reckoned, almost five years.

After his call to Arno, life at home had continued as if nothing had happened. That was true for his wife and son but not for him. No one else knew how he felt and how he fared. Mostly he avoided thinking about it, because there was no point. He had made the choice and life, his second one, continued as before.

A couple years later, in 1961, he had a first heart attack, which prompted leaving the ranch and moving into town, closer to medical care. They subdivided most of the ranch, sold off the last parcels and moved into San Diego proper, to the Linda Vista area, only a few miles from Silva's home. After Med retired in 1962, he spent his leisure with friends from the VFW and the Lemon Grove Masonic Lodge. His achievement of Thirty-Second-Degree Mason was especially significant, as its ideal espoused the conquest of fleshly appetites and passions by moral sense and reason. The recipient demonstrated the highest ideals of honor, family devotion and community involvement. His hidden past made this attainment piercingly poignant. He took a few correspondence courses in creative writing. Mostly he was a father to his teenage son and an accommodating husband to his wife. About the time Med had his second heart attack, Scott was graduating from high school and had been admitted to the newly opened University of California at San Diego. Med's second life progressed as if nothing from his first was anywhere close at hand.

The dream's images of Silva and the children, however, brought up ancient, tucked-away memories. He sat on the cabin cruiser on the Osage, fishing with Sissie. It was the last summer before his fall. She would have been thirteen; the girl always had caught more fish. That day he told her, "That's it, no more! I am tired of baiting your hooks for you." The next winter, the proverbial manure hit the fan and his life forever changed. *What a life it has been! Who would ever have thought a farm boy from the Bootheel would have done the things I did. Even when I went too far. But I could not admit that to any of my own. Finally I did admit it to my God.*

After this second heart attack, he stopped doing anything but remembering or drifting, or listening to his visitors, Roz and Scott, or sleeping, all of which were interspersed with mealtimes. But he still could talk. Concern about his damaged heart led his doctors to administer lots of drugs. After a few weeks, he slipped into unconsciousness. When he regained awareness, his body felt wrong and strange. He had had a significant stroke, probably from the blood thinners. Partial paralysis staked claims to an arm, a leg and his face, the same places as his war wounds. His compromised enunciation, coupled with his disabled body, ensured that he would remain an observer. Passivity became familiar. He looked out the window next to his bed and noticed the afternoon shadows deepening on the grass. Roz would be by, soon.

This passivity and second silence were different than his prison silence had been. It allowed him to see his past in new ways. Most of his life had been lived. No longer directing his focus outwardly, he reflected upon the whole of his life experiences. Perhaps his most telling perception was that he had treated his oldest child like his father had treated him when he was an adult. When he, too, had brought his children and wife to meet William Marion.

His decision to sever any connection to Silva and her family was to protect his second family. But in a similar way, William Marion had claimed he had left his toddler son behind for both their protection, and included any future family his father might have. At the time of their last visit, he'd felt his father's reasoning made no sense. Yet, ultimately, he ended up doing the same to his oldest child and her family. Having achieved a similar outcome, could he better comprehend his father's decision from long ago? Was this what Ethel had meant about making choices that one might never understand?

The image of Sissie's car coat and loafers recalled his last conversation with Arno. After severing all future contact with his daughter and her family, he'd left the office. His highly charged emotions created a mindless fog. When he regained focus, he noticed he was driving to Mission Beach. His mind began searching for the street where she and Blaine had lived in their beach apartment. *Tangerine, no, Tangier, Tangiers Court.* He parked the Rambler on the boulevard and got out. About a half block away, he saw one of the little concrete walkways, San Rafael Court, that led from the street to the ocean front. He had never visited during the war years. This day he felt irresistibly drawn, as if by going there, he could touch and be touched by what he had irretrievably cut from his life. No, cut from all their lives. On the boulevard's sidewalk, he heard the steady traffic behind him as he faced the ocean. He seldom came to the beach and his senses responded all at once. The smell and taste of the briny air as the delicate, water-laden mist touched his exposed skin. The ceaseless pounding of waves that had begun as a soft sonorous hum from the boulevard increased to a steady rhythmic roar once he reached the seawall. Now visible, the relentless ebb and flow of waves washed the shoreline, marked by the tides' advances and retreats.

He had sauntered along Strand Way, each step marking his heartache. The cool November afternoon was sunny and bright. Few people were about. After a few minutes he found the Tangiers Court sign. He couldn't remember the street number but either one of the two apartments would have been where they had lived. Sissie had been so thrilled to find a place on the beach.

"Med, it's wonderful!" Her silvery laughter had rung with enthusiasm and excitement. "Blaine found it through one of his buddies." She never knew that her husband's buddy was him: he had sworn Blaine to secrecy. Arranging the apartment had been his wedding present to them. After the first time she saw the ocean, she declared, as she stood in front of his desk, that she knew living on the beach front was what she truly wanted. After she left that day, he began calling his real estate and property-owning friends to locate any available beachfront apartments.

"It's right on the beach. We can throw open the front window and hear the surf pound all night long. It's heaven!" Her eyes had danced with delight and she never looked more beautiful. How had he and Ethel made such a girl? None of his women could touch his daughter's beauty. Ethel came close, but she had been a dark looker. Lillian was statuesque and voluptuous with ample silky flesh: sheer chemistry had flashed off her when she came in for her employment interview. Roz had been handsome and her feisty, challenging attitude had drawn him in. But Sissie! In a class by herself. Could have drawn a Hollywood talent scout if she'd been interested.

Everything was fine in her world then. She'd been very happy with Blaine at the beach. Then Ethel's cancer entered all of their lives and her death had changed everything.

Hours after giving himself over to those long-ago memories, he heard the familiar sound of Roz's walking shoes. He turned and saw her shoulders were hunched and her face tense. *What has gotten her all stirred up?* She settled into the chair next to his bed and put her purse down on the floor. Her strained smile signaled that a complaint session was coming. Sometimes he was very thankful for his inability to speak, when before she would have expected him to respond in some fashion.

She leaned closer to him. "How are you, today, Virg?" He nodded his head as much as he could. She stroked the top of his blanket. She lifted her eyes to meet his and he felt the irritation seeping from all her pores. "You would think people would have sense enough to call ahead before just appearing on our doorstep, wouldn't you?" she asked.

Knowing she expected no response or would recognize any reaction on his face, he ducked his head to let her know he had heard her. "Buddy showed up, out of the blue! I was getting ready to come here. He wanted to see you but I didn't have the time to explain what was going on, where you are and what happened. He got very irritated and marched off."

That's not like Buddy. Not too much puts his nose out of joint. Wonder what really happened?

"Why couldn't he have called ahead? To just suddenly show up with no warning. It's been years since he last visited. A little warning, just some, would have been considerate." She shook her head in exasperation. Then a more relaxed look came over her face. "There, that's better," and she patted his bed and then his arm. "Just guess I needed to blow off some steam. You know us redheads, it doesn't take much." Med tried to smile, and she stroked his arm. "Ah, Mister, you always tried to take my mind off my blowups back in the day, didn't you?" He heard a mixed tone of yearning and regret in her voice, and tried to move his arm closer to her. She looked down and sadness crossed her face.

"Virg, what a mess, eh?" She paused. "I miss your voice, Virg, I really do. Funny how things go, isn't it? Your voice, what a talker you could be and all the stories you'd tell. I didn't understand how I'd miss the sound of it. The house is so quiet, now. Scott's never been a talker and I never realized how much you kept things flowing between you, him, all of us, really." She dropped her eyes and he felt the shift in her mood.

Roz, to everything there is a season. No telling for sure but I'm not seeing my sticking around much longer. Probably sooner is better than later. He motioned again towards her. She looked up, her eyes watery with tears. "I didn't think we'd end up like this, separated, with you in the hospital and me with Scott. I don't know what I thought our later years would be like. But not like this. Mister . . ." and tears rolled down her cheeks.

I don't know how to make this easier, Roz. I don't. He suddenly felt very tired and motioned with whatever he could: arm, head, leg.

Her mood shifted again. "I'm being a big crybaby, aren't I? It's not that bad. I'm just a little blue today." She smiled brightly, uncharacteristic for Roz, and slapped at his blanket. "Scott is getting his things ready for starting classes at UCSD in a couple of weeks. Big doings, our boy, your son's moving into what you and

I never pulled off—he's going to be a big man on campus! We did it, Virg. We did well, raising our boy. I never said anything to you, but keeping Silva and hers out of his life. It was, it truly was the right thing."

She stopped and looked into his eyes. "That was really hard for you. You never said anything, but I knew. You stood by us all the way. Not only have you been a good dad to Scott, you made me see that you were completely committed to us, your second family. You've been the best husband to me you could've been. Thank you, Virg." She was not given to expressing gratitude.

Is she saying goodbye? Something got to her today, must have been Buddy's visit. Once more he motioned with his arm and he grimaced in an attempt to smile. She sat with him a little bit longer. At the sounds of dinner carts rolling down the hall, she leaned over and pecked his cheek and left before his tray was brought in.

After his meal tray was removed, the room became quiet again. *Buddy had stopped by and she wouldn't tell him where I am.* The day had been filled by his first children, whether in dreams, memories or attempted visits. Visits with Roz were one-way streets.

It would have been good to see the boy. The last time, surely. A sort of completion from that other part of my life. Then a sudden awareness: *I am dying.* Not a shock; rather it offered a clarity about what his waiting was. The doctors had always been clear that his present condition wouldn't improve.

"Sometimes we know ahead of time, Virgil, and sometimes we don't."

"It's been a spell, Ethel." For the first time he was glad to feel, to hear her. She knew more about getting over to "there" than he. Regardless of what the Scriptures said.

"I didn't know it was my time when I crossed. That day I told Sissie I was looking forward to going back to Missouri and fishing." He remembered Sissie had told him this. *"It's different for each of us."*

"Buddy came to see me today." He felt sad as the words flowed in his mind. "She wouldn't tell him about all of this."

"She's not going to tell anyone, Virgil. She's weary from your illness and sensing you're dying. She has to keep things going for your— and her—son." His sadness grew. He wished these two disparate parts of his life could come together when he was gone, that these

different parts of himself could make peace. Ethel's pronounce-
ment felt true.

"You're telling me this for what reason, Ethel?" He wanted to
know.

"*Each of us has our own fate. Some of it we choose because of our
actions. Some of our fate comes from our kin, from those who brought us
into this life. Part of your fate is to see and feel the weight of what your
actions cast for and cost your own children. You leave your life knowing
you created some of your children's suffering. While you do see and feel
this, many don't.*" His heart felt heavier but he accepted the truth
of what she spoke.

"I didn't live my life considering consequences until I left Missouri."

"*But when you started over you became more thoughtful. Your heart
became tender. You started accepting limitations and you flourished,
even when you didn't get your way. You became the person you could've
been when you lived with me and our children.*"

"I didn't know how, then." He felt her compassion surrounding him, comforting him.

"*I knew that. I lived with the shame of how I treated Sissie when she
was a small child. None of us are your victims, Virgil. Each of us chose
and chooses how to carry our fate. So, too, will our children and grandchildren. What we can hope is that they may see their lives with some
clarity and move forward boldly.*"

"I am dying, then." He felt her smile.

"*That's why I am here.*"

"Why *have* you kept coming, Ethel, all these years?" Amusement flowed from her essence.

"*That's the best part. I chose to. Within our family, you were always
working for something or to be someone. But I saw how you looked at
Sissie and I knew she could bring out your best. Because you and I are
parents together, enough remained between us that I could come to you.
Because you started to behave like a grown man, I kept coming. What
someone else wanted and needed, your new family, became your life's direction. You started to live, knowing someone else's needs would decide
your life, as I did. What was best for your son was the most important.*"

Her words didn't change his sadness. But neither did he feel cheated and deprived. He had had a second chance to start over. Beyond death, Ethel, his dark-skinned beauty, had stayed the course with him. A welling of gratitude mingled with his sadness. It has been one hell of a ride! And he felt her gradually depart. Soon they would see one another on the other side.

The door creaked open and he woke up in the dark. He looked out the window next to his bed and saw the parking lot lights shining. The orderly flashed his night lamp on the floor as he made his way to Med's bed. His pulse was checked; pulse checks happened a lot, now. The darkness outside was either day's end or early morning before dawn. After Ethel's last visit, he began to lose his sense of time and the sequence of events. Roz came each day and Scott most days but he couldn't remember his son's last visit or what he had talked about. Before Ethel, he could recall a day's events, its meals, bathroom visits, which orderlies were on what shifts, who checked in with him and visitors. Now each day bled into the next with increasing vagueness.

After the stroke, he had drifted through his memories but each one had had very specific details of location and people and how he had felt emotionally or physically. When he was awake now, not much of anything he remembered, or anyone present, felt substantial. Only in dreams. There, he still wrestled, searched for and pursued. Sometimes it was someone he had known in that ancient part of his life he had jettisoned. He tried in vain to find, to reach them. He could see their form but it felt elusive and out of focus. What he sought out might appear ephemeral but his attempts were focused. Dreams are queer things, but now they felt more real than what went on when he was awake. The creaking door signaled the orderly had left as it slowly closed.

There was less of him now. Little by little he was becoming transparent. He noticed that when either Roz or Scott came, he drifted in and out; their visits became sketchier and full of gaps. At times he thought they were in the same body when either one or both visited. Because he had stopped talking for months, his increasing confusion was not obvious to them. Or so he felt. His inability, rather, his refusal to try to talk, wore away his precision for just the right word in his thoughts. Outside of Roz and Scott, he was rarely spoken to except when orderlies fed or helped him to the bathroom. Not being talked to eroded his sense of being present. Mostly, he heard familiar sounds that were part of his environment. Where did he go during these mental absences?

If this was dying, it wasn't so bad. He had no pain and his care was enough. Would it have been different if he had kept talking? His years in the Pen required silence and that had been his life's most potent experience. The silence there had disarmed him and reduced his focus to only what were his crimes and misdeeds. His self-scrutiny became relentless and uprooted who he had been when he started his sentence.

This second silence became pivotal in his final metamorphosis: his life's first and second chapters would be no more. His weakened mental grasp, however, registered emotions: when feelings swept through him he felt a sharp clarity.

Sometimes, his heart clenched at not seeing his first children. Ethel's appearance was his only contact from then. Thoughts of her, during these bursts of longing, eased him. He wasn't afraid. All these years he had read the Bible. It had remained his emotional raft after his conviction. And he felt forgiven and blessed by God in his second life. Now, though, his sense of God's guidance had been fading. A few of his VFW and Masonic friends had stopped by and spoken of God and faith. He understood why they said these things but connection to his faith was lessening, too. Their increasing discomfort felt almost tactile and he knew they wouldn't return. Would he have done any differently?

He felt his life's fullness. Success and public recognition had accompanied him. He had tasted deeply and assuaged his appetites. Overreaching ambition and disregard for the law had brought him great shame, mortification and loss. In his new life, he'd kept those legal and social consequences at bay. When he and Roz found each other, they were two damaged people who forged a good second chapter together, and she gave him his second son.

Through Scott, he recast his previous rejection of fatherhood. His second family summoned his sobriety and maturity. He became a good father. What he failed to calculate, however, was the additional costs from his first life that would be exacted by his second. To protect his second heart-love, Scottie, he had to refuse his first heart-love, Sissie and his grandchildren. When he let his heart tell him what he needed to do, he knew both great suffering and great joy.

He knew Roz had truly loved him, as he had her. His leaving was destroying her world. She would figure it out because she was as much of a survivor as he had been. He hoped she could continue without bitterness. These concerns lessened as he let go. His old resentments and anger at her biting comments and tirades had evaporated. Letting go was what he did now, bit by bit, second by second, breath by breath, heartbeat after heartbeat. Finally he would be gone. Maybe Ethel would be there to greet him.

The summer sun blazed above the clearing where he lay on the crest of the woods' slope. His front shoulder cradled the stock of a cocked rifle, and he aimed at the distant hole in shaded, leaf-covered soil. Both his Dunn uncles, Will and Jim, lay on either side of him. They'd been tracking a buck, but it had caught their scent and bolted. They needed to bring something back for supper and they had spotted a scrawny male rabbit, which scampered down the hole. Now they waited.

His heart pounded and suddenly he was on the Siberian permafrost wrestling, not with the Russian, but with a large opponent cloaked in flowing black robes. His two arms were pushing back against its upraised arm. No face was visible where a face should have been. His eyes looked up at the towering appendage and this time, no knife threatened to pierce his face or throat. Rather, it was a scythe and then he was sitting next to the faceless being on his prison cell bed. Its hood slipped back to reveal Ethel's face, looking as she had when he first knew her, working in the fields with her long black hair bound back. She looked at him with her dark, penetrating eyes and she began to smile. She reached out both hands for him to take. His heart slowed. He felt calm and soft as he placed his hands into hers.

Epilogue

My grandfather died on September 4, 1964, a couple of weeks after his sixty-fifth birthday. He was buried in Fort Rosecrans, San Diego on September 11, 1964. His widow, Roselle, never notified my mother, Silva, of his illness, death or funeral. She did, however, write to Buddy. On October 3, my uncle wrote these words:

> My heart is very heavy—I received a letter from
> Roselle today. <u>Dad is dead</u>. I will quote that part of her
> letter. "Honey, I will tell you, as much as it hurts, Dad-
> dy is now <u>free</u> and in another world, almost a month
> now." She wrote the letter 27 September, so Dad must
> have died about the time I left San Francisco, 2 Sep-
> tember. I know how you feel but it makes me sad.

From Vietnam, Buddy's letter traveled 8,000 miles to inform his sister of their father's death, which had occurred five miles from our home. She visited their father's grave the following Memorial Day, in 1965.

Thirty-six years later, in 2001, my mother's half-brother, Scott, contacted her. He was researching his father's previous life and family ties in Missouri.

Family Trees

Ethel's family tree

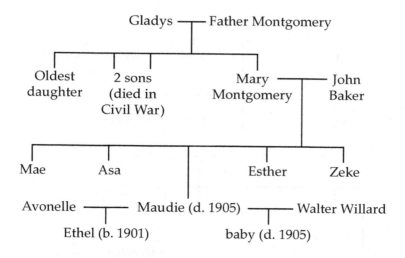

Virgil's family tree

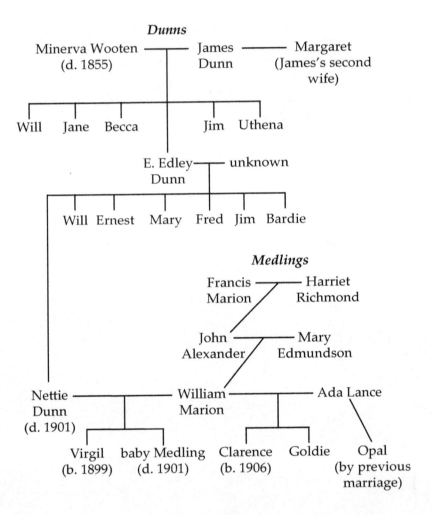

Dunns

Minerva Wooten ——— James ——— Margaret
(d. 1855)   Dunn   (James's second
                                    wife)

Will   Jane   Becca   Jim   Uthena

E. Edley——— unknown
Dunn

Will   Ernest   Mary   Fred   Jim   Bardie

Medlings

Francis ——— Harriet
Marion   Richmond

John ——— Mary
Alexander   Edmundson

Nettie ——————— William ——————— Ada Lance
Dunn   Marion
(d. 1901)

Virgil   baby Medling   Clarence   Goldie   Opal
(b. 1899)   (d. 1901)   (b. 1906)   (by previous
                                                  marriage)

Ethel and Virgil: marriages and offspring

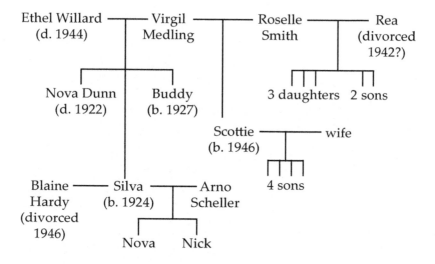

Photo Gallery

An engagement photo of Virgil in his uniform and Ethel,
before she cut her hair.

Virgil and Ethel at 1221 Jones Street in St. Louis. The back of the photo identifies him as a teacher.

The Dunn brothers.

Ethel and Virgil with baby Silva.

Virgil and little Sissie.

Sitting portrait of Virgil during his teaching years.

Sitting portrait of Ethel during Virgil's teaching years.

Virgil's Sunday school class in Hornersville, 1927.

Group photo with William Marion. Goldie is next to her father and Virgil is in top row at right end.

Buddy and Silva, ages 4 and 7 respectively.

Buddy and Silva with their dog Snowball,
during the Jefferson City years.

Silva and friend at the river house. She is about twelve years old.

Ethel fishing at the clubhouse on the Osage River.
(Perhaps Goldie is the woman on the left.)

Ethel in Campbell during Med's incarceration.

Silva in Campbell during Med's incarceration.

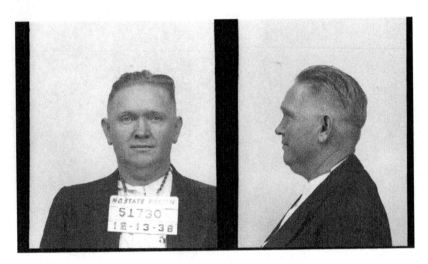

Virgil Medling's State Penitentiary prisoner mug shots.

Silva Avonelle Medling Hardy collage. Put together for Blaine Hardy when he was deployed. Pictures also include their wedding photos and his parents.

Virgil Lee Medling Jr., aka "Buddy," after joining the Army Air Corps.

Virgil Lee Medling's grave in Fort Rosecrans.

Acknowledgements

The process of writing a book includes a multitude of influences and resources. Among the influences were friends' feedback and support, and professionals in different fields. Resources included numerous books, trips made to Missouri's Bootheel, old newspapers on microfiche, genealogy from a distant cousin and from an active member on ancestry.com. I was startled by how many outstanding websites exist, created by Missouri citizens who do so out of their sheer love of capturing the unique details of southeastern Missouri's history, topography and culture.

Influences include:

Erin Sullivan, astrologer. Working with Erin, after my mother's death, was the first research for this book. She performed a dynastic analysis of my maternal line.

Eileen George, who believed I had the talent to tell my stories.

Beth Abernathy and Victoria Prater. Both listened to long sections of my writing and made me feel what I was writing was worth listening to.

Jane Leonard, who told me, more than two years before I attended my first writing class, that this story had to be told.

Judy Hogan, my writing teacher. She believed in the story and was a stern but supportive mentor. She always believed I would write well enough to do the tale justice.

My ancestors. They have been with me throughout this slow, faith-driven path. Telling their stories with emotional veracity allowed them to be seen in their imperfect but complex humanity. I come from a powerful family line, as do all of us.

My muses. The creative process has moments of transcendence. To be gripped by a scene, or conversation between characters, a flash of realization, none of which were planned but spontaneous, are guises of spiritual epiphany. In their absence, diligence and trust has kept the writing process moving forward.

Time. Sometimes the writing needed to sit, for either days or weeks. Clarity always reappeared whenever I returned to revise or edit.

Resources

ancestry.com

Charles Jones and his personal family tree that tracked the Medlings back to Cornwall in 1550. Charles knew all about the Medlings: he is married to one.

Jacqueline Dunn and her family tree notes that tracked the Dunns back to the British Isles and their arrival in America in the mid-1600s. Unfortunately her information was not available on a website. She generously communicated what she had by phone in 2011 while I was visiting Missouri.

thelittlerivervalley.com. A formidable output of the history, geography and topography of this unique region. Almost anything I might want to know was available somewhere in this series of monthly blogs. A tour de force and ongoing effort.

archives.gov/education/lessons/hines-photos/ Teaching with Documents: Photographs of Lewis Hines: Documentation of Child Labor. 1906–1916

Southeast Missourian newspaper. On the road blog, which features unusual historical features of the region.

Dunklin Daily Democrat. Several centennial articles written about life in Dunklin County.

Missouri State Archives in Jefferson City. Repository of Sanborn Fire Maps and phone directories from the 1930s. I was able

to find the house and school during my grandparents' years
there. I also found records of my grandfather's sentencing
hearing. Included in the evidence against him were witnesses,
including his boss Forrest Smith, later to become Governor
of Missouri in 1948, and his secretary/lover Lillian Wadlow.
The Archives located his mug shots and prison records at my
request.

Old Missouri State Penitentiary. I visited cell blocks where most
likely my grandfather was assigned. My visit to the dilapidated prison campus made it clear what his life there was like.
The tour guides, former prison guards, talked to us about the
Auburn prison system.

Osage River in Lake of the Ozarks. My few hours there helped me
understand my grandmother's love for the river.

St. Louis. The garment factory district is long gone. Many of the
old streets have been torn up and replaced as St. Louis mod-
ernized sections close to the river. The address of the Clay
Street Boarding house exists but the structure burned down
years ago. The First Baptist Church is an imposing structure
with an active congregation that is devoted to meeting many
inner-city needs. The large sanctuary is impressive with a
sweeping upstairs balcony. I felt Ethel's hopes when I stood
in that space.

Scott Medling, my half-uncle. Scott kept all the emails between
himself and my mother. He sent them to me when I contacted
him about my mother's passing. I could not have recalled all
the details she confided to him in her messages. His responses
helped me understand the man my grandfather became. Both
Scott and I feel that harsh judgment of any of the people in this
story is pointless. Understanding the context in which they
acted allowed each of us to be impartial and curious.

Nick Scheller. My brother has a prodigious memory, perhaps a
gift from our grandfather. He was able to recall things I had
forgotten or never heard from my mother. A few of these gave
me information used in a few crucial scenes.

Books

Mingo: Southeast Missouri's Ancient Swamp and the Countryside Surrounding It. Cletis Ellingworth, 2008. EBook

Canalou: People, Culture, Bootheel Town. Dan Whittle, 2013, Center for Regional History, Southeast Missouri State University

Thad Snow: A Life of Social Reform in the Missouri Bootheel. Bonnie Stepenoff, 2003, The Curators of the University of Missouri, University of Missouri Press

Pendergast! Lawrence H. Larsen and Nancy J. Hulston, 1997, The Curators of the University of Missouri, University of Missouri Press

America's Siberian Adventure, 1918–20. William S. Graves, Kindle Books original copyright 1931

American Soldiers in Siberia: The Forgotten War. Sylvian G. Kindall, 2014, Kindle Books

The Orphan Trains: Placing Out in America. Marilyn Irvin Holt. 1992, University of Nebraska Press

Delta Empire: Lee Wilson and the Transformation of Agriculture in the New South. Jeannie Whayne, 2011, Louisiana State University Press

The Big Muddy: An Environmental History of the Mississippi and its People from Hernando deSoto to Hurricane Katrina. Christopher Morris, 2012, Oxford University Press

Poor Whites of the Antebellum South: Tenants and Laborers in Central North Carolina and Northeast Mississippi. Charles C. Bolton, 2003, Duke University Press

History of Southeast Missouri. 1888, Goodspeed Brothers

History of Dunklin County, Missouri, 1845–1895. Mary F. Smyth-Davis, Nixon-Jones, St. Louis, Missouri

A Revolution in the Heartland: Changes in Rural Culture, Family and Culture. Rex R. Campbell, with Mary Campbell and Coleen Hughes, 2004, Department of Rural Psycholgy, University of Missouri, Colombia, Missouri

History of Malden. Kennett County Library. Informal collection and oral history about Malden and surrounding area. 1875–1945

CPSIA information can be obtained at www.ICGtesting.com
Printed in the USA
BVOW06s1555230815

414624BV00004B/6/P